PRAISE FOR THE UNDERWATER INVESTIGATION UNIT SERIES

Sea Castle

"The plot comes together like the prove adding a bit to a disturbing big picture. executes a familiar formula with panache

"Mayne combines a brilliant, innovative female lead with a plausibly twisty plot. Kinsey Millhone fans will love McPherson."

—*Publishers Weekly* (starred review)

"Mayne creates a world that blends the crime writing of Michael Connelly with high-tech oceanography in his Underwater Investigation Unit series . . . The series never ceases to be fascinating, making characters sink or swim as lives are on the line and the story veers in unexpected directions. Required reading for any suspense fan."

—*Library Journal*

"This is an above-average thriller that never ceases to surprise readers . . . [T]he experience that Andrew Mayne has created for us [is] one to truly savor."

—Bookreporter

Sea Storm

"The fast-paced plot is filled to the brim with fascinating characters, and the locale is exceptional—both above and below the waterline. One doesn't have to be a nautical adventure fan to enjoy this nail-biter."

—*Publishers Weekly* (starred review)

"Strong pacing, lean prose, and maritime knowledge converge in this crackerjack thriller."

—*Kirkus Reviews*

"Fans of the Underwater Investigation Unit [series] will enjoy this installment, and those who love thrillers will like this too."

—*Library Journal*

Black Coral

"A relentless nail-biter whether below or above the waterline. Even the setbacks are suspenseful."

—*Kirkus Reviews* (starred review)

"Mayne's portrayal of the Everglades ecosystem and its inhabitants serves as a fascinating backdrop for the detective work. Readers will hope the spunky Sloan returns soon."

—*Publishers Weekly*

"As with the series debut, this book moved along well and never lost its momentum. With a great plot and strong narrative, Mayne pulls the reader in from the opening pages and never lets up. He develops the plot well with his strong dialogue and uses shorter chapters to keep the flow throughout. While I know little about diving, Mayne bridged that gap effectively for me and kept things easy to comprehend for the layperson. I am eager to see what is to come, as the third novel in the series was just announced. It's sure to be just as captivating as this one!"

—*Mystery & Suspense Magazine*

"Mayne creates a thrilling plot with likable yet flawed characters . . . Fans of detective series will enjoy seeing where the next episodes take us."

—Bookreporter

"Former illusionist and now bestselling author Andrew Mayne used to have a cable series entitled *Don't Trust Andrew Mayne*. If you take that same recommendation and apply it to his writing, you will have some idea of the games you are in for with his latest novel, titled *Black Coral*. Just when you think you might have things figured out, Andrew Mayne pulls the rug out from under you and leaves you reeling in fits of delight."

—Criminal Element

"The pages are packed with colorful characters . . . Its shenanigans, dark humor, and low view of human foibles should appeal to fans of Carl Hiaasen and John D. MacDonald."

—*Star News*

The Girl Beneath the Sea

"Distinctive characters and a genuinely thrilling finale . . . Readers will look forward to Sloan's further adventures."

—*Publishers Weekly*

"Mayne writes with a clipped narrative style that gives the story rapid-fire propulsion, and he populates the narrative with a rogue's gallery of engaging characters . . . [A] winning new series with a complicated female protagonist that combines police procedural with adventure story and mixes the styles of Lee Child and Clive Cussler."

—*Library Journal*

"Sloan McPherson is a great, gutsy, and resourceful character."

—Authorlink

"Sloan McPherson is one heck of a woman . . . *The Girl Beneath the Sea* is an action-packed mystery that takes you all over Florida in search of answers."

—*Long and Short Reviews*

"The female lead is a resourceful, powerful woman and we're already looking forward to hearing more about her in the future Underwater Investigation Unit novels."

—Yahoo!

"*The Girl Beneath the Sea* continuously dives deeper and deeper until you no longer know whom Sloan can trust. This is a terrific entry in a new and unique series."

—Criminal Element

DARK
DIVE

OTHER TITLES BY ANDREW MAYNE

TRASKER SERIES

Night Owl

UNDERWATER INVESTIGATION UNIT SERIES

Sea Castle
Sea Storm
Black Coral
The Girl Beneath the Sea

THEO CRAY AND JESSICA BLACKWOOD SERIES

The Final Equinox
Mastermind

THEO CRAY SERIES

Dark Pattern
Murder Theory
Looking Glass
The Naturalist

JESSICA BLACKWOOD SERIES

Black Fall
Name of the Devil
Angel Killer

THE CHRONOLOGICAL MAN SERIES

The Monster in the Mist
The Martian Emperor
Station Breaker
Public Enemy Zero
Hollywood Pharaohs
Knight School
The Grendel's Shadow

NONFICTION

The Cure for Writer's Block
How to Write a Novella in 24 Hours

DARK DIVE

A THRILLER

ANDREW MAYNE

THOMAS & MERCER

Published by Thomas & Mercer, Seattle

www.apub.com

Amazon, the Amazon logo, and Thomas & Mercer are trademarks of Amazon.com, Inc., or its affiliates.

ISBN-13: 9781662506451 (paperback)
ISBN-13: 9781662506468 (digital)

Cover design by Shasti O'Leary Soudant
Cover image: © WaterFrame / Alamy

Printed in the United States of America

DARK
DIVE

PROLOGUE

Central Florida, 11,867 BCE

She was scared.

Niqua's heart pumped through her chest, and the muscles around her abdomen were inflamed. The fibers of the moccasin on her left foot had already been worn down to a few threads beneath her toes.

The sharp edges of shells and broken rocks had never bothered her feet before, but since the blessing and the changes that had happened to her body, even the slightest sensation could cause discomfort. When she slept on her back, she felt every stick in the bedding under her. When she slept on her side, it felt as if she would roll over and crush her blessing.

The lack of sleep and constant discomfort were why she'd had words with Akil. When she went to her mother for advice, she'd been told to go collect snails and spend some time with her thoughts.

As she walked along the creek, poking a stick into the water, hoping to find a turtle—knowing that would please Akil—she thought about her ancestors and the fact that every mother in her line had to endure what she was going through. It gave her some measure of peace . . . until she realized she'd strayed too far.

There had been signs of others recently. Distant campfires and strange words echoing across the marsh at night. In this vast land, her people rarely encountered others. So, two of Niqua's tribemates had gone off to find out who these people were and whether they wanted to trade.

The last time they had done this, they'd traded turtle meat for beautiful stones the color of the sky and the sea. Niqua had been eager to see what Lno and Riqua would bring back.

But they never returned.

That had been days ago, and there had been no sign of the others since. Lno and Riqua might have gone on exploring or been called to the ancestors through some accident. Three moons prior, K'Ra, one of the strongest in the family, had hit his head when he slipped crossing a stream and was gone like a fire doused with water.

The moment Niqua heard the twig snap behind her, she knew it was no misstep or accident that had caused Lno and Riqua to disappear.

Now she could *smell* the other. This was no panther or bear. Her nostrils recoiled at an acrid, oily scent that came from burnt flesh and unclean animal skins.

As she waited for another sound, she counted breaths that felt like a thousand days.

She didn't know if it was a sound or something she saw in the twisted maze of mangrove shadows that made her run. Whatever it was, the air by her neck fluttered as something reached out for her and missed.

Niqua dashed along the creek, jumping from dry patch to dry patch, avoiding the sucking wet mud that would slow her down.

She had no idea how far back her pursuer was until she heard him shout something in a tongue that sounded like a frog and a bird in an argument. The words weren't clear, but the anger was unmistakable.

He was ten paces behind her. Niqua had a good lead, but it wouldn't be enough. She had been a good runner before the blessing. Now, she waddled like an armadillo.

Niqua cradled her belly with one arm and kept running. The one advantage she had was that she'd been creek-walking all her life and knew how to spot the best rocks and landings to keep from falling.

She bounded to the other side of the creek and spied a small, dry boulder in the middle of the stream. As she leaped across, she caught her reflection in the water near the nostrils of a small alligator.

As she landed, something sharp hit her shoulder. The other had thrown a rock or used a sling. She kept moving, ignoring the pain.

Niqua saw an opening in the brush and decided to run through it where the mangroves overhung the creek: a small and difficult passage. She squeezed onto an animal trail carved by deer and peccaries. She could move more quickly again, but so would the other.

A grotesque shout came from behind as her pursuer made his way through the opening. Niqua felt another sharp pain, this time on the back of her skull. It felt like a small pebble, the kind you would sling at a bird.

She knew that she could only run for so long. She was already exhausted. Only terror kept her moving.

Niqua's nose realized where she was before her eyes did. It was the fetid, rotten smell of the Darkland. She'd been near it before, but from the opposite end. Never from this side.

Her earliest memories were of stories about what fates befell those who came too close to it. The Darkland was filled with the worst kind of death—the kind that made you disappear, never to meet or become an ancestor.

One only had to draw near to the Darkland to feel the strangeness of it. Trees grew oddly here. Animals behaved erratically, and only birds that ate dead flesh flew over it. There was an older tribal name for the area: Demon Mouth.

The tribe-father said that when he was a boy, several men decided to penetrate the heart of the Darkland and perform a ritual to cleanse it. Only one returned. He babbled about demons crawling from the ground and pulling the other men into their lair below. His madness never broke, and he eventually wandered into the swamp, never to be seen by anyone in the tribe again.

The tribe-father forbade anyone from going into the Darkland. Especially curious teens who wanted to prove their bravery through defiance. Anyone else with half a brain could tell by the smell alone that the Darkland was to be avoided.

Unfortunately, Niqua had no choice. She was trapped between the deadly stranger and the twisted black branches of the Darkland before her.

Niqua put a hand to her belly and felt her blessing. She could live with madness and exile as long as her blessing could live on with the tribe. Her sister N'Bri would take care of the child. She'd lost one of her own and watched Niqua's belly with envy.

If she could keep running, she might be able to make it through to the other side to Akil and the tribe. Madness was better than death, she decided.

Another hoarse scream came from behind her, granting Niqua the courage she needed to plunge into the void.

CHAPTER 1
THE DEEP END

"We got a fun one for you here," says Forest Linderman.

His grin doesn't fill me with joy. Linderman, a trapper who contracts with Florida Fish and Wildlife, can't contain his glee. His smile reaches almost ear to ear on his leathery face, his teeth gleaming in the dark.

Pushing seventy, Linderman is a bit of a Florida legend. From the rifle slung over his shoulder to the gray hair that sticks up from his scalp like steel bristles, you'd have no trouble picking him out in a police lineup as a hunter—or mob hit man.

Behind him, the flashing lights of the swarm of police cars reflect off the surface of the small lake. The unmistakable eyes of alligators shine back like tiny stars in a black sky.

Two hours ago, I got a text from my boss, George Solar, head of Florida's Underwater Investigation Unit, which was only reinstated earlier today. He said to meet at our office first thing in the morning. Forty minutes later, while eating dinner with my boyfriend and daughter, I got another text:

Meet at Belt Road marker 33 ASAP. Sorry.

"McPherson!" shouts Solar from near the edge of the water as he spots me.

He's in the middle of a group of people from different agencies. I spot a few familiar faces from Miami-Dade Police, Florida Department of Law Enforcement, and Florida Fish and Wildlife, as well as two FBI agents. I wouldn't say some of the faces are hostile, but they clearly hold a few grudges against the UIU—some maybe deserved.

Our little unit has made quite a few waves since Solar brought us together. We've sent a handful of crooked public officials and law enforcement agents to jail and ruined the careers of others—deservedly so.

What started as a law enforcement unit tasked with handling various unsolved crimes committed along the thousands of miles of Florida waterways turned into an investigative team with a free hand to go after public corruption too challenging for other agencies to handle.

Political pressure caused us to be disbanded. Public outcry and a string of successes put us back together.

"What's going on?" I ask as he breaks free of the huddle and walks toward me.

"Earlier today, some kayakers spotted two bodies wrapped up. Miami-Dade was handling it. We think it's connected to the Snake Trail Killer. I wanted us to go over it tomorrow in case it was connected to something we were looking into," he explains.

I can tell there's a lot more to this. "Uh-huh," I reply, waiting for the other shoe to drop.

He knows I can tell this is going somewhere . . . complicated. "Yeah. So, they loaded up the coroner's van with the bodies. And the driver got a little distracted."

My eyes dart to the lake. "How distracted?"

Solar takes a deep breath. "Enough to land the van smack in the middle of an alligator breeding ground."

"The driver?" I ask.

"He managed to swim to shore but got a little chewed up. Two deputies killed one alligator and wounded another that slipped back into the water. They airlifted the driver to the hospital."

"What's the plan?" I ask.

"We're going to try to send a boat out and wrap a cable around the van and pull it to shore before it gets too settled into the mud."

"I have a suggestion," Linderman interjects. The trapper has been standing off to the side, listening in on our conversation.

"We'd like one that doesn't involve shooting every reptile in a square mile," says a woman walking up to us.

"Dr. Hastings is looking for a less disruptive solution," Solar translates.

Hastings is a researcher who works with the state to protect and study alligators.

"I'd only put them to sleep for a little while," says Linderman.

"And disrupt the whole mating cycle. This section is already under enough pressure from pythons getting into nests and eating eggs. We don't need you drowning half of them with tranquilizers," Hastings fires back.

Although an alligator can stay at the bottom of a pond for up to twenty-four hours, under sedation it doesn't have the same muscle control and will leave its nose flaps open and drown. Generally, you only tranq them if you plan to pull them ashore. And pulling them ashore is really only an option with one or two alligators.

I see a lot of gleaming eyes out in the water and can hear the sound of them moving around. The combination of mating season and all the flashing lights has them agitated at a time when they would normally be resting.

"Hughes is setting up an ROV to try to wrap a cable around the tow hitch," says Solar.

Scott Hughes, my coworker and friend, is tinkering with an underwater remotely operated vehicle in the bed of his truck. Hughes is a former navy diver who undertook risky underwater operations for his country. For a year or so, he has pursued a new passion: underwater recovery using robotics.

Ever since we had a close call with an underwater explosive on a sinking cruise ship, we've tried to think smarter and not be as impulsive.

Hughes is better at it than I am.

"How's it coming?" asks Solar as we walk over to Hughes.

"Almost ready." He points to a mechanical arm holding a metal loop. "I just need to get this close enough."

The ROV looks more like a sleek turtle than a clunky underwater vehicle. Hughes has been working with a start-up company to integrate AI and other advanced features that will make the ROV more nimble and able to problem-solve.

Hughes presses a button on a control pad, and the ROV lights up.

"Functioning. How can I help you?" says the ROV in a voice that sounds a bit like Keanu Reeves's.

The previous ROV used Hughes's voice, which I found unsettling.

"I need a camera check, Nemo," Hughes tells the bot that he has apparently named Nemo.

"Cameras functional," replies Nemo.

The display pad in Hughes's hand shows a fish-eye view of us staring back at it.

Rectangular boxes form around our faces, and text labels appear. "Bossman 88%" appears under Solar's, "Mechanic 99%" below Hughes's face, "Unknown" below Linderman and Hastings. Under mine, it reads, "Danger 99%."

"Danger ninety-nine percent?" I ask.

"The percent is how confident it is. The AI chose the names," he replies.

"You sound like my daughter blaming ChatGPT."

"Well, I added a chat API so it would be more conversational," says Hughes.

"Just what we need—talking appliances," Solar says with a sigh.

"It's also excellent at problem-solving," Hughes defends his rig.

"We'll see about that," mutters Linderman.

"Sloan, you want to help me put this in the water?" Hughes asks.

Linderman unslings his rifle. "I'll spot you."

"I don't want you anywhere near the water," Hastings tells the trapper.

"Are you going to wish the gators away?" asks Linderman.

"I'll use a pole, like my father taught me, thanks."

It's clear that Hastings and Linderman have a history. Linderman has no hate for alligators and understands their place in the ecosystem, but he knows they're plentiful, so killing one or fifty wouldn't make a huge dent.

Hastings feels differently.

She watches as we bring the robot to the edge of the water, holding the pole limply. I think she's trying to decide if this is a good or a bad idea.

She makes a little headshake, clearly concluding that this is the least worst of a list of terrible ideas and turning toward the water to make sure no alligators decide to lunge at us.

They're normally shy and keep to themselves, but in mating season and with this much commotion, normal doesn't apply.

Hughes and I toss Nemo into the water, and it makes a huge splash, then sinks under the waves.

A thick tail makes an angry slap against the water ten meters away, and we decide to step back from the bank and join the crowd that's gathered at a safe distance.

I watch over Hughes's shoulder as the control pad shows Nemo's point of view.

The water is mostly dark with splashes of light from above, but the LiDAR and sonar sensors create a 3D map that shows what's a few meters ahead.

"Find the van," Hughes tells Nemo.

"Searching," replies the robot's voice over the control pad.

Nemo begins to make a beeping sound every few seconds as it searches.

"No cables?" asks Hastings.

Hughes points to a large plastic case with a cable running into the water. "There's an RF and a laser transceiver in there."

"What about the alligators' eyes?" she asks.

"Harmless," he says, focusing on the control panel.

"Are you sure?"

"The navy tested it."

"The same people who use dolphins for retrieving mines?" she replies. "And kill whales with sonar?"

"I didn't ask," Hughes responds tightly, keeping his attention on Nemo.

"Maybe—" Hastings begins but is cut off by Solar.

"Would you rather we let Linderman drive it?" our boss asks her.

"I've got a truck full of tranquilizers," Linderman puts in, a little too gleefully.

"Save them for the after-party," I tell him.

Nemo starts to beep faster.

On Hughes's display, the outline of the van comes into view. A rectangle appears around it with the word "Van" below it.

"Van found," says Nemo.

"Find the tow hitch and put the loop around it," says Hughes.

"It'll understand that?" asks Hastings.

Hughes points to an antenna on the edge of the console. "Cellular antenna. It talks to a smarter AI in a server farm somewhere that breaks it down into simple instructions that are sent to the smaller AI."

I can tell that Hastings's concern for the alligators is balanced out by her curiosity about the process. She's probably wondering what she could do with something like Nemo to promote wildlife conservation.

As Nemo moves around the van, the beeping picks up in intensity. I can tell by the expression on Hughes's face that this isn't supposed to happen.

"What's wrong?" I ask.

"I'm having it orbit at a distance, but it says it's getting closer," says Hughes.

"Something is getting closer," adds Linderman as the sound reaches a steady pulse.

"Oh shit," mutters Hughes.

Nemo's POV shakes, then goes dark. A moment later we hear a loud thrash from the lake, and the head of a huge alligator breaks the surface, the robot clenched in its jaws.

Apparently realizing this was not a turtle, the massive reptile flings the robot over its back, sending it splashing into the far side of the lake, where it rolls over on its side blinking red warning lights.

Linderman lets out a huge laugh behind us, unable to control himself. "Alligators one, robots zero."

Hughes is staring at his control pad, trying to process what just happened. The others in the crowd realize what just took place, and phones are pulled out to snap photos of the bobbing robot.

"I need to get that out of there," says Hughes.

"I'll help," I reply. "We can probably throw a rope around it."

"I got it," he says as he walks over to a storage box in his truck.

"Excuse me," says a man in a blue long-sleeve shirt with the US Army Corps of Engineers logo on the pocket.

"Yeah?" asks Solar.

"We might have another way." He points to a small pillbox-shaped building almost obscured by the foliage. "That was a test pumping station. It connects this lake to the canal on the other side. There's a meter-wide conduit that runs between them. Right now, the gate is up. I think the end of the channel's about three meters from the van."

"What are you saying?" asks Solar.

"Well, maybe someone could swim through there and connect the van to the hoist?"

"No," says Solar. "We'll wait until we can get a crane here and pull it out."

"Solar," says a man in a Miami-Dade Police jacket. "We might not be able to wait. The driver left the door open. We don't know how long before the bodies get contaminated or—well, eaten."

"No way. The alligators won't eat them. Right, Dr. Hastings?" says Solar.

"Well . . . ," she starts to say.

"Damn it." Solar looks at me regretfully.

"I'll do it." Of course I'll do it. I had a feeling I was going to be in the water the moment we pulled up.

"It's not worth it," says Solar.

"We don't know that. We have no idea who killed them. There could be forensic evidence that makes a difference. I'll be fine. I have the advantage of not looking like a turtle. To be honest, I'm more worried about the pump than the alligator."

"It hasn't worked in years," says Antonio. "You'll be fine."

"I'll be fast," I reply.

"Did you see how fast that alligator was?" asks Solar.

"I've got some raw chicken I can throw into the opposite end to lure them away for a while," says Linderman. "That is, if Dr. Hastings isn't worried that I'll give them indigestion."

"This is a stupid plan," she says.

She's not wrong.

"McPherson, you don't have to," Solar tells me.

I don't want to. But one DNA sample or bite mark could be all it takes to get the killer. One simple dive. Just three meters. Nine feet. I can make that in a few seconds. Simply grab a cable that's dropped near the hitch. I've done more challenging dives. No problem.

"I'll suit up," I say, trying to hide any quaver in my voice.

CHAPTER 2
DANGER IN THE WATER

I'm in my diving suit, sitting on a concrete wall above the canal on the other side of the lake. Linderman has been trolling the water with a raw chicken on the end of a rope, seeing if there are any alligators sitting out the mating frenzy. So far, no bites. However, that doesn't mean no alligators. For all we know, the chicken dragged across the bottom might have awakened a big bull.

I keep that out of my mind and focus on the dive. I've got the route mapped out in my head.

While I'd like to free dive it in order to move fast, Hughes talked me into using a small one-liter tank built into a hydrodynamic backpack that won't slow me down much.

"Is that thing shut down?" Solar asks Antonio about the gate.

"For years. I don't know what's living inside of the tunnel, but Stafford never had a problem."

"Fred Stafford?" I ask, recognizing the name.

"You know him?" replies Antonio.

Every serious diver in Florida knows who Stafford is. He's a dive instructor and technical diver who's done some extremely thorny dives, like fixing leaky pipelines and repairing undersea cables at extreme depths. I've watched Stafford and my father drink each other under the table, telling wild stories.

"He's a family friend," I reply.

"Tell him to return a call, would you? We could have had him out here doing this instead of . . . um, you."

"Just my luck," I reply, moving past the potentially awkward moment.

Solar is standing back, watching as I get ready. I don't have to see his face to know what he's thinking.

"I'll be fast. In and out. No big deal," I say as I slip on my flippers.

"Uh-huh," says Solar. "Didn't we buy some armor for this kind of thing?"

"It's back at HQ," I reply.

"Maybe we should get it."

"No. It'll slow me down."

A group of police and emergency personnel have started to gather on the ridge, separating the canal from the lake. In the distance I can see the blinking mast of a TV news satellite-uplink truck. Overhead, two helicopters circle, their spotlights aimed at the water.

I don't know if that will make the alligators skulk away or agitate them further.

"Where's Hughes?" I ask.

"Fishing his robot out of the water," says Solar.

"Uh, okay."

"Want me to get him?"

"No. We're good. Hey, Linderman, you ready to ring the dinner bell at the opposite end?" I ask.

He looks up from the rope he's been dangling in the canal to check for alligators. "Sure thing. I'll keep them back. If not, I've always got my rifle."

"If you see me struggling, hold off. I'd rather take my chances with a gator than your rusty aim."

The old hunter scowls at the insult.

"I'm just kidding. But seriously, don't point your rifle anywhere near me."

He reels in his chicken. "It'd be a quicker death than letting them get you."

"That's not helpful thinking."

He walks away to bait the alligators. I retrace the path in my head.

The entrance is directly below me. I just have to dive down, slip in, swim like crazy past whatever hasn't been startled from there already, then make it out the other end, where the van should be visible under a spotlight from a helicopter.

Then I simply cinch the cable that's already near the tail hitch around it and swim like hell back through the pipe to safety on the other side.

If I time it right, I can be home in my bathtub sipping a beer in less than two hours.

"You want to call Run?" asks Solar.

My boyfriend is at home with our daughter, Jackie. "No need to worry them. This is just a routine dive."

In alligator-infested waters during mating season . . .

One of the first things you realize when you're a rookie cop in a dangerous situation is that there's no one else to call. Sure, you can ask for backup, but you don't do that when some old lady phones in about growling coming from her backyard or thinks there's someone hiding in her attic.

I have been in a long list of situations that sound like the start of a horror movie. This one tops the list. Although to be perfectly honest, intentionally swimming into a lake full of dangerous reptiles has precedent in my family. While this isn't the first time I've done a recovery from a vehicle in a lake with alligators around, my dad has me beat. He swears that he was once paid by the CIA to sneak into Cuban waters and steal a man-eating crocodile from a swamp filled with them.

Although the real purpose of the crocodile-napping depends on how drunk Dad is, I'm fairly sure there's a grain of truth in there. There always is with his stories. Even the tallest ones.

I've heard him claim the gator snatching was so a US spy could study its anatomy so he could pass himself off as an expert or—I kid you not—to see if they could breed Cuban crocodiles to kill Castro. While I have my doubts about the purpose, I've seen the photos of the crocodile they caught tied up on the deck of the boat with the lights of Havana in the background and my father smiling as he flipped off Fidel.

Compared to Cuban crocodiles, Florida alligators might as well be geckos. Plus, Dad had to deal with a lot worse, including Castro's gunboats. He kept cases of Cuban cigars on board in case their vessel was seized because it was safer to tell the Cubans you were a smuggler than let them think you worked for the CIA.

I check my tank pressure and give my regulator a squeeze. Everything is in order.

"Ready, boss?" I ask.

"I'm pretty sure the answer is no," he replies, then calls into the radio. "Agent Danger is getting into the water. Be ready."

Someone calls back, "Affirmative."

I can tell from Solar's voice how he feels about the whole situation. He's taken his fair share of risks, from personally going undercover in prison to facing down corrupt politicians who would see him destroyed. But putting others in harm's way weighs heavily on him.

"Let's get this done," I say before lowering myself into the water.

I'm grabbing the edge of the pipe before my body has even adjusted to the change of temperature.

The light mounted to my mask casts a narrow beam into the dark.

I can see the flicker of tails as sleeping fish startle awake and swim away.

I kick my legs hard and pass an oscar trying to flee from me.

Too slow. Sloan McPherson is the fastest thing down here.

I'm almost at the halfway point when my light illuminates an obstacle—a rusty metal gate that blocks half the pipe.

While I might be able to swim through the gap, I don't want it to slow me down if I have to make a fast exit after putting the hook on the van.

I grab the edge of the gate and try to push it up. I can feel it budge a little, but not a lot. I take the mini-crowbar from my belt and use the hook end to pull at the edge. The gate gives a little more.

Okay, that will have to do. Solar is probably pacing on the other side, waiting for my bubbles.

I pull myself through and continue down the narrow passage, my tiny light showing the way. I click it off and see a faint glow at the other end. That would be the light from the helicopter.

Okay. This is good. The van should be just beyond the end of the pipe. I got this. I'll be there and back in just a few seconds.

I reach the edge of the pipe and see the shadow of the van and the glimmer of the light on the cracked windshield. The driver's door is wide open.

I swim close to the bottom of the lake—or what looks like the bottom. It's so filled with muck the real bottom is probably several meters below the mud.

The van has already sunk almost past the tops of its wheel wells. Getting it out is going to take a strong tow truck.

Not my problem. Just lasso the tail hitch and get out.

I swim close to the side of the van, curving my body around the door and coming within inches of the metal side panel.

I read the letters C-O-R-O-N-E-R as I pass them.

My left hand grabs the bumper while my right hand reaches out for the hook to wrap around the tail hitch.

I keep an eye on it to make sure I don't feed it to something.

Being underwater with apex predators has many of the same rules as amusement park rides: *Keep your arms and legs inside at all times.*

I once took a submersible (basically a crab cage with an electric motor) to the bottom of shark-infested waters. I was wearing long fins to help me swim faster. When we got to the bottom and I climbed out of the cage, I realized that slight tug I'd felt on the way down was a shark taking a piece out of the fin.

The carabiner isn't hard to find—the cable connected to it is wrapped in bright yellow tape. We call it "yum-yum yellow" because great whites like to chew on it.

Thankfully, alligators are indifferent to the color.

I grasp the buckle with my right and feel around the bumper for the tail hitch.

Then it hits me . . . Did anyone actually check to see if this van had a tail hitch?

As I shove my hand into the muck, the answer becomes clear—no. *Great plan.*

I reach under the bumper to see if I can find a tow hook. The muck and the lack of light aren't helping.

Wait . . .

What happened to the light?

CHAPTER 3
Shadow

I feel my breathing increase and try to calm myself. The lack of light doesn't mean there's a gator directly overhead. There could be lots of explanations—like there being several alligators overhead.

Stop it. Just focus.

Maybe the helicopter got called away.

Right. Just hug the van and wrap the cable around the tow hook.

Slow and steady. We don't want this coming undone.

A wave pushes me close to the van.

Damn. Something swam close.

Alligators are territorial critters. This could have been a warning pass.

Or maybe it's only a wave, I think wishfully.

My hand feels the flat plate of the tow hook under the van. *Thank god.* It took me shoving my arm all the way under the muck to get to it, but I have the hook in the mouth.

Mouth. Don't think about mouths right now.

I have to find the other . . . loop. Otherwise, there's no point. The van will never come out without both tie-downs connected to the cable.

I slide my body under the bumper and feel along until I come to the other loop and try to pull the cable through.

I notice the light is back.

Uh, okay.

Focus.

I have to pull hard on the cable to get it under. The exertion puts me on my back, and I get a glimpse upward as a long and agile alligator swims overhead.

He doesn't seem interested in me—but he also doesn't seem not interested in me.

I pull myself closer to the bottom and push my arm as far as it can go to get the cable around the hook.

I feel something on my belt clang against the bumper. So much for being stealthy.

There! I feel the hook catch the second loop under the van. I clasp the carabiner around the other end and pull it tight.

If the tow operator knows what he's doing, he should have no problem getting the van free. It's officially no longer my problem.

Time to push off and sneak back into the pipe.

Damn it. Something on me is caught under the bumper. I reach down and feel a loop on my utility belt wedged into a gap.

It's not coming loose.

I unhook the belt. All I need is my air tank now.

Which reminds me to check the gauge.

Christ. I'm almost out of air. Once, I leisurely sipped my air supply. Now I'm getting older and taking huge gasps.

No good, Sloan. Five feet or fifty, you have to double-check.

Okay, save the recriminations for later. My daughter will let me have it when I tell her what happened. There're few punishments worse than having your own child scold you for something you told them never to do.

Oh crap! Jackie has her learner's permit test next week.

Stop panicking yourself, Sloan.

You see, there are things more frightening than a pond full of frisky alligators—like your only child getting behind the wheel. The same child who it only seems like yesterday was convinced she could walk through walls if she concentrated hard enough.

I'm free of the belt. Time to hightail it back into the pipe.

I swim around the van—the opposite direction of where I saw the overhead alligator swimming. I instinctively look over my shoulder as I turn, then face forward as I make the bend and come face-to-face with a leathery snout.

Instinct takes over, and I use my already outstretched hand to push down on the snout and swim up and over it.

This may have been a dumb or brilliant move. I'll know the answer if I still have my legs a minute from now.

As I kick past what appears to be an endless highway of scales and ridges below me, the thick tail starts to twitch upward.

People forget that alligators are dangerous at both ends. The jaws may bite you, but the tail can knock you out long enough for the mouth to find you.

I feel a surge of water and keep going. The end of the pipe is close. I plunge straight into it, praying that the gator won't try to chase after me.

I swim as hard as I can through the metal barrel. It's completely dark. I'm swimming too fast to turn on the light on my mask. I remember the metal gate almost a moment too late and keep my head from cracking open by slowing myself down with my hand.

The impact sends a wave of pain from my wrist to my elbow. I ignore it and try to make my way under the metal gate.

I realize turning sideways is not the answer as my slim backpack gets wedged between the bottom of the pipe and the gate above.

I feel a current and begin to panic. My air tank's only giving me weak puffs.

I'm out of options.

I unfasten my pack and push my knees against the surface of the pipe below, trying to dislodge myself from the gate.

Suddenly everything begins to shake, and I hear a metallic grinding sound.

Something is pushing me.

Pushing me back into the lake.

I'm hit by something with the force of a cannon, and my head strikes the tunnel wall.

I see stars.

Then I see nothing.

CHAPTER 4
TURBULENCE

My chest is in agony. It feels like I'm being punched. Actually, I am being punched.

Hughes is leaning over me, soaking wet. He's pumping my chest, pushing the water out of me.

A paramedic tries to take his place, but his powerful arm pushes the EMT away without breaking stride.

I feel a gush of water come out of my lungs, and my nose begins to burn.

He pushes my head to the side so the water has an easier path out.

I start coughing and gasping for air, then convulse and spit up what I estimate to be a grande-size amount of pond water.

Well, I can't be that dead if I'm measuring water in Starbucks cups.

"Sloan!" yells Hughes.

"Scott," I say through coughs, using his first name.

I start to get up. He pushes me back.

"Stay down, for crying out loud," he commands.

"Not my first resusci—" A mouthful of disgusting water completes my sentence. "Giving or receiving," I finally say without any of the confidence I'd intended.

I realize that my wetsuit is open, with my bra visible to the crowd gathered around me. If the alligators and being drowned didn't kill me, the embarrassment might.

Hughes lets a paramedic bring me oxygen. I take a deep breath, make a cough like a chain-smoker, and try to sit up.

It takes all my effort, but damn if I'm going to lie here like a helpless resuscitation practice dummy.

"Miss, you really should . . . ," the paramedic starts as he pushes on my shoulder.

I pull his hand away and avoid making a rude comment. I simply nod and ignore him. I still see stars, and everything is a bit fuzzy.

"What happened?" I finally ask. I can't remember much after going into the pipe.

"Hughes got you," says Solar.

I realize my boss has been kneeling behind Hughes the whole time.

I look at Hughes. He's wearing his polo shirt and slacks, soaked head to toe.

I glance at the lake. Shiny eyes stare back at me.

"You dived in? From here?" I ask.

"You would have done the same," he tells me.

I hear the sound of thrashing tails. "Um . . . I hope you aren't counting on that."

"Miss . . ." The paramedic reaches a hand toward me.

"I'm fine!" I say, ready to swat him away.

Hughes points to my head. I touch my hair and look at my fingertips. They're covered in blood.

"Let him do his job," says Solar.

I let the paramedic tilt my head forward so he can inspect the wound.

"This may sting. God knows what's in that pond," he tells me.

I feel the burn of antiseptic and embarrassment at the gathered crowd. More than a few phones are recording me—and these people are supposed to be professionals. God only knows what's being texted right now.

"What happened?" I ask.

"We're still trying to figure that out," replies Solar.

I look down at my arms and legs. The suit has some scuffs and tears, but nothing that looks like an alligator bite.

"Did it hit me with its tail?"

"That wasn't an alligator. It was the pump," he says.

I turn to look at the pillbox pump house. "I thought it wasn't on. What the hell?"

"I said it wasn't working," replies Antonio from somewhere outside my field of view. "Technically, there's a difference."

"Technically?" Hughes asks.

"If she'd been more careful around the gate, this wouldn't have happ—"

Antonio's words are cut short by what sounds like a punch followed by a body hitting the grass.

"Medic!" somebody shouts.

Oh lord.

I turn around to see who delivered the punch. Solar is shaking his head while Hughes is standing over Antonio's unconscious body. Someone reaches a hand to restrain him. Hughes glares at them, and they back away from the former special operator.

"Hughes, why don't you escort McPherson to the hospital," Solar says as calmly as possible. "I'll tend to Mr. Antonio."

The Army Corps of Engineer comes to his senses, sits up, and yells, "I want him arrested!"

I see Solar's nostrils flare. He's about to say something but thinks better of it and kneels instead, whispering something into Antonio's ear.

I don't know what he said, but the look on Antonio's face suggests that it was a threat he knows Solar will deliver on.

"I'm fine. Just a misunderstanding," mutters Antonio.

I let the paramedics put me on a gurney. I would have fought this a few minutes ago, but the situation has gotten too far out of hand. Making a quick exit seems like the best solution.

As they put me into the back of the ambulance, Hughes climbs inside. He watches me like a concerned brother. I can tell by the redness in his cheeks he's embarrassed by what he did.

"Thank you for saving me from the gas chamber. I was about to take my fish knife to his throat," I joke, trying to lighten the mood.

Hughes shakes his head in disbelief. "Heck of a first day back on the job."

CHAPTER 5
SIDELINED

My boyfriend Run—"partner" is the more contemporary term, I guess—sits on the edge of the hospital bed, looking down at me. Jackie stands at the foot of the bed, arms crossed, resembling my mother more and more every day, her face frozen in a scowl.

"Do I give her the lecture? Or is it your turn, Dad?" she asks in a voice far too mature for just having turned fifteen.

"I know," I reply.

"First off, if you want to be an influencer, we need to talk about your choice of underwear," my daughter tells me.

My cheeks burn when I realize what she's talking about. "It's on the news?"

"TikTok, Reels, everywhere, Mom."

"But that was only a few hours ago."

"Welcome to the twenty-first century," she says in that disdainful way that makes me feel like a character out of *The Flintstones*.

"Don't worry," she adds. "Uncle Scott decking that guy is getting more views."

"Where is he?"

I lost track of him when they pulled me into a room for skull X-rays.

"In the waiting room talking to his wife," says Run.

"Did you speak to him?"

"I thanked him for knocking that guy out for me. I can tell he feels bad, but he shouldn't."

My stomach is in knots. "He could get into a lot of trouble."

"We'll hire him a lawyer and make that other guy's life a nightmare. We stick by our friends," says Run.

Run has never shown the slightest hint of jealousy over my friendship with Hughes. We're both at that place in our lives where we know we're with the person we want to be with.

In truth, Hughes is like one of my brothers—in fact, more like a brother than my actual brothers. My siblings and I love each other dearly, but I'm the only one who stuck with the family tradition of working on water.

"How are we doing?" says Dr. Nadella as she enters the room. She's a compact woman who has been attending to me since I showed up in the emergency room.

Sadly, this is not my first run-in with her. A diver herself, she's an expert in diving-related accidents and has used Hughes and me for many textbook examples of things gone wrong.

"Fantastic. I was just getting chewed out by my daughter," I tell her.

"Good for her. Maybe you should listen. Don't they have robots for this kind of thing?"

"The alligators ate the robot."

"And that's what made you decide it was a good idea to go into the water?" my daughter asks with a sarcastic tone.

"We're in the every-adult-in-my-life-is-an-idiot phase," I explain.

"No, Mom. Just you. Dad doesn't even come close."

Well, I could tell her stories about Run as a teenager, but I keep my mouth shut.

Dr. Nadella flashes a light in my eyes to check for a concussion. "The X-rays looked fine. No new fractures. Although I'm surprised you don't wear a helmet when you dive," she says casually.

"That's only for technical dives," I defend myself.

"Uh-huh," says Dr. Nadella. "And going through a drain pipe isn't a technical dive?"

"Point taken. I'll make sure it's on the next time."

"The next time?" Jackie asks, exasperated.

"That's the 'underwater' part of being in an Underwater Investigation Unit."

"Maybe focus on the 'investigation' part instead? Oh, wait, you get into just as much trouble on land. Remind me why we canceled our trip to Catalina . . . ," she asks rhetorically.

She knows. I had a bit of a shoot-out there.

Dr. Nadella checks the bruises on my arms and legs. They're starting to get a nice yellow color around the edges.

"I'm surprised Solar let you go in there," says Run.

"I didn't give him much of a choice. I should have called up Fred Stafford and asked him for some tips."

"You talk to him lately?" asks Dr. Nadella.

"Stafford? No. Not in forever. You know him?"

"I've been taking care of his bang-ups for years. He's got the record for time spent in the barometric chamber downstairs. He always comes to the Fort Lauderdale Dive Club meetings. I didn't see him yesterday. I assume he's off fixing a pipeline or surveying a cave somewhere. Usually, he tells me when he does so I can forewarn the local hospital." She thinks it over. "I should give him a call, just to check in. He's getting up there."

"I should too," I reply. "Am I good to leave?"

Dr. Nadella lets out a laugh. "Not a chance. Just stay the night so I can check in on you. Okay?"

Run kisses me on the forehead. "We'll come see you first thing."

So much for that hot bath and beer.

Jackie leans over and gives me a hug. "I love you, Mom."

The two of them leave, and I feel a wave of sadness wash over me. Not only because they're going home and I'm stuck here, but also partly out of self-pity: after all, my close calls are so frequent that they've become routine.

CHAPTER 6

BEACHED

After Run picked me up from the hospital in the morning, I decided to drive to our HQ for our first official day back at UIH.

As I enter, George Solar has his laptop open on the table in the center of the Underwater Investigation Unit "office." It's a remodeled boat-repair warehouse on a canal just off the Intracoastal Waterway in Fort Lauderdale that provides quick access via boat to the ocean and the Everglades via the 84 Canal.

It's been weeks since I was here. The table, desks, and filing cabinets are still where I last saw them. The biggest difference is that Gwen Wylder, a recently retired Miami Police Department homicide detective, now sits at a desk in the corner, going through files.

Gwen is working with the UIU as a contractor to help us research cases. Brash, rude, utterly frank, and quick-tempered, Gwen is a genius at what she does. Once you realize you can bark back at her, she isn't such a terror to deal with.

"Hey, look who it is, the underwater crash-test dummy," Gwen says. "Were you blended or pureed?"

I don't have the energy for a sharp comeback. "Nice to see you, Gwen."

She makes a disgusted look at my polite response. I guess she was hoping for a little verbal sparring.

I try out an insult of my own. "I see Solar put you as far away from the front entrance as possible. I assume that was intentional."

Gwen gives me a nod of approval. Sharp remarks are her way of bonding, I've come to realize.

"I wasn't expecting you for another week," says Solar.

I take the seat opposite his. "Run's at work and Jackie's at school."

"That's not how time off works." He slides a folder over to me.

"What's this?" I open it and see pages of lab reports.

"Early forensics from the bodies in the van. Kind of clear-cut. Spoiler alert—the guy spotted with a bloody T-shirt buying lottery tickets at the gas station near the site of the second murder has priors, and there's a DNA match."

"I'll check it out anyway. Anything to take my mind off the news."

"About that . . ."

My stomach lurches. We haven't had a conversation about what happened yet. I've been dreading this since the moment I woke up on the shore of the lake.

"We're going to take a week or two before we officially announce we're back in operation," says Solar. "I think we need to get a few things in order. I've asked Hughes to take some time off. I'm pretty sure I told you the same thing in my text this morning."

"No. You said it might be a good idea if I took some time off. There's a difference. That's a suggestion."

Solar is not amused. "Okay. Then how about an order?"

"How about something to work on?" I point at Gwen. "What's she doing? Can I help?"

"Cleaning up the mess you chimpanzees have made of your case-work. Thank you, no," Gwen calls from across the office.

"I need some time to let things settle down," Solar tells me.

"The brigadier general from the South Atlantic Division of the Army Corps of Engineers called to yell at George for letting Scott knock out their dimwit. So, what he's trying to tell you, for Scott's sake, is to stay home," Gwen translates.

Solar has a hand to his temple. A gesture he makes in frustration. Well . . . I assume it's what he does when he's frustrated, but I've only seen him do this when talking to me . . . and now Gwen.

"Let me talk to him," I tell Solar. "I'd like to give him my opinion on the fine work the Corps is doing down here. We can also talk about the polluted runoff they've been discharging from the lakes. Have you seen what that does to the seagrass?"

"McPherson, these people literally move mountains and change the course of rivers. Along with that comes connections that go a lot deeper than anything I've got. The governor is on our side only as long as we don't start any new battles for him. We need to take a breather for a week. That's all."

"But Hughes shouldn't be on administrative leave or punished on my account," I insist.

"Actually, he should." Solar holds up his hand to let me know he's not finished. "But that's not how we work around here. It was justified in my book, and I'm not going to throw him under the bus. I need the general to cool down and move on to something else.

"In a day or so, the media is going to lose interest in the punch and start asking why this happened in the first place. The general wants to postpone that for as long as possible by distracting from the fact that their incompetence almost killed you."

"Fine. Just let them know that if they go after Hughes, Run and I will hire an attorney—one of those jerks down in Miami you hate so much—and make their lives hell."

"Let's not let it come to that. Okay?"

"Fine." I let go of the chair I've been clenching.

"Since sitting still is impossible for you, I have a project you can work on while you're not here. After what happened last night, I realized that part of our problem is that we have no set procedures."

"Each situation is unique," I reply.

"Sure . . . but, being a diver, you have certain safeguards you always follow—or rather, most divers do. For example, last night you should have had on a helmet."

"I have one," I reply.

"And?"

"I left it at home."

"It's a miracle you're alive."

I feel the same way. "Understood. So, what do you want?"

"A manual. I want you to take a look at the different situations we've been in and put together a guide to best practices."

"Can't I just write 'don't be stupid' on a sticky note and put it on my dashboard?"

"Will you pay attention to it?" he asks.

"Uh, sometimes? Seriously? A rule book? That's never been your style."

"Maybe some things have to change. And don't think of it as a rule book but more of a curriculum." Solar watches me closely as the words set in. "Underwater Investigation 101: Would this be an online thing or something taught at a community college? How about a MasterClass? We have a lot of practical knowledge we can pass on."

"Pass on to whom?" I ask.

"Other agencies. Other departments," he replies.

There's hesitation in his voice. He's leaving something out. I catch a glance at Gwen, who's pretending to study the blank side of a folder.

A disturbing thought hits me. "Are you looking to replace me?"

"No, McPherson. At some point I'm going to have to *promote* you. That means finding someone younger and dumber to do what you and Hughes do."

"I thought that's what robots are for."

"After last night, I'm pretty sure we're far from that being a reality. Either way, if we're going to expand, we're going to need more capable people. Ideally ones that can learn from our institutional knowledge and not make the same mistakes."

"So, an employee workbook for new hires?" I ask.

"And something we can share with others to build relationships," he adds.

My anxiety goes down a notch, but I can't shake the feeling that if Solar wanted to ease me out or have me step aside, this is exactly the way he'd break it to me.

From the look on Jackie's face, Run's indifference, and Solar telling me to make way for a replacement, I'm getting some very strong signals here that scare me almost as much as . . .

CHAPTER 7
DREAMERS

My chest is contracting. It's dark. There's a feeling I can't quite place. Everything is closing in.

"Sloan!"

I feel so small.

"Sloan!"

I feel like I forgot how to breathe.

"Sloan!" Run shouts.

My eyes open. I'm sitting up in bed. Run's arms are around me. I can see the antenna mast of my boat swaying outside in the water. The bright lights of the Fort Lauderdale high-rises glimmer in the background. I remember when I could count them in one glance as a little girl.

I'm breathing semi-normally now. Run is rubbing my back.

"Are you okay?"

"What?" I'm still confused. "What happened?"

"You were having some kind of nightmare."

I put a hand to his face and stare into his eyes and feel his skin. This brings me comfort. I don't want him to let me go. I try to think of what happened, but it's already fading. "I don't remember."

"Probably just reliving what happened in the pipe, hon."

"It's not that. I don't think so. Maybe I just hit my head harder than I thought." I look at the clock and realize it's past midnight. "Happy birthday, babe."

"Oh, that," he says. "I hope you didn't plan anything."

"I didn't," I answer with a twinge of guilt. Actually, something is planned, but Jackie did all the arranging. I just said yes and gave her a budget to work within.

In my defense, arranging a party in my family only takes a phone call. We have almost monthly bashes at our home that usually start off spontaneously on a Saturday afternoon when Run invites a few friends over and calls my dad.

When your friends are avid anglers, fresh mahi-mahi will likely appear on the grill. And lobster, if it's in season.

I had a friend in high school who once lamented that she never got invited to our parties. I had to explain to her nobody ever got invited. People just showed up. It's a tradition that Run inherited from my family. His parents' parties were fancy social affairs with valets and staff serving from silver platters. Whereas we McPhersons crack crabs on newspaper alongside bowls of chips and beer. Lots of beer. One side of our four-car garage resembles a beer cave.

"Why don't you go back to sleep," he suggests.

"Sure." I crawl over and lay my head on his chest. "This okay?"

"Perfect."

When I wake up, Run has already left for his office. He brokers and remodels luxury yachts—which means having to take phone calls at all hours of the day, depending upon the billionaire he happens to be dealing with.

Run and my father are a lot alike in some ways and complete opposites in others. My dad has gone boom and bust his whole life—mostly bust. Run was born into one of the wealthier families in South Florida, but despite having a trust fund that could finance a small navy, he's worked since he was twelve.

When I brought Run home from high school to one of our parties to meet my parents, I found out Dad had known him before I did. Run would drive a little Zodiac raft around the marinas and offer to clean bottoms of boats. Some people appreciated his moxie and hired him whether they needed a cleaning or not.

Run ran the numbers and soon had two other kids on rafts performing the same service. He then got a knack for finding out what kind of gear people wanted and who had something good to sell. He progressed from fishing rods to yachts by the time he was nineteen.

As his clients and his fees went more upscale, I noticed the similarity between Run and Dad.

My father is a deep-sea treasure hunter who does whatever he can to support that habit. His biggest unclaimed prize is a gold-laden Spanish man-of-war somewhere off the coast of Florida. To finance his expeditions, Dad gets wealthy clients to invest in the endeavors. He sells them on the dream. That's his real product.

The same goes for Run. His clients hire him because they want to be Run: a handsome, happy-go-lucky guy who catches marlin in the morning and sits back and watches the sun go down in the evening while eating his catch and drinking a beer on the porch of a beautiful home overlooking the water.

The biggest difference between them is the number of zeros in each transaction. Also, one of the two activities earns you something tangible afterward.

Oddly enough, it's usually my father's. He takes his investors on expeditions, and they get to experience the thrill of the hunt. While he hasn't scored the big one—and giving him money means you'll likely never see it again—his clients get a story to tell.

Dad got sued once by the upset family of a man who helped finance one of his expeditions. When the judge saw the meticulous records (thanks to my mother) and realized that Dad not only had spent the money on exactly what he said he would but also had spent his *own* money and run a loss, he threw the case out.

While Dad is a bullshitter extraordinaire, he's got a reputation as a straight shooter. He gives his investors exactly what he promised: adventure.

By contrast, Run's clients are never satisfied for long. If he suggests a more modest watercraft, they invariably want something bigger and better, thinking that's how they'll access the best inventory he has.

A Qatari businessman once tried to offer Run an enormous sum to buy his home and boat. Run declined. He didn't need the money, and he knew the man wouldn't find the happiness he was after. There was also some ambiguity as to whether I was supposed to be included in the deal.

Both Run and Dad know who they are and what makes them happy. I envy them.

I know I'm happy in the water, but if that were taken from me, I'm not sure what I'd have left.

Deep down, I know Solar is right. I can't keep doing the dangerous dives forever. I don't have to put up my fins just yet, but I shouldn't be swimming into alligator-infested waters when I'm a grandmother—at least not professionally.

In other words, I need to figure out who I am besides Danger.

CHAPTER 8
SEA PEOPLES

I'm standing by the wooden railing at the far end of the dock away from the party. I said my hellos and worked the house back to front, welcoming everyone, then came out here to catch my breath before making another round of small talk.

The fading golden ripples of light from the setting sun dance in the Intracoastal. Water always relaxes me. In the plans for our new house, we have water in some form in every room. Reflecting pools, waterfalls, massive aquariums . . . Run already has the property picked out, but I can't quite pull the trigger on it. It's one thing for me to live in his mansion that he acquired while we were apart. It's another to tell him to spend more than I'll ever make in my lifetime on something as extravagant as that.

We're a devoted couple in every sense of the word, but I still have my boat, the *Eclipse*, tied up at the dock. I use it as my office and quiet space. While there's plenty of room in our seven-thousand-square-foot house, it will always feel like Run's house.

My boat's my own little kingdom. When the world is too much, I can sail away to wherever I want. Not that I do that anymore, but it comforts me to think that I could.

"How you doing, sis?" asks my brother Robbie.

He's two years older and resembles our father more and more the older he gets. A practical businessman, Robbie doesn't have the capacity for bullshit like Dad. He's a good husband and father and treats Jackie like she's his own daughter.

After I gave birth to Jackie and pushed Run away, Robbie was there for me, helping out his teen sister and her child. Actually, nobody in my family ever passed judgment on me. They referred to Run as "That Bastard Run" for a while—mostly in his presence—but I was never made to feel ashamed.

"I'm good," I reply.

"Is that a polite 'good' or a sincere 'good'?"

"Both?"

Robbie leans on the railing next to me. "Well, if you ever want any bad advice, you know you can come to me."

"Are you happy?" The question comes out of nowhere.

"We're great. The kids aren't assholes. Yeah, I'd say I'm happy," he says.

"That sounds like a dodge. You didn't directly answer the question."

"My sister the cop. I don't know. All the parts are there, I guess. We have our ups and our downs. I have nothing to complain about."

"Another dodge. It's me—Sea Monkey. Tell me how you feel."

He laughs. "I haven't called you *that* in a while. Although it *is* still your contact name in my phone . . . I don't know, Sloan. To be honest, really honest, the first thing I think when I see your name in the news is, 'Oh my god, I should be there protecting my little sister.' Stupid, I know. But that's my first reaction."

"We're looking to expand. I can put in a word," I joke.

"Maybe. That's the other thing. I also feel pride. You have no idea how proud you make me feel. The kids, you're their hero. Robbie Junior once made the comment that you were 'one of the cool ones' in the family. And that kind of brings me to the third thing I feel—jealousy.

Not that my kids look up to you. They also look up to a YouTuber who threads spaghetti noodles through his nose. I'm jealous because not a second of you is wasted. You are one of the cool ones. You're like Grandpa and Dad. Maybe even a bit of Uncle Karl, whether you like it or not. You're the most-McPherson McPherson possible."

Uncle Karl did time for trafficking narcotics. It took me a long time to forgive him for that and make my peace. It wasn't easy being in law enforcement with the same last name as a man the DEA and FBI had brought to justice.

Robbie stares out at the waves. "I miss the adventure a little, I guess, but I don't feel it in my blood like you and Dad. I guess that's what I envy. Not that work on the water—but that you have it. I knew it wasn't in me by the time I was twelve, and I'd find any excuse to stay home or hang out in whatever tiny library was on the nearest island."

Some kids collected comics. Robbie collected library cards from all the different places we docked at. If he wasn't checking books out when we got to port, he was mailing them back to where he'd borrowed them from.

Dad once told him, "You don't have to use your real name when you get the card."

Robbie was mortified at the insinuation and made some comment about Dad being no different from the "Sea Peoples" he obviously inherited his morality from.

I thought that was just some generic term he'd invented. I had to go to the library and look it up. Reading about an ancient group of mysterious mariners roving the Mediterranean and wreaking havoc was one of the many sparks that kindled my own interest in archaeology.

"Are you considering dialing it back a little?" asks Robbie.

"Fearing it, to be honest."

"Aren't you almost done with your PhD?"

"Almost. Nadine has cut me way more slack than I deserve." Nadine Baltimore has been my doctorate adviser for the last four years. She's let me change my thesis multiple times to adapt to the work I've been doing for the UIU.

I've had people tell me that they can't wait to read my thesis. Neither can I. I've started it over and over multiple times. At first it was going to be a fairly standard assessment of the different underwater archaeological sites in South Florida. But then a couple of grad students with ROVs built in their dorm were able to map out most of the sites I'd planned on including.

This took a bit of the wind out of what I'd thought would be the most thorough survey to date. No hard feelings, but I'd like to introduce their robot to a certain alligator that likes to eat ROVs.

"From my perspective, going from thrill-seeking underwater cop getting shot at to scuba-diving archaeologist not getting shot at sounds like an upgrade."

"Fair point. It's just . . ." I can't find the words.

"You want to leave when you decide it's time. Not be shoved out the door?"

"Sort of. Nobody is shoving, other than fate. I don't know. Thanks for talking to me about it."

"Hey, Mom!" Jackie comes up to the deck with her friend Claire following behind.

"What's up?"

"Claire and I were talking to Kayla and Josie, and we had an idea. You know they all got PADI certified. What if we all went on a night dive?" she asks excitedly.

"An all-girl night dive!" says Claire. "We could totally get that in the school newspaper!"

I look at Jackie's excited face, and I start to get dizzy. Something punches a hole in my stomach straight to my spine, and my knees buckle.

Robbie grabs my elbow. "You okay?"

"Yeah. Fine. I didn't eat all day," I lie.

Jackie is confused and stares at me. "Mom?"

"We'll talk about it, sweetheart. Okay? I'm going to get something to eat and sit down."

I make a beeline for the house, ashamed of the lie. Well, not a lie, but a cover-up.

I run into Wendy Quintez, the owner of a dive shop on US 1. "Hey, Sloan, I was hoping I could catch you. Do you have a second?"

I want to brush her off, but there's a tone in her voice.

"What is it?"

"Do you know Fred Stafford?"

"Yeah. How is he?" Fred's the expert diver who they would have called instead of me, if they could have reached him.

"I don't know. Nobody has been able to contact him," she explains.

"Could he be on an overseas job?"

"We keep his backup gear at our shop. He always picks it up on the way to the airport. Fred was in the shop a week ago, and nobody's seen him since," she says.

"No mention of a dive?"

"None. We were talking about doing a tour group dive this week. Then nothing. I'm a little concerned."

The shakiness in my knees is gone, and the pit in my stomach has faded. I take a cleansing breath.

"Can you make me a list of everyone you can think of who knows Fred?"

CHAPTER 9
DEEP BACKGROUND

The UIU office is supposed to be closed on Sunday, so I'm in the empty office, reading the missing-persons report that Fred Stafford's girlfriend, Stacy Carlota, filed with the Broward Sheriff's Office.

Although I have the report in front of me, I decide to give her a call in case anything was left out.

"Hello?" Stacy answers the phone sounding exhausted.

"Hello, Stacy Carlota? My name is Sloan McPherson. Do you have a moment?"

"I'm so glad it's you!" she says enthusiastically. "This is about Fred, right?"

"Yes. I'm calling more as a favor. Wendy Quintez asked me if I could look into locating Fred. Can I ask you some questions? Again, this isn't an official call. I'm just trying to help out," I explain.

"Yes. Of course. What can I tell you?"

"First, I have to ask you the basics. I'm sure you already went over these with the police, but just for my satisfaction, I want to ask you directly. Okay?"

"Sure. Of course."

"First, has Fred ever disappeared like this before? I know he travels quite a bit."

"Not like this. We don't live together, so I don't know where he is every day, but Fred doesn't make plans and break them without letting you know. That's not the kind of guy he is."

"Did he have money problems?" I ask.

"Did Fred ever *not* have money problems? The moment he got paid for a job, he'd spend it on some new toy. Fred's always struggling with bills, but he got better about that recently. I think he finally got smart."

A tiny red flag waves whenever someone's financial situation dramatically changes. I have to tread lightly.

"Do you think he could have been involved in something illegal that might have made him need to lie low?" I ask.

"Like drugs? Are you serious?"

"I have to ask."

"Fred would never harm anyone or do anything like dealing drugs. You know him, Sloan."

I've thought I knew a lot of people . . . "I understand. But like I said, I have to ask."

I make a note that Stacy insists Stafford isn't involved in drugs.

"When was the last time you saw him?"

"Last Wednesday. We went to a movie that night, and he fell asleep. He'd been diving earlier in the day and was exhausted."

"Did you two argue?"

"Argue? No. We drove to my place and he passed out on the couch. Older guys, you know."

Actually, not really, since Run and I are almost the same age. But I get her point. A good night's sleep has become a key part of my own idea of a romantic evening.

"You said he went diving. Do you know who with?"

"He didn't say. It could have been alone. He's always testing out new gear. That's what kind of has me scared and why I'm glad you called. I'm worried that . . . well, something could have happened. Just the idea that he's . . ." Her voice fades.

"I'm sure he's fine. Fred is an excellent diver. The best." Although I can name more than a few of the best that the sea took from us.

I hear the sound of sniffling on the other end of the phone. "I'm sorry. I've been having nightmares about him being alone."

I can't think about that too much. I need to deal with my own trauma later. "Any idea who he might have dived with if he wasn't alone?"

"Liza, Pete, Ed. It could have been any of them," she replies.

"Who are they?" I ask.

"Oh. They call themselves the 'Dive Rats.' Fred dives with them almost every week. At least one of them. Well, Liza always dives with her husband, Pete. But Fred and he have dived together as just a pair. Ed too," she explains.

I take the names and contact information and add them to the list that Wendy Quintez gave me.

"Sloan, be honest with me. Is he dead?"

I can tell by the tone in her voice she's spent the last several days preparing herself for this possibility. I don't want to cause her any undue stress, but I also don't want to give her false hope.

"Sometimes people don't want to be found. Other times, well, the worst happens. But I'll do my best to find out."

I hear the front door of the UIU office creak as someone enters.

"Stacy, can I put you on hold for a moment?" I ask.

"Of course."

Gwen Wylder walks into the office and sees me sitting at my desk. "You really are bad at taking a hint."

"Fred Stafford has been missing for several days. I'm talking to his girlfriend. He's a diver."

"Oh. Stafford with two *f*s?" asks Gwen.

"Yes."

"I'll get right on it. If Solar gives you a problem, let me handle it," she offers.

"You are the best and the worst, Gwen."

"It's what I call life balance," she says as she plants herself at her desk.

I unmute my phone. "Hey, Stacy. We're going to ask around and see if we can find out anything. Can you tell me a little more about those friends you mentioned?"

"Sure. I don't know them that well. Fred has been trying to get me to dive, but I hate the water. But anyway, Liza Yurinov and Pete Langshire run a dive shop up near Orlando. Ed Buelman, he's some kind of real estate agent. I think he handles island properties, that kind of thing. I really don't know much else about them. I've met them a handful of times when Fred brought them into my restaurant."

"That's the Tarpon Café?" I ask.

"Yes. I'm the manager. That's where I met Fred, actually. He'd just come back from some pipeline in Guatemala or somewhere."

"Have you talked to any of them?"

"I texted Liza. She said she hadn't seen him for a few days but didn't seem worried."

"Okay. I'll follow up with them. If you need anything, you can reach me at this number. Even if you just want someone to talk to. Understood?"

"Yes. Thank you, Sloan. You know, Fred was very proud of you. He put you up on quite the pedestal."

"Well, Fred's a legend. He taught me more than a few things that saved my life."

I immediately regret my choice of words but can't do anything to unsay them.

"What scares me is that he might have died trapped down there," she says.

"Like in a wreck? Fred knows the layout of every sunken ship on the East Coast. I doubt that could stop him."

"It's not the ocean diving that scared me. It's the caves."

"Cave diving?"

"Yes. That's mostly what Fred and the Dive Rats do—dive underwater caverns," she admits.

I feel my chest tighten. "Understood. I'll call you if I learn anything." I end the conversation abruptly.

"Everything okay?" asks Gwen.

"Fine. Poor woman. I can't imagine what she's going through," I reply.

I excuse myself to go to the washroom and splash cold water on my face. I've done cave dives before, but the thought of them never gave me this much anxiety before. Getting tossed around a dark pipe two days ago probably didn't help.

But it's the thought of something happening to Fred that is most unsettling.

If he's mortal, we all are.

CHAPTER 10
DIVE RATS

I find a group photo of the Dive Rats on Liza Yurinov's Facebook page. Fred is instantly recognizable as they pose in their dive suits, standing in front of a truck before a backdrop of mangroves. Liza appears to be in her late thirties. Her husband, Pete Langshire, looks like he's in his late forties, and Ed Buelman seems midthirties. Ed and Pete have the same close-cropped haircut, while Fred has long, wet hair that hangs down almost to his sunglasses. Fred is considerably older and grayer but just as fit as the rest.

They're all smiles and look like they've just finished an exciting dive. Liza is holding a helmet—actually a bike helmet—in her right hand, and there's a bunch of gear, including a rebreather, in the back of the truck.

I've posed for hundreds of photos like these. There's something special about them. They show that you were part of a group that shared a memorable adventure.

I'm sure a thousand years from now there will be photos—or holograms or whatever—of people in suits smiling before a huge borehole on Europa or some other celestial body.

Fred has no social media footprint of his own. The only way you'd know he existed was from posts of other people mentioning him. Liza and Pete have personal pages and one for their dive shop, the Diver's Bell. Their posts show dive trips in the Atlantic, Florida lakes, underwater caverns, and overseas. The Diver's Bell sells and rents equipment as well as offering classes and dive vacations. From the photos, it would appear that Fred served as dive master on a number of them.

I went to Fred when I wanted to learn how to use a rebreather—a system that scrubs the CO_2 when you exhale and periodically adds in a bit of oxygen so you can stay down longer and go deeper. This is the same way they keep the astronauts from suffocating. As you exhale, your breath is fed through a canister filled with soda lime that absorbs the carbon dioxide. Sensors keep track of how much CO_2 is in your air and how much oxygen you need.

They're pretty simple machines other than the fact that too much oxygen can cause a seizure, and if the soda lime gets wet, it can release a fatal gas.

Although I'd used a rebreather before I could legally drive, I took classes from Fred because nobody knew more about the systems than he did. He'd even worked on exotic liquid-oxygen systems and helped develop air mixes for deep-sea diving.

Fred was a good teacher because he was so methodical. While you could learn a lot in my family, sometimes the explanations were along the lines of "Doing it that way is stupid," rather than technical advice.

Most of us tend to develop bad habits over time as we get away with more and more careless actions. Fred was consistent and precise—at least when I knew him.

I didn't know him during his Dive Rat phase, as far as I'm aware.

The biggest mystery is Ed Buelman. His social media shows various vacation properties he's listed and sold. There are a few shots of him in Miami clubs with affluent-looking people, but not much else. His bio says he grew up in the Northeast and moved to Florida in the early 2000s. He lists diving as his hobby, and his profile picture is him in scuba gear at the bow of a boat.

I decide to call him first.

His phone goes straight to voice mail, so I leave him a message. "Hey, Mr. Buelman, my name is Sloan McPherson. I'm calling about Fred Stafford. Could you give me a call back when you get a chance?"

I try my luck again and call the number for the Diver's Bell.

"Diver's Bell, how can I help you?" asks a female voice.

"Hello, is Liza Yurinov there?" I ask.

"Speaking. How can I help you?"

"My name is Sloan McPherson. I'm calling about Fred Stafford."

"Oh, hey. I think I spoke to you about eight years ago at your dad's place. I see your name in the news all the time. What about Fred?"

"I'm trying to locate him. Nobody has seen him for several days. I was wondering if you spoke to him."

"No. I haven't seen him in about a week," Liza says. "Fred is like that. Some undersea cable will get cut and he'll fly out in the middle of the night to fix it."

"I spoke to Stacy. She seemed very concerned."

"Uh-huh. Stacy is sweet, but she's a bit of a worrier. He might have needed some time away from her. I mean, that's just Fred. Always with the mysteries."

"The dive shop down here says he didn't stop in," I explain. "Police couldn't reach him for a job either."

"We go weeks without hearing from him. I know he's been using more gear from us and purchased a lot of new equipment. He might just not need their help anymore."

I wouldn't describe Liza as indifferent. "Unconcerned" is the better term.

"Maybe so. Let me know if you hear from him. Is your husband around?"

"No, he's out running some gear to Tampa. I can give you his phone," she offers.

"Thank you."

I call her husband next.

"Hello?" Pete Langshire answers.

"Hi, this is Sloan McPherson. I'm a friend of Fred Stafford."

"The famous Sloan McPherson. What can I do for you?"

"I'm trying to track down Fred. He's been missing for a few days, and his girlfriend is a bit concerned. I wondered if you knew anything."

"No. I haven't heard from him either. He didn't mention a job, but that wouldn't be unusual for him. Did you call the shop and speak to Liza? He might have dropped in," he suggests.

"I just did. She hasn't seen him either," I reply.

"Come to think of it, I remember hearing something about him getting some last-minute job working on an oil rig," says Pete.

"Do you remember when that was? Or who it was with?"

"No. I just remember it coming up in conversation. Maybe a week ago?"

"When was the last time you spoke to him?"

"Let me think for a second . . . Maybe last Thursday? He drove up from Fort Lauderdale to the shop to get some air tanks refilled."

Stacy said he spent Wednesday night with her. That puts him up in the Orlando area late Thursday afternoon. After that, his whereabouts are a mystery.

I'll have to see if I can get his phone records to find out where he's been, but that could be tricky. Meanwhile, I'll have to keep searching the old-fashioned way.

"Do you think Ed Buelman might have some idea?" I ask.

"Possibly. He and Fred have been palling around a lot. Liza and I call them the Odd Couple," he says with a laugh.

"Why is that?"

"You know Fred. He's worn the same pair of pants for twenty years. I don't think Ed has ever worn the same shirt twice."

"How did you meet Buelman?"

"He wandered into our shop one day and bought one of just about everything. That's a good guy to know in our business."

"Had he dived before?"

"Ed? Some. More like resort diving. He was interested in doing more adventurous stuff."

"Cave diving?" I ask.

"Yep. You do much?"

"Not lately."

"You should come with us next Friday. A bunch of us are going out to Neptune's Labyrinth. You ever dived there?" he asks.

Neptune's Labyrinth has long been the stuff of Florida urban legend. It's reputed to be a pristine cave deep in Central Florida and known to only a few people. I would probably know more about it if I hadn't spent my life and career in South Florida.

"No. It's hard to get to, isn't it?"

"It is if you don't know the secret way."

"Sounds interesting," I respond, although my knee is suddenly shaking. "Maybe if Fred turns up, we can all go."

"Well, Fred or not, count yourself invited. You should really see it before it gets ruined," says Pete.

"We'll see. Do you know how I can get hold of Ed?"

"He's got two numbers. Let me give them both to you."

"Any luck?" Gwen asks after I hang up.

"No, not really. I've got one more person to talk to."

I dial Ed Buelman's other number.

"Yo!" says a friendly voice.

"Hello, my name is Sloan McPherson. I'm calling about Fred Stafford."

"What did he do?" Buelman jokes.

"Nothing. Nobody has seen him, that's the issue. I was wondering if you've talked to him."

"Probably not since last week. Is everything okay?"

"Stacy's worried about him. She hasn't heard from him in days."

"Ah. Poor gal. I don't think she ever understood Fred's lifestyle. He could be six hundred feet below the ocean welding a pipeline or in the arms of another woman right now. There's no telling with Fred. He likes to live on the edge a bit. Too fast for me, sometimes. You're bound to crack under pressure at some point, you know."

"Maybe so. If you hear anything, please let me know."

"Of course," says Ed. "I like Stafford."

I click off and stare at the photo of Fred with the others. They all look happy. Like they all have each other's backs. But after talking to his friends, I'm not sure how true that is.

"Can I give you a couple people to look into for me?" I ask Gwen.

"Liza Yurinov, Peter Langshire, and Ed Buelman?"

"Yeah . . . ," I say, a little puzzled.

"I took a look over your shoulder and looked them up."

"Um, thanks. I'm going to go talk to Hughes."

"You going to pull him into this too?" asks Gwen.

"No. I just want to check in."

"Uh-huh."

CHAPTER 11
Locus

When I pull up to Hughes's house, his garage door is open and he's holding his daughter, Callie, in his arms as he stares down at the different parts to what looks like a disassembled underwater robot on a table.

"Training your apprentice?" I ask as I step into the garage.

He's still staring at the robot, then realizes I mean his daughter. "Oh, her. I could only hope so. You want to build robots that get torn apart by mean alligators?" he asks her.

Callie decides she'd rather grab his nose and giggle. "Down," she commands.

"Remember what happened the last time I put you down in the workshop? Mommy found you playing with the welder. Daddy got in *big* trouble. He didn't get to watch what he wanted on TV for a whole week," he explains in a singsong chant that sounds surreal coming from the mouth of a former navy diver.

"My childhood was different. My family would have taken it as a sign of interest and hung me over the stern to weld a mount." A slight exaggeration, but not by much.

"She loves the toy tool set you bought her. She bangs that plastic hammer on everything. Cathy's been meaning to thank you."

"Well, I owe her for taking Jackie into a Kate Spade. We were getting on just fine with Forever 21."

I've tried to explain to Jackie that even though she lives in a huge house and stands to inherit her father's trust fund, money has value, and she can't feel entitled to everything she wants. To her credit, she understood and asked if she could work at Run's marina. The thought of her spending that much time around a bunch of drunks on pleasure boats didn't put me at ease. She's fifteen going on . . . I don't want to think about that.

I suggested she work in his office instead.

"Anyway," I tell Hughes, "I want to thank you."

"Thank me? I was going to apologize. If my little gator chew toy had worked, you never would have had to go in there. And if I hadn't been so focused on salvaging it, I would have checked out that pump house."

"Hey, you were there when it counted," I tell him. "That's what matters. You always are."

"So are you." He uses a free hand to pat the controls for the robot. "But if I can get these things working, we won't have to do that as much."

"Here's hoping. You talk to Solar?"

"Not for a few days. I took his suggestion that I take some time off to heart. Although I just spent a lot of time off. Whatever it takes to stay on his good side," he says with a shrug.

"Are you kidding? You're his golden boy. You can do no wrong."

"Are *you* kidding? I can think of a few wrongs off the top of my head."

"The asshole you dropped? You saved me the trouble. If he comes for you, I'll go for his throat with the most vicious lawyer I can hire." The threat feels hollow when I realize I would have to do it with Run's money.

"Thanks. Any news on Stafford?" he asks.

"Gwen told you?"

"I never reveal my sources," Hughes says with a smirk. "Especially ones with a mean streak a mile long."

"Yeah. Nothing yet. I spoke to some of his friends."

"The Dive Rats?" asks Hughes.

"Yeah . . . Why did I even drop by if Gwen's already given you the details?"

"That's all I know. That and something about Neptune's Labyrinth."

"You've heard of it?"

"Dive spot near the Devil's Cauldron, isn't it?"

The Devil's Cauldron is a bit of Florida hokum. It's the alleged center of all things weird, from Skunk Ape sightings—our version of Bigfoot—to alien encounters and a hole in the ground from which the devil is said to crawl up from hell to do evil on Earth.

"I guess so," I say. "But technically I think there are a couple Devil's Cauldrons. Basically, any sinkhole in a remote area gets that title. Geography be damned."

"It certainly does have a spooky factor. I remember an old survival instructor I had in the navy. He said they'd drop guys off by themselves in the middle of the swamp at night near the Devil's Cauldron, and they'd have to find their way back. Apparently, they eventually started using a different part of the Everglades because guys kept coming back with weird stories. He said a super-rational guy he knew swore a pair of orange eyes followed him everywhere he went. He convinced himself it was a runaway orangutan to keep from driving himself nuts."

"I've seen plenty of weird things, and Dad would have you believe he shook hands with the Loch Ness Monster, but that's pretty damn creepy."

"The other stories were even stranger," says Hughes. He turns to Callie. "But you don't believe in monsters, do you?"

Callie shakes her head and giggles.

"Apparently Neptune's Labyrinth is supposed to be an amazing cave-diving spot nobody knows about," I tell him.

"You believe that?"

"It wouldn't surprise me. I know of a few spots like that myself that don't appear on any map and you won't see in a documentary."

I can tell you a spot in the Pacific where you'll see more great white sharks in an hour than you can any other place on the planet. I know a cove where you can almost walk from one side to another on the backs of dolphins that are smarter than any I've ever encountered. The sea is still full of mysteries; you just have to look harder to find them.

"I think I see where this is going," says Hughes. "If it's a missing motorcyclist, you check the morgue. A missing lumberjack, you check the forest. A missing diver . . ."

"Yeah. That's what I'm afraid of."

"Is he the kind to dive alone?"

"You mean stupid like me? Yeah. He's more cautious because he does a lot of technical diving. I rarely go down more than thirty feet on most of my inland dives. There aren't a whole lot of places down here that go much deeper. But if he's doing cave dives in Central Florida, who knows?"

"Gwen said she checked all the hospitals. So there's that."

Of course she did. That was my next step, but Gwen is speedier and more thorough.

"Well, obviously I'll have to ask Solar first, but I'm thinking of accepting the invite to dive Neptune's Labyrinth with the Rats on Friday. George wants me taking time off, but this is too good a chance to pass up in terms of nosing around about Fred."

"Let me handle it," Hughes offers.

"Aren't you even more in Solar's doghouse?"

"That's exactly why I should ask. How much more trouble can I get into? If anything, he'll appreciate the brazenness of the request."

"Look at you. This isn't the clean-cut ex-navy guy we hired from Fort Lauderdale."

"I guess you've been rubbing off on me."

"Ha. I think Solar hoped the influence would go the other way. Joke's on him. So, yeah, ask him and tell me what happens. And let me know if you need a job reference when he fires you."

"Will do. Where are you heading now?" he asks.

"I'm going to ask for a key to Stafford's house from his girlfriend to check it out," I reply.

"Let me take Callie back in and I'll come with you."

"What about your . . . creation?" I ask, gesturing to the robot parts.

"That can wait. I'd much rather go chasing after Bigfoot in the Everglades."

CHAPTER 12
DRY DOCK

Fred Stafford's house is at the end of a road in an unincorporated area near Davie, Florida. A tall chain-link fence stretches across the front of the property with a gate in front of the empty driveway. The lawn is a little high but not out of control. The house itself is a single story painted blue with a gravel path that leads to the backyard.

I rattle the gate in case Stafford has a dog Stacy forgot to tell us about. Nothing barks or comes running at us, so I unlock the gate using one of the keys Stacy gave me.

Hughes and I walk up to the front door and put on latex gloves. If we find ourselves in a crime scene, we don't want our fingerprints making a mess of things.

I knock on the door. "Fred? Are you there?"

I wait a beat, then try again. "Hey, Fred, this is Sloan McPherson. I'm coming in."

The door shows no sign of forced entry, so I grab the handle and give it a twist.

"Locked," I tell Hughes as I find the right key.

Hughes puts his hand near his gun. Neither of us expects to have to draw our weapon, but you can never be too sure.

I push the door open and reveal a dark living room. The blinds are down, but I can see a television, coffee table, armchair, and TV console. The furniture is basic. The kind of thing you buy at Walmart when you're single and don't expect to spend much time at home.

"Very bachelor pad," says Hughes. "Looks like my place when I was in the navy. I thought Stafford made good money."

"Fred was paid well when he did underwater construction jobs, but he also spent his money quickly. You'd see a fifty-thousand-dollar watch on his wrist and then a hundred-dollar one six months later. I don't know if he gambles, but it wouldn't surprise me."

I turn on the light switch so Hughes and I don't have to walk around in the dark.

"Fred? You home?" I call out.

There's still no answer.

Hughes and I make a quick sweep of the kitchen area directly ahead and then into the two bedrooms and bathrooms. One of us enters while the other covers. It's a bit routine for us, but an essential procedure.

After giving the laundry room and garage a quick inspection, we return to the living room so we can perform a more thorough search.

So far, I've seen no signs of violence. The house looks like Fred walked out the door and never came back. But that's based on a quick inspection that was only intended to make sure he wasn't lying unconscious or dead here. We also needed to make sure that there wasn't anybody else lurking around.

I once did a search of a trailer home, helping another agency with a fugitive roundup. We'd heard the suspect was last seen inside, but after searching every corner of the small dwelling, we were ready to give up.

However, something told me to look closer. I don't know if it was intuition or OCD, but I went back into the bedroom and opened up the closet one more time.

There were scattered shirts on hangers and a pile of clothes on the floor. We'd searched the closet before and moved on. This time I gave the clothes a kick and felt my foot hit something . . . or rather someone.

"Don't shoot," the suspect shouted from under the pile of dirty clothes.

It didn't seem possible that someone could hide under there, but someone did.

Point is, you can't let yourself get lazy and treat this like a normal job. Lives are at stake, most importantly your own. A half-assed search so you can get back to the office and finish your paperwork is not only sloppy but dangerous.

"I'm going to check outside. You good in here?" asks Hughes.

"Yeah," I reply. "I'll see if there's anything we missed."

I take out my flashlight and inspect the walls and dark corners. Just because you don't see a pool of blood doesn't mean someone wasn't killed there. It can take a forensic team and fluorescent dyes to pick up traces of blood after even the most gruesome murder.

One of my instructors told us about a case in Plantation, Florida, where a woman reported her husband missing, and then a few days later his head showed up on the front lawn in a garbage bag. Something seemed odd, so detectives had techs do a search of the house. Sure enough, they found blood spatter where the man had his head severed from his body.

The husband and his wife were involved in drug trafficking. She and her boyfriend had decided to rip him off and take him out of the picture. They'd scoured and cleaned the walls and floor, but that only made the techs more suspicious—enough to look in tiny crevices in the baseboards and find the victim's blood.

I don't have the ability to do that kind of search in Fred's house. I can only look for anything out of the ordinary and proceed from there.

On his coffee table are a small tool kit and the parts to a pressure gauge. Fred does occasional work for companies that want him to test their dive gear. His methodical nature and willingness to go deeper and stay down longer than most make him a good judge of equipment quality.

At the edge of the table is a stack of dive logs. This is helpful for monitoring time spent underwater as well as recording where you've been. I pick up the top book. The last entry was two months ago.

Either Fred stopped keeping track or his current dive log is somewhere else—possibly in his truck.

On his kitchen table there's a mask sitting on a newspaper next to some bottles of silicone spray and lubricants. The newspaper is two weeks old, so this doesn't look like a recent project.

I walk into his bedroom again. The bed is unmade and the top drawer to his dresser is partially open. I peer inside and see eight watches in cases. One of them is identical to a watch Run wears. Jackie called it the "Tesla" watch after she heard how much he paid for it.

If Fred had been the victim of a robbery, these would be long gone.

I open the dresser drawer wider and see wads of money from different countries Fred has dived in, alongside assorted coins, household documents, and his passport.

I pick up the passport and take a look at the stamps. The last one was three months ago for a trip to Aruba. I put it back and search the rest of the house.

In the laundry room I notice a stack of plastic containers of various sizes and bottles of liquid I can't identify.

These could be used to clean equipment pieces. I also notice several packages of brushes of different sizes sitting on a shelf.

Back in the kitchen, I spot a patch of dirt next to the sink. I scrape a sample of it into a plastic bag, then pull out my phone and start taking photos of his house. I'm not trying to capture anything specific, but maybe Stacy can tell me if there's anything out of the ordinary—like a huge metal safe that's no longer here.

His garage is lined with metal racks filled with tubs containing dive suits, tanks, gear, and enough equipment for a small dive shop.

In the corner is a washbasin with an air compressor used to fill air tanks. Next to that is a metal cabinet.

I open it and find shelves full of parts for rebreathers. To the side there are several buckets of laboratory-grade soda lime—for scrubbing the air. He's also got a few pure oxygen cylinders sitting on the floor.

In the center of the garage stand two folding tables, pushed up against each other. They look brand new. A box of plastic sheets sits under the tables. Here I see more dirt like what I found by the kitchen sink.

Diving inshore can get muddy. I might be looking at what he cleaned off his equipment. I scrape another sample into a baggie, just in case.

"McPherson?" Hughes calls out.

I walk through the back door and into the backyard. Hughes is standing next to a large aboveground pool—the kind you usually see in YouTube videos when they burst open with too many people inside.

"Testing pool," I say.

"Yeah. That's not what I wanted to show you," says Hughes.

He leads me to the corner of the property where there're two small storage sheds. He pulls open the door of the nearest one.

"The other one has lawn equipment. This one, just this."

Inside is a row of four sawhorses with a sheet of plywood lying on top of them. There's nothing else except an empty box of plastic gloves on the floor.

"What do you think was in here?" he asks.

"I don't know."

"Here's the other thing." Hughes kneels and points to a metal lock and hasp sitting in the grass.

I kneel with him to look at it. There's a padlock key on the key chain that Stacy lent me. I try to slip it into the lock, but it doesn't fit.

"I think it was pried open," he says. "And another thing, if you look at the dirt and grass, you can see that a large truck was backed up in here a few days ago. Whatever was in here, it was moved around the same time Stafford went missing."

"Interesting." I study the top of the plywood. "There's a large table in the garage. I assumed it was a worktable."

My mind races through all the things that might have been on either table. Lots of things. Too many things.

"We'll have to ask Stacy," I conclude.

"Curious, isn't it?"

"Yes, it is. Either Stafford moved something from here in a hurry or someone else came looking for it."

I look down at the key ring Stacy lent me and notice something I hadn't paid attention to before. It's one of those things you see a million times until it becomes background noise.

The key ring is attached to a square piece of foam. I hold it up for Hughes to see.

"A floating key chain?"

These are pretty common in South Florida, where there's a nonzero chance your keys will fall into a pool or canal or the ocean on any random day. I hand him the key chain to look closer at it.

"Oh," he replies. "Think it's a lead?"

"I don't know, but it's one more place to check."

I've owned dozens of key chains like this and rarely paid attention to what was written on them. I almost missed this one: RIVER CREEK CASINO.

It's a Native American gaming resort in the middle of Broward County. Only a twenty-minute drive from here.

A key chain is no proof of anything, but it might be an indication that there's another side to Fred Stafford we didn't know about. Heck, Stacy might not even have known—or didn't want to tell us.

"I'm going to grab a few things for Gwen to look at, then we can head over there. Sound good?" I ask.

"As long as there's a fried Twinkie in it for me," says Hughes, referencing one of River Creek's famous snacks, borrowed from Las Vegas.

CHAPTER 13
RED FLAGS

Lonnie Warren, River Creek Casino's head of security, is a tall, lanky man who still dresses like he's back in Nevada, where he grew up and started working in gaming in the early 1980s. He's guiding us past the slot machines and poker tables to a doorway that leads to the upstairs office.

The casino is clean and modern in contrast to the clientele, who look old and worn out. Exempt from the indoor-smoking laws, cigarettes and cigars burn everywhere, but thanks to advances in HVAC technology, I can barely smell them.

We pass a lounge where a young woman with a beautiful voice is singing a bluesy version of Taylor Swift's "Blank Space" to an almost empty audience.

It's got to be rough performing for two passed-out drunks, but from what I understand from a friend, the pay is good and the work is steady. Singing in an empty Florida casino is probably better than solo karaoke in your apartment.

"I'm actually glad you called," says Warren. "I'd wondered where Staff had been. We hadn't seen him in a while."

"Do you know him?" asks Hughes.

We called the casino to let them know we were coming. I'd mentioned asking about Fred on Warren's voice mail, but that was the extent of what I said.

Warren was waiting for us at the front entrance and greeted us with a toothy smile. He's been in the business long enough to know it's good practice to treat the police like your best friends. When you're running an operation that's illegal only a few hundred meters away and sucks money out of a community that can't afford it, you need to be on good terms with local law enforcement.

Though the casino is federally protected, the surrounding area is county and state property. If the sheriff or governor were inclined, they could put up twenty-four-hour DUI stops at the entrance and exit and scare off a substantial amount of the casino's business.

Because of this, casinos like River Creek go out of their way to be good citizens and sometimes overly accommodating to the police.

Right now I want to lean into that accommodation and find out what happened to Fred Stafford.

Warren takes us up a flight of stairs to his office.

Hughes nods to a door with a sign that says TRIBAL POLICE. Although the tribe has a contract with the Broward Sheriff's Office, the tribal police department is the true authority on the property.

Having them literally next door to the head of security for the casino is convenient.

We enter Warren's office. It's a large room with a wall of monitors and a man and woman in uniforms at desks at one end.

"Nate, Becca, this is McPherson and Hughes from the Underwater Investigation Unit," says Warren.

Becca leaps up from her chair to shake my hand. "It's a pleasure! You made me take up diving."

"Did somebody drown?" asks Nate as he shakes our hands.

"Excuse Nate. We keep him around to annoy the drunks," says Warren.

"And everyone else," adds Becca.

"Why don't you two go make the rounds," he says, dismissing them.

Warren directs us to two chairs while he takes a seat on a couch. A mural of what looks like a Seminole warrior wrestling an alligator hangs over his head.

"What do you want to know about Fred Stafford?" he asks.

"I take it he's a regular?"

"Just about every week." Warren points to a monitor showing an empty poker table. "Table eight. That was his favorite."

"Is he good?" asks Hughes.

"Did he leave with more money than he came in here with? Some days. Most days not. He's no heavy hitter. A few thousand here and there. We try to keep an eye out for people on a real losing streak. Stafford had some big losses but didn't raise a flag in the system."

"A flag?" I ask.

"We use computers to track players. We look for signs of addiction. Believe it or not, we steer them to counseling," he tells us.

"How kind of you," says Hughes.

I suspect the whole operation offends him a bit.

"Not out of kindness. It's bad for business. The last thing we want is for the news to say some poor asshole killed his wife and kids and then himself because he wasted their savings on our slots. I've seen it happen back in Nevada. We had a cozier relationship with the press there, but not so much here. It's bad business to bleed people dry—especially when they're locals.

"If some guy loses his house in Vegas and flies home to Cleveland and blows his brains out, nobody cares. If that happened here, we'd have protesters surrounding the building. Like I said, it's good business to keep track of that." He shoots his cuffs and points to the table in front of us. "That folder contains his win and loss statements. It's not signed; you'd need a court order for that. But nothing is stopping you from having a look."

"We should probably . . . Never mind," says Hughes as I pick it up before he can finish his sentence.

I scan through the pages. They show a pattern of small wagers getting larger seven months ago. His win-to-lose rate didn't change much, but he was losing way more money in total. Hundreds of thousands of dollars in the last two months alone.

"When *do* you flag losses like this?" I ask.

"When it looks desperate. Irrational wagers or using a credit card at ATMs near the casino to get a cash advance to pay for chips. Stafford was using cash from elsewhere. That's generally not a sign of distress. He paid for a few items in the gift shop with his credit card last month, and there was no problem with the charge. When I see credit cards getting declined, I know they're in trouble. Stafford acted like a guy who's earning lump sums and then spending them here. From diving, I assume."

"What did he tell you about that?" I ask.

"I didn't speak to him much directly, but I talk to our staff about people. It helps me keep an eye on this place. The bartenders told me he did underwater construction and that kind of thing. I've got a few guys like that in here. They risk their neck on some dangerous job, then spend it here. I think it's different sides of the same coin."

"Did he ever come in here with anyone?" I ask.

"We can check the tapes, but mostly just alone. I remember a girlfriend, or a woman he knew, coming in with him a year ago."

I pull up a photo of Stacy on my phone. "Her?"

"I don't think so. Same type, but maybe a little younger."

"Do you think he could have been in trouble? Was he gambling outside the casino?"

"You mean illegal games? I make it a point not to know about what happens outside of here. We had some Guatemalans trying to run a poker game in our presidential suite. That lasted all of one day until room service saw the card table. We let tribal police handle them before turning them over."

"Could he have been borrowing money to gamble?" asks Hughes.

"Not from anyone who does that kind of thing for a living. If you want to borrow money from the mob to gamble, they make sure you spend it in their places. That way they can steal it back faster from you. Somebody else? Maybe. There are some people who stake poker players in tournaments. Stafford wasn't that good. I don't know who'd want to back him. Is there anything else I can help you with?"

"Any photos you turn up showing Stafford with other people, like that woman, that would be helpful." I lift the folder. "Can I take this?"

"Take what?" Warren winks.

Outside, Hughes and I stand outside my Chevy Suburban to talk it over.

"What do you think?" asks Hughes.

"Well, we confirmed that there's another side to Fred we didn't know about. The money is suspicious. As far as I know, Fred's work was pretty steady. We could ask Stacy."

"Did Warren seem a little overeager to share?" asks Hughes.

"Possibly. Or he just has his own suspicions and doesn't want it blowing up in his face."

"Now what?"

"I want to know where he's been, where his money came from, and what the hell was in the shed."

"Mm. I think I know what you're thinking," replies Hughes. "They might all be connected."

"But connected to what? Nazi gold? Pallets of cocaine? Nazi cocaine?"

"You gotta suggest that to Solar so I can see how he reacts."

"He'll just give me that look," I say sourly.

"Well, if he does, you'll still know what he's thinking because Gwen will blurt it out for him."

"Oh damn. I never realized that: Gwen is like Solar on truth serum."

Hughes nods. "But seriously . . . we're in deep enough now that we have to take it to him."

CHAPTER 14
DEAD RECKONING

The next day, Hughes, Gwen, and I are sitting at the table in our warehouse headquarters when Solar walks in. I wouldn't describe his expression as happy.

"Most bosses have trouble getting people to come into the office. What is it with you guys?"

"We wanted to talk to you about—" I begin.

"Fred Stafford. I heard," Solar cuts me off.

Hughes and I look at Gwen.

She shakes her head. "I didn't tell him."

"Lonnie Warren called me after you left the casino," explains Solar.

I'm about to blurt out my surprise that Solar knows him but then realize my stupidity. George Solar is a nexus of Florida information. Lord knows how many drug dealers and lowlifes walked through that casino while Solar was keeping tabs on them—including his own people. Clearly, Warren made a courtesy call and maybe also wanted to do a little prying of his own.

I get my argument ready in my head, including how to handle Solar's response.

"Do it," says Solar.

"Uh. What?" I ask.

"I was only keeping you on the sidelines to wait things out. But that doesn't mean we stop policing if there's something important to handle."

"Uh-huh," I reply, skeptical.

"And Miami police just arrested that suspect in the Snake Trail murders. They got fingerprint matches from the bodies you recovered in the van."

"That's it?" I ask.

"That's it. The press won't forget about what happened, but it will just be a footnote as they drool over their latest serial killer, Christopher Lark Armad."

"And the Army Corps of Engineers?"

"I'm going to call the general and ask if he wants to be on the stage while we pat each other on the back for catching the killer or watch from home. I have an idea which way that will go."

The Snake Trail murders case was never ours. We were providing assistance with evidence recovery in the water. However, Solar has enough pull that he can influence who gets credit and who doesn't.

"I hope Antonio doesn't make a fuss."

"He hasn't been an issue since I talked to him that night," says Solar.

"What exactly did you say to him?" asks Gwen.

"It's not important. Tell me about Stafford," he says as he sits.

"We were at the casino because we had a hunch that he might have a gambling problem," I explain.

"And?"

"It was enough for Warren to pay attention to him. Not enough to discourage him from patronizing the casino."

"Yeah. That sounds like Warren. He'll tip me off if suspects are at the tables—but only after they've lost everything."

"Stafford's truck was gone, and it looked like he'd been storing something heavy in the shed and the garage."

"Any idea what?"

"None. I did get some dirt samples," I add.

"Anything?" asks Solar.

"I couldn't find a match for anything."

He nods. "We'll send it out to a different lab now that it's an official case."

I should be happy, but I feel uncertain. "You know," I tell Solar, "there's a chance he's chilling out in some bar in Bermuda, drinking Red Stripe."

"Not without his passport," says Gwen. She's clearly reviewed the inventory list from Stafford's place.

"He could have two," says Hughes.

"I checked the State Department. He doesn't," she responds.

"Either way, there's also the chance that he's floating out in the ocean somewhere because a boat hit him or something else," Solar theorizes.

That's a horrible but realistic thought. Sometimes the biggest hazards in the ocean are the two-legged kind. I worry more about a speedboat pilot ignoring a dive flag than I do about sharks.

"I checked with the parking violations departments from the Keys to Jacksonville. Nobody has seen Stafford's truck in any of the beach lots," says Gwen.

Hughes and I exchange glances.

"Oh, look, they're giving me the 'Oh my god, Gwen knows how to use a computer and email people' look," she tells Solar.

"That brings me to another point I need to make," Solar says. "Especially to you, McPherson. I get that Stafford is a friend of your dad's and that you know many of the people involved, but we have to treat this like real police work. That means everyone is a suspect. Even people you've known. I want you to go back and talk to Stafford's girlfriend, push a little more. I find it hard to believe she didn't know about his gambling."

"I didn't ask," I point out.

"And she didn't offer it," he completes the thought.

It was right there on that key chain. Maybe she didn't realize? I don't know. But Solar is right. I need to speak to her again, in a more professional tone.

"I'll bring her in and talk to her in the side room. Make it more official," I tell him.

"Sound good. Gwen, I see you typing, so I can assume you're already looking up Stafford's cellular accounts. While I can't get a warrant for the records yet, we can see what towers he may have made calls through. And for fifty bucks we can see what phone calls he made from just about anywhere in the Caribbean. If he's alive and well, I want to find out sooner than later," he concludes.

"Stafford's Dive Rat pals invited Sloan to go on a dive," says Hughes. "If the cellular data doesn't lead anywhere, it might not be a bad idea to get up close, see what they know or don't realize they know."

"When is the dive?" asks Solar.

"Friday," I tell him.

"If we think they need a little more scrutiny, I might agree to that. But it has to be both of you. No more stupid solo stunts."

"Actually, that'll be double the stupid," I answer, instantly regretting it.

Solar raises an eyebrow. "Uh-huh."

"What can I do in the meantime?" asks Hughes, covering for me.

"I want you to go back home and repair your toys. I have an uncomfortable feeling we'll be needing them."

While I appreciate the serious attention that Solar is giving this case, I'm a little surprised by it. I walked in here convinced I was going to have to twist his arm. Instead, he's issuing marching orders for us.

"Solar . . . what's up?" I ask him. "All we have is a person who hasn't been seen, yet you seem to be escalating things."

"Part of this business is recognizing patterns, McPherson. It's why you and Hughes started digging in. Between him going missing, what was going on in the shed, and the money problems, I'm seeing an uncomfortable pattern."

"Could you explain a little more?" asks Hughes.

"I hate to say it, but my gut is telling me Stafford didn't bump his head on a boat propeller. He's not relaxing on some beach. He's dead because someone killed him."

CHAPTER 15

SUSPICION

Solar's words bounce around in my head as I sit across from Stacy in the small conference room in the back of our office. A decade ago, this room held blueprints for the boats built and repaired here. A filing cabinet with long, thin drawers still rests against the far wall under the frosted glass that lets in light from the center of the building.

Stacy is nervous. There was a bit of a tremble in her voice when I called and asked her to come in. I could have gone to her, but as Solar pointed out, this is real now, and I need to treat her like a potential suspect.

If she's involved in his disappearance, why would she be the one to call the police when he went missing? Because that's what a guilty person might think an innocent person would do. There are so many podcasts and true crime shows on television now, everybody is an amateur detective and a murder theorizer.

In the same way that medical shows made people think they understood medicine, courtroom dramas and live court TV convinced some people that they can get away with murder if they're smart enough—and everyone thinks they're smart.

The only flaw in that thinking is these shows generally show the methods of people who got caught. The ones who got away don't sit around doing interviews; podcasts don't interview police explaining why they never caught the culprit.

"Did Fred ever talk to you about gambling?" I ask straightaway.

"What do you mean?"

"Did he mention going to casinos?"

"Maybe. I don't recall. Why?"

"Fred was a regular at River Creek Casino. The key chain you gave me? It was from there," I explain.

"Oh. Maybe. I never noticed. He sometimes watched poker tournaments on television, I guess."

"He lost over two hundred thousand dollars there in the last three months. Did you know that?"

Stacy's face freezes. "I knew he was having money problems. Sometimes, we . . . it was a discussion."

That's code for "an argument." Although couples who don't live together don't usually argue about that as much. Unless . . .

"Were you and Fred talking about moving in together?" I ask.

"It's something we talked about a while ago. Nothing ever came of it. Fred was into it, then seemed hesitant."

A couple taking one step forward with that discussion and then pulling back feels like a breakup waiting to happen.

I have to ask an uncomfortable question.

"Did you and Fred break up?"

Stacy looks down at her knotted hands. "We've had arguments. We'd separated before, then came back together. Fred has his ups and downs. We do, I guess."

"And the night he slept at your house, where did he sleep?"

Stacy's eyes begin to water. "The couch. We'd had a fight. He drank too much and was too tired to drive home. He slept on the couch. He was gone before I woke up." She starts to hyperventilate. "And that was the last time I saw him."

I give her a moment to compose herself. This is supposed to be an interview and not a full-on interrogation. I'm pushing a little too hard because I don't want to be duped . . . again.

On my last case, I took a "victim" into protective custody only to realize she was actually who I was after. From the outside, it looked like I was playing a long game to get her to expose herself—at least that's how the media described it. The reality was that I was fooled like everyone else and made serious mistakes that almost enabled her to get away. I still haven't fully processed it.

I reach out and clasp Stacy's hand. "Take your time. I'm just trying to understand Fred's life. That can help me know where to look."

"I know. I know. Thank you, Sloan. It's not easy ending on an argument. I would have told you, but I didn't want you thinking he was gone because he was avoiding me."

Or that you might have killed him.

"Do you know where he got the money he was gambling?"

"He didn't say. I assumed it was from undersea work."

"He was using cash at the casino. They don't normally pay divers that way. Could he have been working for someone else? Someone local who might have paid him in cash?"

"For scuba diving? Maybe? I don't know."

"Perhaps for something illegal?" I gently suggest.

"Like what?"

"I don't know. Sometimes drug traffickers will anchor their loads down and drop them into the ocean and have divers retrieve them."

Stacy appears mortified. "Fred? Are you kidding?"

"I have to explore all options. I want to find Fred too."

She nods quickly and sits back, but her breathing remains accelerated.

"Next question: It looked like he had been storing something heavy in his shed and garage, on sawbucks and on that big table. Any idea what that could have been?"

"No. I actually haven't been in his house for a while. He gave me the keys, but we always met at my place. He said his house smelled because of all the dive gear," she explains.

I didn't notice a scent, and dive gear mostly smells like metal and neoprene with a little oil. Maybe it was an excuse to not have to entertain her in his home—and to keep her from seeing something she shouldn't.

"What about family? Did you ever talk to his relatives?"

"No. He took a call from his sister Petra one night," Stacy recalls.

"Petra? I don't think I ever heard of her." I've never heard Fred talk about any family at all.

"I think she lives in Europe or somewhere."

"What did they talk about?"

"I don't know. He just said that it was his sister and stepped outside. That was all I know. It was months ago," she tells me.

"Did he sound excited or upset?"

"Does Fred ever sound excited or upset? I once saw him get stung by a bee, and he just said, 'Oops.'"

That sounds like Fred. It's one of the reasons he was such a good dive master. Nothing fazed him.

"Do you know any of his friends, aside from the Rats? Maybe people he grew up with?" I'm grasping for any kind of lead now.

"No. I think he moved here from Minnesota when he was a teenager. But I don't know anyone else besides the Dive Rats. Did you talk to them?"

"I talked to Liza, Pete, and Ed, the three who seem closest to Fred. They claim to be as baffled as I am. Tell me, what do you think of them?"

"Um, they're okay. Not my crowd. But Fred loved spending time with them," she explains with a shrug.

"Not your crowd?"

"I'm not a diver. I didn't fit in with them. I only met them a couple times, and all they did was talk about their dives. I felt so excluded. I was upset with Fred. I shouldn't have been. But I was," she admits.

"Be honest. What did you think of them?"

"I thought they were assholes. Fred was different. But they were obnoxious. Maybe more Ed and Pete. Liza's okay. But they'd get a little drunk and just be the worst kind of person you want in a restaurant. I asked Fred why he spent so much time with them. He said they shared his love of diving and they were his friends. But I also know that Ed was paying him for dive lessons. So I don't know if he really thought of Ed as a friend or a customer."

I think she's being forthcoming, but I'm not sure what else to ask her, other than one very delicate question.

"Has there been anyone else in your life?" I ask.

"Have I been seeing anyone else? No. Just Fred. I'm not that type. Nothing like . . ." She fades off.

"Like who?"

"She was perfectly nice to me, but it was hard to tell if Liza was with Peter or Ed, okay? Nothing happened, but the way they joked, I sort of thought they might be, what, swingers?" she concludes.

Interesting. "And Fred?"

"With her? No, of course not. She's not his type," Stacy says with the conviction of a woman who's worked extremely hard to convince herself of something.

"Okay, let's talk again when I have more updates," I tell her.

After Stacy leaves, I reflect on what we talked about. The case keeps going in new directions. Unfortunately, none of them is the direction I want.

What *was* Fred mixed up in? Gambling? Drugs? Underwater swinger parties?

I'm getting the strong feeling that the answer is with the Dive Rats. But I'll need to speak with them in person to confirm the hunch.

"Hey, McPherson. Can I show you something?" Gwen asks as she pokes her head into the room.

CHAPTER 16
LATITUDE

Gwen has laid out Stafford's dive logs in the middle of the table. The log that ended two months ago lies wide open. She's standing next to it as if for a dramatic reveal.

"Look," she says.

I pick it up. The log entries are pretty standard, if not methodical. Who was in the dive party, what equipment was used, where he got the air from, how much time was spent at what depth. How much time he took between dives. It's all in Fred's familiar handwriting, including the way he writes the numeral 7—with the line through it.

Gwen left sticky notes on some of the pages. When I examine them, I notice something odd.

The locations are the names of stars: Polaris, Sirius, Arcturus, Deneb, Vega, and Albireo.

"Is that kind of denomination a normal thing?" asks Gwen.

"No, it's not. It's what you do when you don't want anyone to know where you've been diving."

I have some familiarity with this, having grown up in a family of treasure hunters. When we'd find an interesting spot, Dad would note it in his logbook, using the name of whatever movie we'd watched on board the night before.

For expeditions that included nonfamily members, Dad would shut off the navigation instruments and outright lie to people about where we were. His foolproof plan in case disaster struck was an envelope taped above the radio that said "Open in case of emergency" and contained our actual location.

I think that alone tells you quite a bit about how I was raised.

The fact that Stafford used the names of stars instead of fake or incorrect places indicates that he was trying to obfuscate, not actively deceive anyone—which sounds more like the clear and direct Stafford I know. It's a polite way to say, *None of your business.*

"Any ideas?" asks Gwen.

I take a seat and study the six suspicious log entries. There's no mention of other people on the dives. That stands out. I also see that Stafford used a rebreather and took backup oxygen and soda lime with him.

"Whatever he's doing, he's staying down a long time," I explain. "Without knowing the locations, this could be under an Antarctic lake or in his backyard pool."

"So it's a code?" asks Gwen.

"Maybe? It could just be something in his head."

"From the looks of these books, this man is thorough. I don't think he'd leave something to memory."

"Funny . . . he doesn't mention chartering a boat, and I don't think he owns one."

"I looked up boat registrations," says Gwen. "He hasn't owned one in over ten years. Does that mean these are places he could reach from the beach?"

"Maybe. But you said they haven't found his truck," I reply.

"That doesn't mean he didn't do a beach dive, drown, and have someone steal his truck after they noticed it for a few days." Gwen picks up the log and flips to the front. "Huh." She turns the inside of the cover toward me. "What do you see?"

It's a list of names and phone numbers. Some of them are international.

"A contact list?"

"Look closer."

I study the names and numbers more closely for a clue.

"Fake?" I ask.

"That or Stafford likes to keep track of spammers. Area code 290 hasn't been assigned. The only people who have it in their numbers are telemarketers."

"Or it's a country code," I tell her.

Next to the first number is the name Simon Iswald.

"Hmm." Gwen taps on her computer. "Interesting. It's also the country code for Saint Helena and Tristan da Cunha. Is that a dive spot?"

"Yes. It's one of the most remote ones that has an airport nearby. I've never been."

"Let's ask Solar what we have in our air travel budget," says Gwen with a slight grin.

"Or we could just call the number," I suggest.

"Where's your spirit of adventure?"

"I left it at the bottom of a lake."

I take out my phone and dial the number. My ears are immediately greeted with an annoying tone and a message that says the call cannot be placed.

"Well?" asks Gwen.

"Fake number, I think. Let's look at the others."

We make our way through all twelve, and only one connects. The rest are not in service. The one that does definitely does *not* belong to a person named Angela Reynolds.

"Hey, look at this," says Gwen. "The area codes are pretty close to either the number two-nine-zero or eight-one-five. This has to be a code."

"They might be in pairs. Let's assume one of them is latitude and make up a longitude for the other."

When I type a number pair into WolframAlpha.com, a dot appears in the middle of the Atlantic Ocean.

"Interesting," says Gwen. "That's not that far away from Saint Helena and Tristan da Cunha."

"Actually, the point is about eight thousand miles to the north."

"At least it's in the same hemisphere."

"Um, you mean the Western one?" I respond. "Then, yes, that island is the same hemisphere as South Florida. The Northern one? No."

"Sorry, I forgot you were raised by Blackbeard."

"He was only an uncle," I reply. "But if you draw a line around the earth where the dot is, the line runs through Florida . . . as well as just about every continent. Now let's try one of the other numbers."

I add that as the longitude, and the dot is now in Nepal.

"Yetis—I knew it," says Gwen. "I'll tell Solar to book us tickets."

"Hold on. Latitudes and longitudes can be negative numbers too. Stafford may not have felt the need to add that detail."

I make the longitude a negative number and the dot jumps across continents and right onto Florida. Central Florida, to be precise.

When I enter the coordinates into Google Maps, an aerial image of Ocala National Forest appears. The dot lies atop a small pond in the middle of the forest.

We apply the code to the other number pairs and find five other locations in Central Florida that are all tiny ponds or close to them.

"I think I cracked the other part," says Gwen. "Simon Iswald—S-I— matches the first two letters in Sirius. Angela Reynolds—A-R—Arcturus. The others match up as well."

I see ChatGPT open on her phone. "*You* cracked it?"

"Well, I was smart enough to consult an expert code breaker."

I take a map from a drawer and lay it out on the table. Gwen puts Xs on the spots from Stafford's log and labels each with the code name he used.

"You want to call the park rangers? I'm going to head home and get a change of clothes and then drive up there so I can have a look first thing in the morning."

"Yeah, sure," says Gwen. "Don't forget your bug spray."

CHAPTER 17
Terra Incognito

Parts of Ocala Forest resemble an alien landscape. Patches of green grass and bushes stretch to the horizon with sporadic spindly trees reaching into a blue sky dotted with clouds.

Without mountain ranges or buildings in the distance, one spot looks just like another ten miles away. It's easy to get lost if you're not keeping track of the time and can't see the sun.

Thankfully, this part of Florida isn't quite as swampy as southern Florida. There's plenty of marsh and wetlands, but you can walk miles without getting soggy socks if it's not raining. But, since it's Florida, it's a good bet you'll get rain at some point.

I checked out of my motel room before the sun was up and drove to the first location on the list—an unnamed pond a short walk from National Forest Service Road 77. There's nothing else for miles in either direction, and I'm curious as to how Stafford selected this spot—assuming this was his dive location and not some unpopulated rock in the middle of the Atlantic Ocean.

The Park Service said they had no sign of Stafford but promised to keep an eye out for him. They gave us the radio frequency to use to reach them if I had problems with cellular. Thankfully, I have a satellite phone as part of my everyday carry.

I park my vehicle by the edge of the road and grab my backpack with my gear and a small case with a quadcopter that has come in handy on multiple occasions.

I didn't spot Stafford's truck from the road, but the vegetation is so thick that it could have been ten feet from me and I wouldn't have known it.

My plan is to find my way to the pond and make my way back, looking for any signs of a trail or his presence. He's not the kind of guy to leave empty beer cans and Frito-Lay wrappers lying around, but it's not too hard to spot a trail a person has used if you know what to look for—especially if they're carrying dive gear.

I remember Stafford using a folding cart to carry his tanks and equipment. It had fat tires and a handle. I called it his wagon, but he had the last laugh when I reached the end of a long pier completely winded from carrying all my gear and he hadn't even broken a sweat.

I sidle through the trees lining the road and enter the vast expanse of the forest—which turns out to contain open space rather than thick foliage.

While not as scenic as Yellowstone or other wilderness, this eco-sphere has its own beauty. You just have to look and listen. In the warmer months the cicadas buzz nonstop, and you hear the constant croaking of frogs. As I walk along a thin trail that could have been made by deer, boar, black bear, or all of the above, I hear things scurrying away in the brush. Most creatures here will keep their distance from loud bipedal apes, but not all of them.

Snakes are everywhere, and panthers will track people as they move through their territory. This part of Florida also has the state's highest density of black bears.

Most of the encounters between bears and people in Florida happen when someone is out walking or hiking with a dog. Bears have no concept of what a pet or a leash is, so they just see some clumsy ape following around a small mammal and decide they like their odds.

The last time a bear attacked a person near here was three years ago. There was no dog involved, as far as I heard. A woman was leaning up against a tree and a bear came at her. It turned out the bear had cubs nearby.

A more recent human and bear encounter went the other way when several people were charged with animal cruelty for using their dogs to torture and kill bears. Those poor creatures just can't get a break.

I keep my eyes open for any sign of them, hoping we don't come anywhere near each other.

According to my GPS the pond lies just beyond a stand of trees ahead of me. I've seen no sign of Stafford or any other humans. This makes me feel good. There's nothing worse than finding some spot that looks like it's been untouched by creation and seeing a pile of cigarette butts.

I walk around the trees and find an opening that overlooks a pond. The small body of water is almost perfectly round and maybe ten meters across at its widest point. On one side there's marshy grass; dry earth on the other. I step through the muck to the dry area and inspect the dirt.

I see faint footprints and indentations that might have come from Stafford's cart. None looks like it was made since he went missing, though.

If he died in the pond, he would have had some gear left behind—unless somebody stole it. But that would surprise me at this location.

I take out my camera to get some photos. I want to make sure I didn't miss anything.

When I first started working for a local police department as a recovery diver, we still used film, and every roll was precious. Now the phone in my pocket can take 4K videos and thousands of photos without making a dent in the storage.

Solar admonishes us to use what's cheap. If you can take ten photos, take a hundred. Sometimes the clue isn't what's in the photograph—it's what's not.

The one thing I really want to photograph I can't without getting wet or going back to my vehicle to grab my underwater ROV—and that's what's in this goddamn pond.

Why did Stafford come here? How did he manage to spend four hours at the bottom? What made it so interesting—or why did he decide that it wasn't?

Out of curiosity, I take a reel of string and a fishing weight from my backpack. I unwind five meters of string, then toss the weight into the middle of the pond.

It falls straight down and the string goes taut. That's at least ten feet from the top of the pond to the weight.

I let out another yard.

Almost thirteen feet.

I let out some more.

Twenty feet.

And more.

Forty feet.

Sixty and the string goes slack.

That doesn't mean the hole goes down only that far. It might mean the weight hit a ledge or slope.

The Blue Grotto is an underwater cavern in Williston, Florida, that goes down one hundred feet—at an angle. Sinkholes don't usually run straight down. The erosion of limestone that forms them can go in any direction, including sideways: whichever direction the water runs. Like terrestrial caverns, water-filled sinkholes sometimes can form entire interconnected systems, with two separate caverns linking up at some spot.

I use my satellite connection to see if there's any info online about this hole. Something we might have missed. My search comes up empty.

This pond only has a number for a name and little other information. It could be one of the deepest in the area and nobody would be the wiser.

"Fred, what the hell were you doing down there?"

My question is mocked by cicadas and frogs.

Not too long ago, I'd have grabbed my gear from my Suburban and taken a look, but I'm not ready for that. Whatever is down there, I don't think it's Fred.

I walk back, studying the ground again for clues and wondering how Fred found this sinkhole in the first place.

CHAPTER 18
WISHING WELL

It takes me two hours to get to the next location. I have to take a side road that's barely drivable and may or may not allow nongovernment vehicles. It was hard to tell from the rusted sign full of buckshot holes.

This location, Arcturus, is ten miles south of an old bombing range. It's a pain to get to. There's much better hiking and kayaking north of here. This is the kind of place where only wild animals and biologists are likely to wander.

I find a spot due west of the sinkhole and park my vehicle. As I turn off the ignition and look around, I accept that finding any sign of Stafford will be more challenging than I expected.

Unlike me, Stafford likely would have avoided parking alongside the road. He would have cared about being seen by park rangers, whereas I don't.

This means he'd still need a clear path to the sinkhole and wouldn't want to haul his gear across creeks or through thick vegetation. He'd have found a parking spot that allowed him to hide his truck but easily access Arcturus.

I stare down at the map on my iPad and realize Stafford probably looked at the same images I'm seeing and chose where to park based on it.

There's a strip of forest to the north of me that grows thicker the farther it goes. Pulling into the brush close to the tip of the woods would give him some cover without turning the hike to the sinkhole into an ordeal.

I get back on the road and drive another mile, then park.

I grab my bag and walk along the side of the road, studying the trees, looking for some point where Stafford might have driven straight through.

I find a few dead ends that lead only to more trees and decide to give up this pursuit and simply head for the sinkhole. But my feet have other plans and take me another thirty meters.

Clear as day, I see thick tire tracks in the dirt leading through a narrow gap. Somebody pulled off the road here.

I follow the tracks into the trees and find myself on a narrow path enclosed under the forest canopy. You'd never see any of this from the air.

I round a bend and see the familiar blue of Stafford's truck. The tailgate is open, and several air tanks resting on a stand are visible.

I feel no joy at the sight. Based upon the leaves and palm fronds scattered on the truck, it's been here for as long as Stafford has been missing.

This is not a good sign.

I take out my phone and call Hughes.

"How's it going?" he asks.

"I found his truck," I reply.

Hughes understands this could be both good and bad news. "Any sign of him?"

"No. I'm about to head over to the sinkhole. Here are the coordinates."

"Okay. I'll load up and head your way. Need me to call the Park Service?"

"Yeah. Could you?"

"Sure thing. And McPherson . . . I get it."

That's all he has to say. Moments like this are filled with mixed emotions. When I was hunting the Swamp Killer, finding his victims in a spot where we expected to find them wasn't exactly a high point.

I stow my phone and focus. All we have is a truck. He could have had engine trouble and had someone pick him up. The vehicle could have been stolen—and then randomly left in a spot noted in his dive log.

Yeah, right.

I take a few photos of the truck, then move on through the trees and to the sinkhole.

When I reach a clearing that stretches for almost half a mile, I can finally see the small copse of trees under which the other sinkhole lies.

Feeling nothing but dread, I find a small path that Stafford may have used and head through the trees.

This part of the forest feels different. The spaces are more closed in, and the trees feel . . . darker. They say that we design parks and golf courses to please our Paleolithic brains. We're happy when we see greenery, water, and a few trees we could climb when in danger. This area has all the right ingredients but in all the wrong proportions. The ground is firm enough and not difficult to walk on, but the farther I go, the more I feel like I'm being swallowed up.

I reach the edge of the small wooded area and turn back to look for a moment. The stillness of the grassy field unnerves me.

I find a gap in the trees and enter. The sinkhole is visible within just a few paces.

So is a bright yellow rope tied to a tree. One end is wrapped around the trunk. The other goes straight into the water.

I walk over and give it a tug. There's no resistance. I remember to put on my latex gloves, then keep pulling.

Thirty meters of wet rope are lying at my feet before I pull up the end. It's broken and frayed—snapped.

I spot two dive bags at the edge of the sinkhole that I didn't notice before. One has a spare tank. The other is empty except for a pair of boots, a cell phone, and Fred Stafford's wallet.

Dispirited, I sit by the edge of the sinkhole and ask out loud: "Fred, what the hell did you get yourself into?"

While, internally, I wonder: *What am I about to get myself into?*

CHAPTER 19

DEPTHS

I eventually find the willpower to stand up, take photos of the scene, and use my string and weight to measure the depth of the pool.

It's fifteen meters at one end and more than forty at the other, with no indication that this is the true depth of the cavern.

Although significantly narrower than the Blue Grotto, this sinkhole may be deeper and take the record for Florida. It's far deeper than the last one—and that's saying something.

I'm still curious as to how Stafford found this hole. I've been through all the hydrological records and seen what's been recorded and what hasn't. Measurements I've made have even been used by the state to update their records.

Arcturus and the other locations simply aren't listed anywhere other than as small bodies of water.

And even if they were tagged as deep sinkholes, at most a surveyor would have dropped a weight in at one location, then moved on. That would be the most we'd know about it, short of someone going down and finding out.

Even satellite imaging can tell you only so much. From orbit or a plane, using the latest navy or NASA mapping methods, Blue Grotto would appear to be only ten meters deep because most of it descends sideways.

One theory is that Stafford set out to manually measure the deepest sinkholes. But for whom? It's not something he'd take on himself.

Stafford had to have some way to know to come to these spots. Why?

One possibility is that he was working on some project for the military. It wouldn't be completely out of the ordinary for him to take a contract helping them measure something. My dad has been hired for dives by the navy more than a few times.

Maybe they were looking for places to do underwater training? Testing some kind of long-range sensory array?

I could invent an endless list, but I need to settle on what I know: his truck is parked nearby, and it looks like he went down, snapped his rope, and never came back up.

I call Run while I wait for Hughes to show up.

"How's it going?" he asks.

"I found Stafford's truck in the middle of nowhere. It doesn't look good."

"Oh, Sloan, that sucks. You told his girlfriend?"

"Not yet. I need to be sure."

"What happened?"

"From the looks of it, Fred was diving in a sinkhole that wasn't on the charts. It's at least a hundred feet deep and probably goes back a ways."

"My two biggest fears: diving alone and caves," says Run.

"Mine too. That's what's been giving me nightmares."

"For someone with a fear of diving alone, you sure do it a lot."

I realize he said "diving alone" and not "dying alone." I don't correct myself. I used to love the freedom to go under the waves whenever I wanted. That's changed.

I know the tumble in the pipe still has me rattled, but there's something else that's been bothering me. I used to dive for fun and intellectual curiosity. The water was an enjoyable experience.

Since I joined the UIU, it's mostly been about death. I don't go into the water to study the prehistory of Florida; I dive to recover bodies or look for traces of the most evil acts humans commit.

Water was once my escape from the land. But now only the most terrifying things come from it.

Water once meant life. Now it brings death.

"You still there?" asks Run.

"Yeah. Just thinking about things."

"I know you have to work in the water, and calling it hazardous is an understatement, but I don't worry. Maybe I'm being naive, but you and your family—well, you, your dad, and grandfather—have a knack for things. I'm not saying you don't make mistakes, but some part of your brain always has a backup plan."

"Hmm." I don't know what to say to that, except I hope it's true.

"You're also built differently. It might be evolution at work. All those genetics plus all that experience. You could probably set the record for a breath hold."

"Holding your breath is the worst thing you can do when you're using compressed air," I remind him.

"You know what I mean. The thing I've observed about you and your dad that I don't see in other divers is that you don't get careless and you don't shirk responsibility. When you make a mistake, you call yourself out on it."

"Fred was cautious too."

"Maybe. But Fred wasn't from the water. He didn't grow up in it like you did. I don't think he even scuba dived until he was twenty. You've been doing it since you were two. Your body just knows things."

"Are you telling me this to put *me* at ease or you?" I ask.

"I don't know. Maybe both. I can't tell you to stop. I just have to make my peace with it all. But yeah, I worry like hell," he admits.

"You don't show it."

"We got a kid I don't want to scare. Although I'm sure she feels the same way."

That hurts. "It didn't feel that way at the hospital."

"I know we didn't make a fuss. But I think that was just our way of dealing with it. Jackie slept that night curled up in her bed with that jacket you wear on cold dives."

"Why didn't you tell me?" I ask.

"She made me promise not to."

"Okay. Well, now *I* have to confess . . ."

Rule number one in our house: don't lie or break a promise. Rule number two is to confess.

"About what?"

"I've been thinking it's time for me to consider what's next."

"You mean diving as part of your job?" asks Run.

"Maybe. It's not the way it was before. It's just . . . dark. At first, I thought it was the close calls that were wearing on me. Now I think that the whole thing's kind of been ruined for me."

"We can talk about that. But I have a hard time imagining you being away from the water for very long. Maybe not with so many people shooting at you, though."

"Yes. We should talk," I agree.

"So what was Fred doing out there?" asks Run.

"I have no idea. I've got a lot of theories, but nothing makes sense. There are six such locations in his logbook, and I've only been to two. Both were uncharted."

"Six? What the hell was he looking for?" asks Run.

"I don't know that he was . . ."

I stop to consider what Run asked. I've been thinking more about how Stafford found the sinkholes and why he was looking for them, not that he might have been looking for something *in* them.

Forget a hydrologist—I need to talk to a pirate.

"Hey, I'm going to call Dad and ask him that. Give Jackie a hug for me."

"Will do. I love you."

"Me too."

CHAPTER 20
PRIVATEER

"What's up, Sea Monkey?" my father greets me by phone. "How's your head?"

"Better. I'm up near Ocala looking into Fred Stafford's disappearance."

"How's it going?"

"Not good. I found his truck and maybe the last place he dived. It's in the middle of Ocala Forest."

"Oh man. That's too bad." I can hear the sadness in his voice. Dad knew Fred better than most.

"Yeah."

"You know how people say at least they died doing what they loved? That's bullshit. What I love about diving and the water is *not* dying. That's the worst part. You wouldn't tell the widow of a firefighter who burned to death, 'At least he died doing what he loved.' You know?"

"I can tell you've thought a lot about this."

"Yeah. More than once. Fred was a good guy. A bit mysterious, but a good guy," says Dad.

"What do you mean?" I ask.

"I didn't pry, but he never talked about growing up or anything about his life before he started diving. I got the sense he had a difficult childhood. I never asked. Maybe I should have."

"Did he ever mention a sister?"

"A sister? No. Plenty of girlfriends. That's how he said he learned German."

"German?"

"I think so. He was drunk and his words were slurred. Something like that. He said he dated a woman who taught him the language. There was always something else going on with him. We all have our tics."

"We certainly do. Please keep the news about Fred to yourself until we learn more. We haven't found a body, so I don't want to jump to any conclusions."

"Understood."

"There's another reason I called," I say. "It looks like Fred was diving in some unmarked sinkholes that go really deep. I think he might've been looking for something. Do you have any idea what that could be? Was he treasure hunting? Inshore? Is that crazy?"

"No, not at all. Crazy to expect to find anything, but not crazy to think there might be something. There are tons of rumors of buried treasure across the state. Did you say you were in Ocala?"

"Yeah."

"The treasure of Don Felipe is supposed to be just north of there," he says.

"Who was that?"

"Felipe was a Spaniard who owned a plantation near there in the early 1800s. When the Seminole Wars started, he allegedly hid his family fortune—which would have been gold and silver. The Indians killed him before he could recover it."

"How much credibility do you give that story?"

"There were wealthy people in that area back then. Records show a Don Philip Robert Yonge owning property. They didn't have banks to lock their fortunes in. So, it wouldn't surprise me if there were more than a few buried chests hidden out there over the years."

"But in a sinkhole?" I ask.

"Well, there's the Ponce de Leon Springs a few miles to the east of you. Legend has it that someone once saw a chest at the bottom of the spring but couldn't get to it before it sank further."

"And how do you rate that one?"

"Not too highly. Although Ponce de Leon was convinced there was gold to be found. Poor bastard chose the one state where there's not a single natural gold deposit," says my father with a laugh. "If you really want to find gold, go offshore."

"Did you ever talk to Fred about treasure hunting?"

"If we did, I was the one carrying the conversation. That kind of thing wasn't as interesting to him. Although military history was. Say, you've got the Pine Castle Bombing Range near there, don't you?"

"Yeah. The southern end is pretty close."

"There are a few strange stories about that place. There was a UFO sighting in the '70s. Apparently, they got a radar lock on something out there."

Dad is far more open-minded about such accounts than I am. Although his own personal theory is that, if we do have visitors, they're coming from under the sea. He's got hours of stories about weird encounters he's had while diving.

"So Fred wasn't into treasure hunting but might have been looking for UFOs?"

"No, not that. They still use the range. Live-fire exercises. Have been since World War II. All kinds of aircraft fly through there. Even classified ones. Been a couple crashes near there," he adds.

"I imagine they get all the pieces afterward," I reply.

"Not always. Sometimes planes drop things like sensor packages. But then again, crashing in a sinkhole would be like making a hole in one from a hundred miles away."

"Right. So, no gold, no UFO parts."

"Well, there could have been hidden Spanish gold. Maybe something not widely known. Some account could pop up in a book in an auction and nobody had heard about it before. You know I keep an eye out for ledgers from maritime insurers. You never know what you'll find. But the first gold brought to Florida may not have been with the Spaniards, you know."

"Not the Mayans, Dad. There's no record, just a lot of conjecture."

There's a theory that Mayans may have come to Florida when their peninsula experienced a severe drought in the ninth century. While there are some cultural similarities, such as folklore, and theories that maize may have been planted here in pre-Columbian times, the evidence is thin.

I'm not saying it didn't happen, but at most it would have been a small and likely doomed group. But who is to say? History is based on what we can find, and most of it is lost forever.

"All of this is moot if Fred wasn't the treasure-seeking type," I point out.

"People change," says Dad.

"Did you know Fred gambled?"

"He mentioned poker a bit and tried to get me into a game. I declined."

"Apparently he'd been spending quite a bit at the casino and losing a ton."

"Well, forget what I said about him not being a treasure hunter. A man down on his luck is willing to bet on anything."

"I'm going to send you some coordinates too. I don't know if they have to do with anything, but maybe they're connected to some old pirate map you stole off the table at Long John Silver's." I see the sunlight bounce off a car in the distance. "Hughes and Solar are here. Could you do a little more digging and see what else you can come up with about his sinkhole diving?"

"Sure. Maybe he was after Don Felipe's treasure. If Felipe was on the run, he might have headed south right near where you're standing."

I hang up and look toward the direction of the sinkhole, wondering what else could be down there besides Fred Stafford.

CHAPTER 21
DEPTH FINDER

Solar is staring down at the sinkhole while Hughes unpacks the gear we carried to the spot. Besides the two cases for the underwater robot, Scott brought a large spool of fiber-optic cable to create a connection between the robot and the surface. The acoustic transmitter he used back at the lake is good only for a few meters. Anything more than that and you want the robot to either be fully autonomous or hardwired to the surface. Radio waves don't make it far through water. You can put an antenna under the surface and send signals hundreds of meters, but not at a high bandwidth.

The difficulties involved in learning what's below the water help explain the notion that we know more about the surface of the moon than the bottom of the ocean. Well, we actually know much more about the bottom of the ocean than we do the moon. The problem is there's just so damned much ocean bottom.

I realized while quite young that maps can give you a false confidence about the world. Early explorers made them based entirely on measurements made by unaided eyesight. That's why they were filled with phantom oceans and distorted coastlines.

As our ability to geolocate became more precise with better time-keeping, maps improved dramatically and the broad shape of the world's islands and continents came into focus. But we remained limited in understanding the world beneath the sea. We knew only what we dragged up in our nets and what depth gauges like my little weight and string could tell us.

While that's not a bad way to measure the depth of the ocean floor, you can only measure what you can measure. Millions of soundings have been taken of Atlantic crossing routes and coastlines. The farther you get away from well-traveled routes, though, the fewer measurements we've made. Ships could report an average ocean depth of six hundred feet in one spot and completely miss an undersea mountain ten miles south of a shipping lane.

With the advent of sonar, the world's navies came to a much better understanding of the ocean floor. A sea-change moment in oceanography occurred when the *Meteor* expeditions in 1925 made seventy thousand measurements using an echo sounder—relatively new technology at the time.

Side-scanning sonar and other instruments would increase our knowledge and measure ever greater areas, but to this day, vast reaches of ocean remain largely uncharted and unexplored. While we're unlikely to discover any more giant trenches or massive underwater mountains, we discover new features all the time.

"We're ready to put 'er in," says Hughes as he takes his robot to the edge of the lake. "We should have a constant camera feed all the way down."

"This looks different than the one we used at Belt Road. I take it it didn't survive?" says Solar.

"It's in the robot ICU, being repaired. This is a dumber prototype, but I figure it will work well enough," Hughes tells us.

He's built a large screen into the lid of one of the cases so users can view what the robot sees.

"I've told it to find the lowest depth, using a spiral pattern," Hughes explains.

If Stafford's body is down there, it could be wedged into a crevice. If the robot went straight down, it could pass just a few meters away and we'd never see it if the camera wasn't aimed in the right direction.

Hughes points to several spherical domes on the body of the robot. "We have 360-degree coverage and a simple AI looking for anything unusual in case we're not looking in the right place."

The robot propels itself to the middle of the pond, then starts to make a whirring noise as the air is compressed from a bladder into a tank, then submerges as its propellers drive it down.

Even with all of the air out of the bladder, the robot is still slightly buoyant. This is in case there's a catastrophic mechanical malfunction. The device will float back to the surface without its propellers pushing it down.

As the robot descends, onboard computers give us a continuous view of the sides of the sinkhole by digitally stitching all the camera feeds together and keeping the viewing area centered on our monitor. The rover's onboard lights illuminate the passage as the unit corkscrews deeper beneath us.

The sides of the walls look dark green. If the water lacked organic debris, they'd appear grayer. This kind of sinkhole forms when rainwater that absorbed carbon from the atmosphere creates carbonic acid and dissolves the limestone.

While the rain may have fallen evenly, all it takes is one depression to gather slightly more water and you get a cascading effect. Surface carbon from wildfires can also contribute to sinkhole formation.

I had a high school teacher who said that Florida could be best understood as a kind of superorganism. She explained that almost all the geology was based on systems that were alive at one point. The limestone underneath most of Florida was created by the accumulation of the remains of sea organisms when the state was covered by a shallow sea. As water levels lowered and the seafloor became land, plant life began to form and started creating the topsoil that covers the peninsula.

Florida, she explained, was built by biology. If you want to understand the land, you have to understand the organisms that made it.

As the robot descends past endless strata of limestone, we effectively travel deeper into the past, going back millions of years.

"It's starting to incline," says Hughes. "Twenty-five meters. Still going strong."

A chart in a window on the screen shows the robot's estimated position in a rough approximation of the sinkhole. The passage is narrower here, but the forward lights reach into blackness. There's clearly more to go.

A square catches my eye. "What's that?"

Hughes spins the view to look down. A weight from a weight belt is sitting on a layer of sediment. This is the first sign of a human presence we've seen.

"Looks recent," says Hughes.

"How did it come off a weight belt?" asks Solar.

"I shove them into pockets in my vest. It's easy for them to slip out if you're not careful," I explain.

"I made a digital marker so we can come back with the arm and retrieve it," says Hughes.

The robot spins around and resumes following the muck-lined bottom of the cave into the void.

It's hard to know how far down the true bottom is because millions of years of debris have covered the floor with sediment.

The passage widens and the walls are no longer visible. The cave is getting wider and deeper.

We're all leaning in, almost with our noses to the screen, trying to spot any sign of Stafford.

The floor of the cave starts to rise and the passage narrows, then comes to an abrupt end.

"Nothing," I breathe at last.

"Let's back up and take a look at the sides," says Hughes.

The robot spins left and follows the side of the cave until it starts to recede into darkness.

"Looks like there's another passage," he observes.

Suddenly the robot comes to a stop.

"What happened?"

"It's too fat," says Hughes. "It can't go any farther. All I can do is increase the brightness of the lights and move the cameras a bit."

More details come into view. The light beam bounces off particles in the water and hits the rear wall of a larger chamber that the robot can't reach.

There's no way of telling how large it is or if it goes off in some other direction.

The camera sweeps around, and the light vanishes into another void.

"This looks like it just keeps going. It may be connected to other sinkholes nearby," says Hughes.

He pulls the robot back, and it begins to turn as he looks for a way through the passage.

"No luck," he says after ten minutes. "Let me back up."

The robot goes into reverse and the passage recedes from view.

The robot makes a pinging noise a moment before I see it.

In the top left corner is the sharp angle of something.

The camera moves and it comes into view: a blue swim fin.

Written in permanent ink on the inside is "Staff," Fred's nickname.

"Can we get the robot to go in farther?" asks Solar.

"No. It's too big to fit the passage," says Hughes.

"Can we get a smaller one here?"

"I can have someone ship one. It will take a couple days."

"I'll go down," my mouth says before my brain can think.

CHAPTER 22
DECLINE

Solar is listening to all the precautions I'm going to take when I dive into the sinkhole. He didn't shut me down the moment I suggested it, but he also didn't exactly jump up and down with excitement.

I try to explain it in technical detail. "The two biggest problems with these kinds of dives are, one, getting lost and running out of air, and two, getting stuck and ascending too quickly because of an emergency."

Hughes nods in agreement.

"That's three things," says Solar. "You're not instilling me with confidence. Didn't three expert cave divers die in one cave in South Africa?"

"That cave was almost a thousand feet deep. This is one-tenth that. I can free dive to the bottom here with enough weight."

"Didn't the world's best free diver have a stroke?"

Clearly, Solar's concern for my diving work has led him to do some deep research.

"He was setting a record and passed out when ascending from an eight-hundred-foot dive. This is much shallower. You've seen me do this before. But I'll be using air and in contact with you and Hughes."

"I could use the robot for recovery," says Hughes.

"You can't get it through the gap. How is that going to help? What happens when you're on the other side?" Solar replies.

"I can use the slimmer backpack. It won't be a problem. If it is, I don't go through," I say with a shrug.

"Walk me through it," he tells me.

"We lower a rope to the bottom and place an extra tank down there. I'll have plenty of air in case there's a problem. We'll have radio contact throughout."

"I'll suit up in case we need backup," says Hughes.

None of this is sitting well with Solar.

"Look at it this way: even if we wait for the other ROV, we're still going to have to send someone down there if there's a body to be recovered. There's no way around that," I argue.

"If the ROV shows us there's nothing down there, then there's no point in putting anyone into the water," Solar rebuts me.

"I'll cover that area much faster. We could spend days trying to send the robot into dark corners. No offense to Hughes's work, but I'm still better. That thing was made to be safer, not more efficient."

"Okay. But we have checkpoints. If I say come up, you come up. Understand?"

I stow a bad joke about getting the bends from coming up too fast. "Understood."

An hour later, I'm suited up and ready to go. We hauled all the gear from our vehicles, not knowing exactly what we'd need. As a precaution, Solar called the Park Service and let them know what we were up to.

I wanted to protest this as overkill, but it wasn't a bad idea. If I come up too quickly or suffer some other problem, having medical personnel nearby isn't the worst idea.

I stand over the edge of the sinkhole and stare down at the rippling surface and wait for my knees to buckle or my stomach to knot up. Instead, I feel perfectly fine.

I've done dives like this a thousand times before. Maybe all my recent anxiety was a passing thing.

Or maybe the adrenaline and the desire to not leave Fred down there in a cold and lonely grave have overruled my deepest fears.

I decide that's a question for another day and jump in.

I grab the rope with my hand and slowly let the air out of my vest, descending feetfirst into the abyss.

If Solar weren't watching, I'd go faster. But I need to do this by the book—at least the book he understands. I know exactly what my body can handle, but there's no point in pushing it.

I look up and the bright mouth of the sinkhole grows smaller.

Every three meters, my hand touches a knot in the rope. Hughes wrote the depth on tape wrapped around the rope so I'd know without having to check my depth gauge.

It's a precaution to make things easier if I find myself in distress. Sometimes the brain can get foggy and it gets hard to focus. Plenty of accidents happen on the way up and not at the bottom. Having reminders and knots like these reduces the amount of thinking required.

My father is a big believer that reducing the thinking required is the best strategy. He writes instructions on duct tape and sticks them to everything from the engine room of his boat to the inside of our freezer. If he'd been an actor, he would have taped the script to the stage.

None of this is for his benefit. He knows his own lines by rote. He wants to ensure that all the other dummies know what to do too.

This dummy knows she has to slowly descend to the bottom—taking time to equalize every few meters.

"McPherson, you hear us?" asks Hughes over the underwater radio.

"Affirmative," I reply into the microphone inside my face mask. "Ten meters," I call out.

I let myself fall a little deeper, hand on the rope. I stop at the next knot.

"Twenty meters."

We'd talked about sending the robot down with me, but given the small space, there was a possibility that its cable could wrap around me and create a complication.

"Thirty-five meters. I can see the slope."

"Take it nice and slow," says Solar.

"Don't worry."

"Worry about what?" asks Solar.

Remembering how the radio can get garbled, I enunciate each word. "I said don't worry."

"Roger," says Solar.

My fins hit the sloping floor and kick up a cloud of particles. When I work at underwater archaeological sites, I have to move super slowly because it can take minutes for a cloud of sediment to settle back to the bottom.

"I'm on the slope. I'm going to start swimming. Bringing the end of the rope with me."

I unhook the spare tank attached to the rope and fasten the end to a carabiner on my belt. It's a last-resort measure in case we lose contact for too long.

I glide down the passage headfirst with my mask lights leading the way. It's much more spacious down here than it seemed when watching the dive video. The camera's fish-eye view and the lack of familiar landmarks made it seem tighter.

I could walk across the muck and still not touch the ceiling, if I had enough weight.

"Going through the passage," I call out.

"—ative," says Hughes.

Swimming down an incline can be dangerous if you don't keep an eye on your depth gauge. Unlike a straight descent following a rope, it's easy to descend too quickly without realizing it. It's even more dangerous on the way up. You need to make sure you're not so buoyant you race to the surface without realizing it.

I count my strokes and track my depth. If my geometry is correct, I've moved about twenty meters from the central sinkhole. Solar and Hughes should be "behind" me now.

"How are you doing?" asks Hughes.

"A-OK. I set down the spare tank. You sound clearer," I reply.

"I lowered the antenna to the bottom," he explains.

We'd kept it near the top when I first ascended so it would be in range. Now that I'm entering the passage, he put it on a line of sight with me.

"I'm entering the first chamber," I call out.

I pan my head around, and my lights fall on the fin we spotted earlier. I swim over to it and get a closer look.

While I can't send video to the surface, a small camera on top of my mask is capturing everything I see. Even though I plan to take the fin back up with me, I want to get it on video before disturbing it.

I move back to the center of the passage and tilt my head all around and inspect the ceiling. My air bubbles float upward and try to find the highest point. You can sometimes use them as a method to find your way out of a cave system. They can also get you lost when they seek some other high point away from the exit.

I don't see any other sign of Fred, so I move toward the end of the passage where the robot couldn't go any farther.

"I'm at the gap. I'm going to move through it," I call into the radio.

"Keep us updated," says Solar.

I grab the walls on either side and pull my body into the next chamber. I can feel the top of my pack scrape the roof.

The only way Fred would have passed through here is if he took off his rebreather.

"I'm through," I call out.

"Re— that?"

"I'm through," I reply.

"—irmative."

This chamber is bigger than the last one. My little lights don't even reach the far end.

I swim down, find the floor, and keep going. A layer of silt lifts in my wake.

I slow to reduce the turbulence and aim my lights at the ceiling. Even though I'm not moving, my body starts to drift slowly.

When I rotate around and aim my light ahead, I see several gaps of various sizes. I also notice the silt is moving toward them.

I swim to the closest gap. It's a narrow passage that goes down at an incline. My light beam fades in it after ten meters.

I pull back and inspect the next one. This goes straight, then curves to the side. Here also I feel a slight current.

"Guys, I think there's an underwater river down here," I say into the radio.

"—eat that?"

"RIVER," I call out loudly.

A river doesn't have to be raging rapids—merely a movement of water from one place to another. This whole section could be draining through miles of crevices into more porous rock.

That also means these passages could continue on and even connect to other sinkhole networks underground.

Fred could be inside any of these narrow channels.

I pull out and aim my light at the different openings. Should I see how far I get down the largest one? What if it keeps going?

Part of me wants to say, *Screw it, let's go*, but the mature voice in my head that sounds a lot like George Solar is telling me to return to the surface.

I know if I surface now, I may not have a chance for a long time—if ever—to recover Stafford.

"Hey, guys . . ."

There's no response. I'm too far away from the antenna.

My chest tightens, and I start to breathe more quickly.

It's not a full-on panic, but I don't feel at ease anymore. I have to surface now.

I'm so sorry, Fred.

CHAPTER 23

DEBRIS

I'm sitting on the edge of the sinkhole, staring at the evidence bags containing what we think are Stafford's ballast weight and fin. Hughes is reeling in the ropes and cables we used for my dive.

"It took discipline to come up," says Solar. "I know it killed you to do that, but you have to know when to call it off."

Actually, panic made me come back up. I gesture to the contents of the bags. "Is this it, then?"

"I don't know. You're the expert. What's the practicality of a bigger search effort?"

"It depends on how far the passages go. It might take a detailed survey. The danger is it means putting more people into what could be a hazardous situation."

"Right, and he might have just had a heart attack down there," says Solar.

"Maybe. I don't know how the fin made it to the first chamber. He might have taken it off to slip into one of the other passages. He could have been disoriented. Sometimes people start stripping off equipment."

My mind races through different scenarios that all lead to Stafford's lifeless body stuck in some unseen, tight passage with no way out.

"That might have been from a different dive," says Hughes. "There are a few other sinkholes near here. He might have gone down one of them after."

"Which only complicates the search more."

"This is a Park Service problem now. We'll let them handle the search," says Solar.

"Do you know who their number-one diver was for search and recovery in the forests?" I ask.

"Stafford?" guesses Solar.

"Yep. The man they sent to rescue folks in dark places is now trapped in a dark place. As far as we know."

The fin and the weight and his wallet carry a lot of credibility, but Stafford's abandoned truck is what's most convincing. As a rule of thumb, when you find the vehicle of a person missing for a week in a forest like Ocala, the smart money says he's dead.

"I can get a smaller autonomous robot to search the narrower sections," says Hughes. "I wouldn't give up on a recovery just yet."

The fact that we're talking about "recovery" breaks my heart. I didn't go down there expecting to find him alive and well. But I wasn't hoping to find a body either.

"Did you see anything down there that explains what he was doing?" asks Solar.

"Geologically, the cavern is interesting. The underwater river is probably new news, or at least hasn't been studied much. We'll need a hydrologist to know more. They can use dyes and other tests to see where the water goes."

"We could improvise an echo sounder too," offers Hughes. "Make a noise in one sinkhole and see if it travels to another through water."

"Different subject," I say. "What do I tell his girlfriend?"

"You tell her we found his truck and gear but no body. It doesn't look good," says Solar.

"You think he could've been exploring the hole for general research?" asks Hughes.

I shake my head. "That doesn't sound like Stafford. I think he was looking for something. And given what we saw at his house, I think he found it."

"What could that something be?" asks Solar.

"Well, I talked to my father about treasure hunting in these parts. He told me the usual Florida bullshit lore but nothing solid enough for Stafford to risk his neck. There's a legend about a family treasure buried near here, but it doesn't mention anything about a sinkhole."

"And because of Florida's geology, finding a naturally occurring precious metal is an improbability," Solar points out.

"That's not quite true," says Hughes as he finishes wrapping a cable around a spindle.

"What do you mean? This is all limestone. You'd have to go through three miles of it before you get to the Florida platform," I tell him. "You might as well be building boring machines and making trade deals with the mole people."

He looks up at me with a smile. "Meteoric metal. I read a paper by a researcher who thinks Lake Okeechobee was formed by a meteor impact in the limestone seabed. There're cracks radiating out from it like a bullet hole in glass. At least that's what he thinks."

"We're a long way from Lake Okeechobee," I point out.

"I'm not saying Stafford was looking for *that* meteor. But deep, round holes could draw folks looking for impact sites."

"Interesting. Both this location and the other *are* very round."

"And named for stars," he adds.

"What's the going price for a meteor?" asks Solar.

"Most often you only find fragments. So, a few grand to hundreds of thousands, depending?"

"It did look like he'd moved something heavy in his garage and shed."

"Let's think about the order of things," says Solar. "At some point, Stafford hauled a big and dirty object home. Then he disappears and we find his truck and other possessions here. So this"—he waves a hand over what remains of Fred Stafford—"was . . ."

"A return trip," I reply. "Which ended tragically."

Solar skewers me with his intense green eyes. "Why return?"

"Looking for more? Whatever he hauled home, it was long gone when we got there. It's not in the back of his truck. I don't think he was bringing it back to resubmerge it."

Solar turns his gaze to Hughes. "Unbox that contraption of yours and get us a soil sample we can send to NASA or whoever you ask about those kinds of things."

The lab we sent the samples from Stafford's house didn't have anything to say other than "unspecified soil with clay composition." Which is why Solar is seeking a higher forensic authority.

"On it."

"McPherson, when you get back, you and Gwen go through everything you have on Stafford. Search his trash, his attic. Look for anything. If he was hunting for meteors, gold, whatever, it stands to reason there would be *something* to indicate it. Like a metal detector tucked away in a closet, or books on the topic."

"I can talk to his dive buddies again too. His girlfriend didn't have much to say, but she wasn't diving with him. They might know more."

"Be subtle. You said the lock had been pried off the shed? If he did find something and talked about it, maybe somebody took it when he went missing. Assume anyone you talk to is a potential suspect."

"What about the other dive locations in his log?" I ask.

"How close are they?"

"Most of them are northwest of here—sixty miles or so," I reply.

"Check in with his friends and re-search his house. I want you to exhaust all the avenues on land before we put you or a robot back in the water."

CHAPTER 24

BACKGROUND

Gwen sits at the big table with stacks of boxes when I arrive the next morning. I recognize some of the items from my cursory search of Stafford's house. Since we couldn't locate next of kin, Solar was able to get a limited warrant to search his house for the sake of Stafford's well-being. Basically, this meant that if we found a kilo of cocaine or a confession that he killed Kennedy, we couldn't use that to charge him with a crime.

"How was the dive?" asks Gwen as I sit across from her.

I look around to make sure we're alone. "Utterly terrifying, to be honest."

"Sounds like you're finally getting some common sense."

"Maybe. Maybe not. I was fine for a while . . . then I had a minor panic attack. I haven't told Solar or Hughes about it," I confide.

"Still getting over the tumble in the drain?"

"I don't know. I've been through worse. Much worse. I might just be losing my nerve."

"Let's take your mind off that with some thrilling text forensics. I took just about everything I could out of his house that might contain clues about what he was up to." Gwen points to a bulging garbage bag. "I also went through his trash."

"Anything stand out?"

"That a human could live on that much take-out Thai food and pizza without getting bored to death. Also, he'd been purchasing a lot of big plastic containers that I couldn't find in the house."

I nod. "We use them to soak our dive gear, rinse off the saltwater, remove the grime. Stafford was meticulous about that."

"Okay. But more than one hundred containers?"

"Oh. That's a bit excessive."

She gestures to the boxes of documents and books on the table. "These tell an interesting story. I found his Social Security card, passports, birth certificate, and deed to his house."

"Anything off?"

"Everything's in order. But it's a little odd. Stafford is sixty-five years old, but almost none of the documents came from later than 1985."

"I think that's roughly when he moved to Florida."

"His birth certificate says he was born in Florida. You said he was from Minnesota?"

"My dad or Stacy mentioned that, I think. He grew up somewhere else. Maybe he was born here, then his family moved up there?" I ask. "Could you reach his mother or father?"

"His mother is deceased and his father is just listed on his birth certificate as 'unknown.' That's not a good sign," says Gwen.

"My dad said something about him having a difficult childhood. Maybe he started over down here. Were you able to find a Petra Stafford? That was the name of his sister, according to Stacy."

"None. It's possible she had a different last name," Gwen says.

"Are the documents real?"

"What do you take me for? I double-checked. Everything is legitimate. But nothing other than the birth certificate is older than 1985. He got his Social Security card that year and his first passport in 1989."

"What about the other documents?"

"I didn't find anything mentioning meteors, lost gold, diamonds, UFOs, or aircraft parts, if that's what you're asking. Lots of diving logs. Boxes and boxes of manuals for different kinds of dive gear and five copies of *Playboy* from the 1990s filed in a folder titled 'Playboys.'"

"Sounds like Stafford. We still haven't found his laptop. That raises a flag."

Gwen nods. "Find anything on his phone?"

"It's a password-protected iPhone. Hughes is seeing what he can do with it. I was hoping you'd find something," I admit.

"Like a manifesto? No such luck. Maybe in the dive logs and maps there's some other story that can be told. I also found this in the trash."

Gwen sets down a crumpled receipt in a plastic sleeve. The ink is so faint it's almost impossible to read. The amount is for six hundred dollars and says something like "Moth Retail." The top of the receipt has a series of lines of faded text that says "Hug . . . Stor . . ."

"I couldn't find a huge store that sells moths at retail," Gwen remarks. "I did find this, though. I thought you might find it interesting." She removes a clear plastic bag from a box and lays it on the table in front of me. Inside is a book. *Life at the Bottom of the World* by Jacques Cousteau. "I guess he's like your patron saint or something, right?"

"It's complicated." I put on a pair of gloves and take the paperback out of the plastic. The cover is worn, and the pages have taken on a brown tint.

The publication date is 1981. I flip through pages and see where passages have been underlined and the names of places circled. I also notice that the book uses the UK spelling for words like "colour." When I turn to the copyright page, I see that it's a British edition.

"I guess he had this for a while. Or bought it used," I venture.

"Turn to the back of the book," says Gwen.

I flip to the back. There's a description of the contents. I read through the text several times while Gwen watches.

"I don't understand," I finally say, setting the book down.

"Didn't you watch *The Hardy Boys and Nancy Drew Hour?*"

"I was more into *Baywatch* and *SeaQuest*."

Gwen takes her phone off the table and turns on its flashlight and aims it at the back cover of the book, then moves it around. The glare on the coating washes out of the text until a number etched into the surface becomes visible.

Someone once placed a piece of paper on the back of the book to make a note and left an impression grooved shallowly into the book jacket.

"He used it as a scratch pad?" I ask.

"A long time ago. I found the book inside the bag, and there's no indention on the bag. At some point he used his most prized possession as a writing surface."

"We don't know if it was his prized possession," I point out.

"Maybe. I got a photo of the number . . . with some difficulty."

Gwen slides a printout in front of me. It's a blowup of the number with the color and contrast adjusted to make it clearer.

There's no mistaking Stafford's handwriting. All the sevens have their little crossbars.

It's a phone number with a 305 area code. That's South Florida.

"You try the number?" I ask, already knowing the answer.

"Yes. It's for a tire shop in Hialeah," she replies. "I couldn't find a connection to him. But I didn't look too hard. Notice this, though?" She points to the "1" in front of the number.

"That's the country code for the US and Canada," I tell her.

"How often do you use it?" she asks.

"Overseas? All the time. But I would never write it down. Maybe if was an out-of-state number . . ."

"He may have written this before he came to South Florida," Gwen observes.

"Some kid in Minnesota reads about Jacques Cousteau and moves to a warmer climate to explore the oceans. That doesn't seem out of line." I shrug.

"Well, here's the other thing . . ."

I know Gwen well enough to know when she's about to drop a bombshell.

"Go on, already," I tell her.

"You were too young for it to faze you, but back in 1995, we had a bit of a telephone apocalypse when they changed the area code for cities north of Miami from 305 to 954," says Gwen.

"Ah . . . I take it, then, that using 954 instead of 305 as the area code doesn't reach a tire shop in Hialeah."

"Correct. It connects to a middle school in Plantation."

"Okay . . ."

"That got that number twelve years ago," she finishes.

"Oh. Well, that doesn't help us."

"It does if I did a search through a records database from 1985 and find out the name of the person who originally had that number," she reveals with a dramatic flourish.

"Say it, Gwen."

"Jerry Reesman."

"Jerry who?"

Gwen looks disappointed. "Jerry Reesman? Seriously? Did you ever read a newspaper before you became a cop?"

"Not unless there was a lobster and a mallet on top of it."

"Jerry Reesman is a South Florida con artist. His name has shown up in everything from bet fixing at the dog track to bribing elected officials."

"Interesting."

"Somehow, he never did any time. The slippery bastard always got away. Witness didn't show up, judges threw out the cases. All those high rollers you exposed in the Bonaventure case? I guarantee Reesman knows who you are."

"What was Stafford doing with *his* number?"

"What was Stafford doing with a notorious con man's number all the way back in the 1980s?"

"Where is Reesman now?"

"He lives in Summer Grove."

"The adult retirement community? The one where they did a drug bust?"

"That one. They may be old, but they still party hard."

"A bunch of retired mafiosos and drug dealers live there, last I heard."

"That's the place. Want to stop in and see what Reesman has to say?"

"Monthly rental!" I blurt out as I reach for the receipt.

"What?"

"Look. That says 'monthly rental.' And at the top? It's not 'store,' it's 'storage.' What storage place starts with H-U-G?"

Gwen pulls it up on her phone. "Hugo Storage in Davie. It's only a few miles from Stafford's house."

I take Stafford's keys off the table and select the small key that didn't fit the padlock on the shed. "I wonder . . ."

"I wonder indeed."

"I'll grab Hughes and take a look. See what you can set up with Reesman."

I'm out the door before Gwen can respond.

CHAPTER 25
FINAL STOP

The owner of Hugo Storage opens the gate in the chain-link fence for my vehicle when I flash my badge at the camera.

His office is a white building at the edge of the gate. Behind it are rows and rows of storage units that look like they've been here since Florida was part of Spain.

"Can I help you?" asks the old man from under an umbrella protecting him from an afternoon shower.

"We're looking for Fred Stafford's unit," I reply.

He looks at me and then Hughes. "Who?"

"Fred Stafford? I think he has a storage unit here," I explain.

He shakes his head. "I don't know him. Are you sure you have the right place?"

"He drives a blue truck. He might have dive gear like tanks inside of it?"

"Oh. That guy. I've seen him. I think he has a unit towards the end that way," the man replies.

"Any chance you can look it up?"

"You cops?"

"Yes. I showed you my badge," I remind him.

"My grandson has a badge. It doesn't mean he's the sheriff."

"We're cops. I assure you."

"Then get a warrant. I don't want to be an asshole, but I also don't want to get sued."

"Okay. We'll just have a look, then, I guess. For what it's worth, Fred's gone missing and I'm a friend."

"Whatever," says the most miserable man in the world as he turns around and heads back into his office.

"Nice guy," Hughes replies.

"How much stomach do you have for attempted breaking and entering?" I ask.

"It's not attempted if we get the right storage unit on the first try."

I drive us down to the end of the rows that Mr. Sunshine gestured toward. As I pass the roll-up doors, I feel a scar itch on my leg.

"Last time I was in a place like this, I got trapped in a pile of crates and had to talk some car thieves into helping me out," I remind Hughes.

"Sorry I wasn't there for you. The FDLE had me doing busy work. It won't happen this time," he promises.

We get out and go up to the first storage unit. The lock fits a completely different kind of key from Fred's. I try it anyway. It doesn't fit.

I move on to the second unit and try the lock. It doesn't open either.

"About how many units are here?" I ask.

"Twenty-four per each row and there are five rows," says Hughes.

"Alexa, how much is twenty-four times five?" I ask out loud and pretend like I'm expecting an answer.

"You should have used ChatGPT now that it can do math," says Hughes. "Let me try the next one. No offense, but your luck hasn't been the best lately."

I toss the keys at Hughes's chest. He snatches them out of the air before they even come close to hitting him.

He leans down and makes a show of placing the key into the lock. "Abracadabra."

He turns it and the lock snaps open. He stands up straight and takes a bow.

"If I find out that you and the geezer back there were in on it, I'll be very upset."

"More important question: What do you think's behind the door?" he asks.

"Anything from an alien spaceship to King Tut," I answer. "What's your guess?"

Hughes looks to the ground for a moment. "I have no idea. I can't get the idea of meteors out of my head. But my gut tells me it's going to be a pile of smelly dive suits and some rusty tanks."

I reach down and lift the handle to the roll-up door and give it a yank. "No more games. Let's find out."

The door slides up and reveals a small room lined with empty metal shelves and something roughly the shape of a body under a blue tarp sitting on a table like the one we found in the shed.

Hughes and I both get serious real fast, slipping on gloves simultaneously.

"You want to get this on your phone?" I ask him.

It's important that we proceed extremely carefully if this is what we're afraid it might be. There will be many questions later.

I walk to the far end of the table and lift the edge of the tarp and slowly pull it off what's on the table.

I see it before Hughes does. "Holy shit."

It's hard to make out the details because it's wrapped in layers of clear plastic shipping material, but the contours and shape are unmistakable. Especially the sunken eyes and hollow cheeks looking back at me.

I let the tarp fall to the floor.

"Jesus," says Hughes as he stands there letting his phone record.
We're both dumbfounded.

"That ain't Stafford," Hughes finally manages.

"No. Not unless he's a time traveler."

We're looking at the remains of a body that's very, very old.

And by "remains," I don't mean a skeleton. I mean a well-preserved body that looks like it's been dehydrated—but not decomposed.

"How old?" asks Hughes.

"A hundred years? More? It's really hard to tell."

I lean in for a closer look and notice something about the left hand—it's clutching something.

I can't quite make out the fine details through the plastic, but it looks like a stone with a sharp edge: like a weapon. The black material covering the tip could even be blood.

"Let's get Solar here and figure out what to do next," says Hughes.

"I'm going to get my professor down here too."

This may be an archaeological matter, not a police one.

CHAPTER 26

SUNSHINE

Reesman is sitting under an umbrella at a table on a pool deck filled with people who could have been background extras in *Scarface*. I mean actual actors in the movie—now almost fifty years older, with tan wrinkles and sagging body parts.

All of that old flesh has me thinking about what Hughes and I found in the storage unit. I have to put that out of my mind for now. The archaeologist in me can ponder it later.

Reesman is a heavyset man smoking a cigar as he scrolls through his iPad while drinking a beer. He looks up as we approach.

We didn't tell him we were coming. Gwen had a friend on the staff who tipped her off on where to find him.

"Sorry, ladies, I don't run strip clubs anymore. I don't have any work for you," he says, then turns back to his iPad.

Gwen warned me to expect this. Reesman is a first-rate asshole with no love for the police—especially me or her, apparently. She also said she could tell when he was lying—which is whenever he's talking.

Gwen takes a seat. "We'd be legal, but I understand that's not your taste."

"You got some sass in you," says Reesman. "How about you, sweetheart?"

I never realized how creepy "sweetheart" could sound until now.

"Hello, Mr. Reesman," I reply professionally. "How are you doing?"

One of the ways to get someone talking is not to ask them if you can ask them some questions but to just start asking them questions. First small talk, then what you really want to know.

"Better since I saw you on the news. Hanging it all out there, huh?" He leers.

I don't take the bait. I know he's got a hate on for me because I put some of his cohorts in jail.

An older waiter walks up to the table.

"They don't need anything, Clive. They'll be leaving," says Reesman, waving the man off.

"How well did you know Fred Stafford?" I ask.

"Fred Staph-infection? Don't know him. Nice way to ease into the question. But pass," he replies. "You now working with her and that scum Solar?"

"In a manner of speaking," Gwen answers.

"I know you think your boss is a hero. But I know stories. Don't believe everything about the myth. You know what I'm saying? He's just as crooked as the rest of them. He was just slightly smarter, then figured out how to use *you* to take out all his enemies."

"Jerry, do you believe half the shit that comes out of your mouth, or does your brain just take a vacation?" Gwen inquires in an innocent tone.

"You are as mouthy as I heard. But I think your former friends in homicide used another word to describe you," he shoots back.

"Then you know I'm not a cop anymore."

"They finally forced you out."

"It's called retirement. It's also called not giving a fuck. I could slap the shit out of you and there's nothing you could do about it," she says, deadpan.

"You mean other than get an erection?" he says with a laugh.

"Would you even know where to look to see if you had one?"

"Hey," I interrupt. "This is amusing and all, but my friend is missing and I'm trying to find out what happened to him. Mr. Reesman, forget the badges for a moment."

"Badge. Just one of you has a badge," he replies.

I ignore the taunt directed at Gwen. "I've known Fred since I was a kid. He wasn't a close family friend, but someone I looked up to. His friend reached out to me because nobody has seen him for well over a week," I explain as earnestly as possible.

"Is there more to you than a pretty face?" asks Reesman.

"They're still scraping the blood off the streets in Catalina from the last group of people who put her to the test," says Gwen.

One person's moment of heroism is another's personal trauma. I don't question what I had to do in that situation, but I don't feel great about it.

"That's right. The crew Ethan Granth hired," says Reesman. "He was an imbecile."

"Could you tell us about Fred Stafford?" I try once more.

"Darling, I know a lot of people. I probably crossed paths with him at some point if he was somebody worth knowing. But I don't know where he is. I can't even put a face to the name."

"Then tell us why he had your phone number all the way back in 1985," says Gwen.

"Maybe he sold me some weed? I don't know. Do you know how many people had my number? I put it on goddamn ballpoint pens."

"What for?" I ask.

"Laundromats, carpet cleaning, nightclubs . . . hell, I don't know. I've had a lot of businesses."

"Racketeering, sports fixing, vote buying," lists Gwen.

"And how many juries found me guilty? Zilch. I've known my share of shady people, to be sure. By 'shady people' I mean politicians, police, and judges." Reesman looks at me. "Here's one for you. The day I opened my first bar in North Miami, do you know who came in right before closing to tell me how much I was going to have to pay to keep my windows from getting broke and my cash register from being robbed? One answer, and it wasn't guys with Italian accents."

"No. I don't."

Reesman is getting worked up. "It was the *cops*. Your people. I go down to the station to complain to the captain. I tell him his guys came in there and told me I had to pay them five hundred dollars a week. You know what he said? It would be a thousand if I didn't mind my business."

"I know that station. Five of them eventually did time, including the captain—Forez was his name," says Gwen.

"'Eventually' is the operative word. They bled me dry for years. And time? Three months, then released for good behavior. It was made very clear to me then how things worked. I've been accused of everything, and nothing ever stuck because I'm not the scumbag you all think I am."

"Then what kind of scumbag are you? 'Cause we ain't buying your 'I'm just a victim of the big bad city' story," says Gwen.

Reesman looks at me. "You have no idea how bad an idea it was to bring her here. If you came alone and I'd've known anything, I'd have told you already."

"If anything comes to mind, let us know." I place my business card on the table.

"Yeah. Sure. I'll get right on it."

"You're a prick, Reesman," says Gwen.

"Why don't you go fuck off now." He picks up my card and tears it in half.

Gwen and I get up and leave. When she gets into the passenger side of my vehicle, I give her a long stare.

"Did you have to press all his buttons?" I finally ask.

"You have your methods. I have mine. Listen, he was never going to tell us anything. There was no point to trying to be little Ms. Sincere. He can spot that a mile away. You don't last that long without being smart."

"So what the hell was the point of all that?"

Gwen's phone rings and she answers. "Uh-huh. Say that again? You sure? Okay. Thanks."

"What was that?" I ask after she hangs up.

"That was the waiter, Clive, my friend on the inside. Reesman has loose lips, so I had him listening after we left. Apparently, Reesman made a comment to the effect of, 'They should look at Skolnick Farm.'"

"Skolnick Farm? What is that?"

"We'll soon find out." Gwen crosses her arms and stares back at me, victorious.

"Well played. Really well played."

"I still got a few tricks," she says with a sniff.

CHAPTER 27
BUDDY SYSTEM

"Does the coroner have any news?" I ask Solar as he sits at the table where Gwen, Hughes, and I are waiting.

"Not yet. They're taking their time. This all got really complicated fast. Your professor, Baltimore, she's working with them. You might hear something sooner than I do," he says. "So . . . you talked to Jerry Reesman. How'd it go?"

I had to leave the storage unit while the forensic team was just getting started. Not that there was going to be much to see. They were going to take photos and fingerprint samples of everything, then carefully move the remains into a coroner's van—hopefully one that wouldn't end up in a canal.

"We don't exactly have a break about Stafford's whereabouts as much as a potential lead," I explain.

Solar rolls his eyes. "This is going to get interesting. You should write down what he told you, set it on fire, and bury the ashes. He's burned more people with bullshit leads than I care to remember."

"This wasn't bullshit," says Gwen. "He didn't say it to us. He mentioned it to someone after we left. I have an informant who's close to him."

"An informant who never got exposed?" asks Solar.

"Yes. Because I'm the only one who knows who he is. And now McPherson." She turns to me. "And she's going to keep her mouth shut, right?"

"Sealed."

"I'm not asking," says Solar. "I just want to know if it's any good."

"We'll know soon enough," I reply.

"About what, exactly?"

"Reesman said something about Stafford and 'Skolnick Farm,'" Gwen tells him.

"Was that the youth ranch up near Port Saint Lucie?" asks Solar.

"It was a boys' home from the 1950s to the 1970s," explains Gwen. "It was eventually shut down after the state moved to a foster care system."

"And he said Stafford was there?"

"He may have been speaking metaphorically. But we think the two are connected and it's worth checking out."

"Okay. But don't let Reesman send you on a wild-goose chase. We shouldn't forget about Stafford's friends." Solar looks at me as he says this, as it was on my to-do. "One or more of them might know something about what we found in his storage unit."

"I'm on that. I just haven't had time since the storage unit."

Gwen speaks up. "Liza Yurinov had a DUI four years ago. Pete Langshire was charged with stealing tools from an employer, but it was thrown out before trial, and Ed Buelman was arrested for selling narcotics when he was in college, but that case was dismissed. He's had a few lawsuits that resulted in out-of-court settlements."

"Clean-cut bunch," Solar observes dryly. "But nothing that screams murderer or grave robber."

"Nothing that screams honest either," says Gwen. "I didn't talk to any of them, but I wouldn't trust any of them farther than I could throw them. If they knew why Stafford drowned, I don't get the sense they have the time to care. But that's just me. McPherson is the one that talked to them."

"I don't know, but I might after I dive with them."

"Which you'll be doing this Friday," says Solar. "With Hughes alongside you," he reminds me. "And, given all we've found, you'll both be exercising extreme caution. Remember: we still don't have Stafford's body. There could be a diving knife in his back, for all we know."

"Do you really think our killer's gonna let their guard down while diving with two cops?" asks Gwen.

Solar stares at her. "What we *do* know is that we can't keep the body from that storage unit a secret for much longer. Once it's public, the Rats and everyone else will know exactly what Stafford was up to—or appears to have been up to," he corrects himself. "Though I'm still not sure why he'd want a dead body. The swamps are full of them."

"Unless there's something special about this one," I reply.

"We'll see. But for now, focus on the living. Anything else?"

"What about looking into the other sinkholes?" I ask. "Stafford could be down there."

"One step at a time. We can bring in more resources, but the state is going to be sending down all kinds of people to breathe down our necks if Stafford's mummy came from state land. Not to mention the Indian tribes. We might end up with recovery teams in all the sinkholes, whether we want them or not," says Solar. "Go check out Skolnick Farm and then find out what Stafford's friends know—which I suspect is a lot."

CHAPTER 28
THE FLORIDA PROJECT

Skolnick Farm isn't even in the middle of nowhere. It's off to the side in some forgotten corner of nowhere.

Only one state road comes near it. There are a few scattered farms and forests in a region carved by irrigation canals.

It's the part of Florida that feels like a video game background that keeps repeating until you have to check your odometer to make sure that you're actually traveling forward in time and space and not stuck in a *Groundhog Day* loop.

"Imagine working out here every day," I say to Hughes in the passenger seat.

"Imagine coming face-to-face with a dead body at any random moment or swimming with alligators," he replies. "I think I could get used to farm life real quick."

"Bullshit. One week in and you'd be adding AI to the tractors and trying to figure out a way to get bees to do your bidding or something equally weird."

"Probably."

"Find out anything else about the boys' home?" I ask.

"The newspapers were kind of thin on account of it being in the middle of nowhere. The Skolnicks were an old Florida farming family. When the last one died off in the 1940s, their attorney turned this into a home for orphaned boys. They were taught agricultural skills. That faded into a more traditional education in the 1950s and '60s."

"I guess people had a problem with using child labor in hazardous industries," I reply.

"Something like that. At some point in the late 1970s, they started doing rehabilitation of young men in the juvenile justice system who didn't have homes to go back to or had behavior issues. Then in the late 1980s, they shut down and redirected their wards to other state programs."

"Any reason why?"

"Nothing specific. But it looks like they stopped getting state grants. It may not have been feasible. The home was owned and operated by a charitable trust. From land purchase records it looks like they sold off most of the surrounding farmland, including water rights, over several years. In one transaction, they sold several thousand acres for ten million dollars to a development company looking to build a planned city between the coast and Lake Okeechobee."

I check the gas gauge when I see the first station in miles.

"Let's pull in here. You want to grab some coffee while I pump?" I ask.

"Sure thing."

I pull up to the pump and start filling the monstrous gas tank. On the side of the road with the gas station, there are clusters of trees emitting riotous birdsong. Across the road lies wide-open land that doesn't look like it's being cultivated for anything, but I'd be the last to know.

The gas tank is almost full when a tractor trailer rumbles by.

"Must be rush hour," I say under my breath.

I love the solitude of open water; this kind of place unnerves me for some reason. I can't tell if it's the isolation of the farmland or the sporadic patches of natural landscape that feel like isolated islands separated by asphalt and man-made canals.

Canals made Florida what it is. I'm not ready to throw myself in front of a dredging machine, but I sometimes wonder what it would have been like to explore Florida when the only way to cross the state was on foot and in a canoe.

Probably too many snakes and too much malaria for my taste. Malaria was eventually eliminated by the 1940s here with better land management, lots of chemicals, and the introduction of fish that eat mosquito larvae.

"Hey, McPherson," Hughes calls to me from the front door of the gas station. "I want you to meet someone."

Sitting behind the counter on a stool is an older woman in the middle of telling some story to Hughes. She nods to me, then carries on.

"In 1942 the army was going to build a bombing range because they heard the navy wanted to use Lake Okeechobee to practice naval aviation without the Germans or Japanese knowing what they were doing. There was even some talk of building an airport right out here. But nothing came of that. After Walt made his deal with John D. MacArthur to build Disney World near where PGA Boulevard stands today, a few people started bidding on land here to build a resort complex between Orlando and Miami because there were going to be two big airports. Of course, Roy put the kibosh on that." She stops and takes a deep breath.

"Anyway, you were asking about Skolnick Farm. It's not much of a farm now and hasn't been since I was a little girl. My family's store provided a lot of their groceries. Although we had to use Mr. Mazer's truck for deliveries. Actually, they were his cousins who had a produce stall near the highway. This was an old truck that could barely make it down the road. My daddy had to go out and help fix it when it wouldn't leave the driveway."

"You ever been to the farm?" asks Hughes, interrupting her multistranded narrative.

"Lots of times. I helped out Ms. Nagle a few times when she was short-staffed in the kitchen. The first time, I didn't know what to expect. You know, we'd heard all kinds of stories about the 'wild boys' and how they were bank robbers and, pardon my language, R-A-P-I-S-T-S waiting to happen."

"What were they like?" asks Hughes.

"Perfect gentlemen," the woman says with emphasis. "'Yes, ma'am. No, ma'am. Thank you, ma'am.' Now they were young boys and I wasn't much older myself, so I got stares, but as soon as I caught one looking at me, he'd turn all red and look away.

"When I got home that first day, I told my daddy how well behaved those young men were and how I couldn't understand why they didn't have homes, now that they were done getting into trouble.

"He said, 'They weren't like that when they came to Skolnick Farm. Mr. Mazer gave them discipline. They're not polite, they're scared.' And ever since, I think about that . . . Is someone being nice because they *want* to or because they're afraid? It's like dogs. Some breeds are naturally good. Some have a mean streak you can never train out of them. That's why you hear all those stories about old ladies getting bit by their pit bulls."

"Do you think these boys were pit bulls?" I ask.

"Some, most definitely. They were only saying 'yes, ma'am' because Mr. Mazer or one of his teachers was watching. You could kind of tell by the look in their eyes. Others, they were just like any other child, only they'd had some real hard luck."

"Did you ever meet a boy named Fred Stafford?" I ask.

She shakes her head. "I never got to know any of them. Mr. Mazer kept them to the farm. I'd see a lot of different faces each time I was there. I think some of the boys ran away. I guess that was a real problem. There were no fences, and if someone didn't like it, they'd just walk away. If they were smart, they'd take the back roads. If they weren't I'd see them in the back of Mazer's pickup truck all sad-faced after they got snatched on the highway and hauled back to the farm."

"About how many boys were there at a time?" I ask.

"I think it fluctuated. They had the main building, and then some Quonset huts Mazer bought real cheap would pop up on the property to house more boys. We could tell when there were more of them by the number of cans of beef stew they ordered. Mother would say, 'Looks like Mazer has a new crop of boys—he just ordered fifty more cans.'"

"Dumb question, but do you have records?" asks my inner Gwen Wylder.

"What would you want that for?"

"Just out of curiosity," I reply.

"Mother kept all the records. I think they might be in the garage. I didn't throw a lot of that out because of tax reasons. I can take a look when I get home. But why are you all interested in Skolnick Farm, anyway? You looking to turn it into a home and raise some kids?"

"Hughes and I work together. We're not married. I think a friend of mine may have been sent there. He went missing recently."

I take out my phone and show her a photo of Fred Stafford.

"I don't think I've ever seen him. He could have walked in here twenty minutes ago and I would have forgot, but nothing rings a bell. Well, let me know if you find him, because that would be a first."

"A first what?" asks Hughes.

"The first time any of those boys ever came back after they left the farm."

CHAPTER 29
CAMPUS

I park my Suburban in front of the metal barrier blocking the road to Skolnick Farm. Trees along the highway hide the buildings and main house from view. You could drive right by the entrance and never realize there was an orphanage hidden back there.

The surrounding farmland that once was part of the property has modern irrigation equipment and well-kept fences. As we walk down the fractured asphalt of the driveway, it feels like we're entering another era. The main building is a two-story throwback to 1930s minimalist architecture. Like many government buildings at the time, it's all straight lines and narrow windows, built on a gradual hill with planks covering windows at ground level.

The rest of the property is a collection of small buildings and Quonset huts spread out across several acres of weed-infested grass.

Gravel paths connect several of the buildings, while the rest of the property looks undeveloped. Whatever lawn-maintenance program they had in place looks like it was halted when Jimmy Carter became president.

Cicadas provide the obligatory soundtrack for any part of rural Florida this time of year. My nostrils pick up the scent of a decaying animal in the brush to the side of us.

We walk toward the building with a thick chain wrapped around the door handles and a No Trespassing sign above it. The windows have aged plywood panels covering them. Likely to keep people out and to provide some protection in case of a hurricane. None of them looks like it's been pried away. I can't see any sign of forced entry.

"Looks like the meth heads overlooked this one," I tell my partner.

"I think it's too out of the way. You'd never know it was here."

We walk around the side of the building and see more covered windows. We find a concrete patio in the back with fissures large enough to shove your hand into. At one end is a rusted pole for a basketball hoop with a backboard that's almost completely rotted away.

The huts are lined up as if on a miniature army base. I walk up to the closest one, which is missing a door. Metal cots are piled up in the back with trash. The mattresses have almost decomposed back into their base elements.

As I step onto the floor, the wooden planks squeak, and I hear the sound of scurrying from somewhere underneath my feet.

"At least it's not going unused," I observe.

All the doors to the huts have been pulled off. Each one resembles the first, with the exception of the last, which looks like it was used to store lawn-maintenance equipment.

The property goes on all the way to a line of trees, where a small path cuts through. We walk to the edge and find a concrete picnic table.

"Lunchroom?" I ask.

"Teachers' lounge," says Hughes as he kicks an ancient coffee can used to hold cigarette butts.

I look around at this desolate place and try to imagine what it was like forty years ago.

In my mind's eye it's equally depressing—but in a different way.

"Haunted" is how I would describe it now.

"Hopeless" is how I see it back then.

"I'm surprised there wasn't more written about this place," I say to Hughes.

"Yeah. It'd be a great location for a teenage *Cool Hand Luke*."

"You mean *Holes*," I say. "That was one of my favorite books as a kid. The desert location seemed so exotic to me, having spent too much time on the water."

We'd only found three news articles mentioning Skolnick Farm. One was a *Sentinel* feature written in the 1950s, showing a group of young boys in a classroom.

Another was an editorial from 1969, promoting how the school instilled patriotic values in rebellious young men.

The last one was written in 1983, announcing plans for an expansion that never happened.

All three articles were light on details and mostly praised the school as a proud Florida institution.

Since it was smaller than other orphanages and youth facilities, it evidently flew under the radar. We found plenty of court documents ordering young men to be sent here. Mostly hard-luck cases without parental support, like runaways picked up for shoplifting.

Mazer, the attorney who ran the trust and operated the property, also served as a ward for the court and sat on the local child-services board.

How Stafford fit into all of this, I have no idea. I wasn't exactly expecting to see him sitting on the steps here, but I was hoping for something. Maybe a parked trailer home or some hopeful sign that he was hiding out here and hadn't died back in the sinkhole.

"You think Reesman pulled a fast one?" asks Hughes.

"It has crossed my mind. He might have sussed out Gwen's informant and decided to make us feel like idiots. Joke's on him, though: Gwen is back in the office in air-conditioning while we're out here. Of course, if Reesman really wanted to be cruel, he could have just named some offshore shipwreck and you and I would be out there trying to find it."

"Worse, he could have mentioned the landfill."

"Gwen isn't the gullible type. She can be a bit overconfident, but I don't think she'd easily fall for one of his tricks. At least I'd like to think she wouldn't. Maybe there's something more here."

"Want to check out the building?" asks Hughes.

I nod. "I'm pretty sure I can get that lock open."

Ten minutes later we're standing inside the foyer. The power has been out for years, and the batteries for the emergency lights have exploded in their cases and oozed out the bottom in a dark-brown goo. The place smells like a rodent mass grave. Ceiling tiles have fallen and formed misshapen piles on the peeling linoleum.

"It's even more cozy on the inside," I remark.

We use our flashlight to guide our way through the first floor. The building is split into two wings, running left and right.

On the left side we find offices with rotten desks, empty filing cabinets, and a cafeteria with an open kitchen.

Torn posters line one wall, including a food pyramid from the 1970s. Hughes lifts up a poster that pulled through its thumbtacks on the top.

Bill Cosby leans on a stack of books and gives a thumbs-up, encouraging kids that reading is empowering.

"Not at all creepy," I reply.

Hughes lets it fall back in place. "I can never look at Jell-O the same way."

We walk toward the other end of the first floor. The doors have been removed from the hinges, revealing empty classrooms with no desks. Only broken blackboards remain.

There's a single dictionary on a bookshelf. The rest are completely empty.

"Do you get the idea that this may have been the only reading material back when it was open?" asks Hughes.

"I've been thinking the same thing."

We take the stairs to the second floor, stepping over more fallen ceiling tiles and going around electrical conduit that's fallen from the rafters.

"The way the humidity breaks things down in Florida, it's hard to tell if this happened a year ago or a century," says Hughes.

"That's one of the problems with archaeology in tropical locations. Everything turns back into jungle in a few decades except stone. That's why we think of Mayan culture as a bunch of pyramids and not a vast empire built on agriculture."

I think about the body we found in Stafford's storage unit. We'll be able to get an approximate measure of age once Nadine does tests. Archaeological dating has come a long way in the last few decades. I have to grit my teeth every time I hear someone say it's not that accurate when it comes to dating really old artifacts as an excuse for why their pet prehistory theory is stupid.

History is weird, and it only gets crazier the closer you look. We don't know a lot about the people who have lived here for ten thousand years. We find new clues all the time. Archaeologists are just now grappling with the idea that there was a vast civilization that stretched from Great Britain to mainland Europe when sea levels were low enough that you could walk across the English Channel.

In Turkey they're finding stone monuments older than we consider the starting point of civilization.

God only knows what was going on thousands of years ago below my feet.

The upstairs contains two large bathrooms and an open area that was presumably where the boys slept. There's no cots or furniture, only linoleum with round indentations where you'd expect bed legs to have been placed.

Hughes moves his flashlight from corner to corner. "I guess this is about what we should have expected. No flashing light that says *clue*."

"Definitely not. Do we call it quits?"

"Do you feel like you've looked enough? Is there anyplace you'd regret not looking after we're two hours away?"

It's a great way of framing a question to prompt a thoughtful response.

"Let's look outside again. I want to make sure we covered the entire property."

Hughes takes out his phone and pulls up an aerial map. "Looks like we missed a building on the other side of the trees by the teachers' smoking area."

CHAPTER 30
THE SHED

The cinder block building is about ten feet wide and thirty deep. It's set up on a concrete foundation that appears to have been hastily poured into a rough ditch. A thick brass and stainless steel padlock is fastened to a heavy-duty latch above the doorknob.

This isn't a symbolic lock; it's the kind a property owner uses when they don't want someone to pop it off with a screwdriver or crowbar.

The front of the shed faces a weed-covered space at the far end of the property, where small bushes grow in clusters. There are too many rocks and hills for the property to be used for baseball or soccer. That might have been part of the planned expansion that never happened.

I use my kit to pick the lock, then pull it from the latch. Hughes and I take a step back as I open the door in case we're about to unseal a meat locker that hasn't been cleaned in decades.

A musty scent greets my nostrils, but I don't catch the reek of death.

Hughes aims his flashlight inside. Rusty rakes, pitchforks, and shovels hang from hooks on the walls. No rotting sides of meat or bodies. It looks like an old toolshed they kept locked so the delinquents couldn't steal the equipment.

There are a few cans in the corner and a milk crate with brushes encrusted in paint. The back of the shed is a row of metal shelves with pipe fittings and plumbing tools. The shelving unit on the far right is empty.

"Well, that's anticlimactic," says Hughes.

"It could have been far worse. Should we take a selfie to send to Reesman flipping him off?"

"I'd rather he never knew we came here, to be honest. Maybe we make Gwen buy us lunch while we go over how she handles informants in the future."

I take out my phone and snap a few photos of the interior with a wide-angle lens.

"Just in case."

I check the photos to make sure the flash didn't ruin things with light glare off a metal paint bucket. Something stands out when I look at one of the images. Not an object or anything obvious, but the near symmetry of the photo. I'd used the widest-angle setting to capture as much of the inside as possible.

The shed is almost the same size as the storage unit where we found Stafford's mummy. Ten by twenty feet is a common-enough size for a storage room. But this room looks shallower.

"Hold on," I say to Hughes.

I step outside and use the virtual measuring tape on my iPhone to get the length of the building.

It's twenty feet, give or take an inch.

I step back into the shed and measure the distance from the front to the back wall.

It's fourteen feet.

"Hughes, I don't think we've seen all of it."

"Yeah. It does look a little shallow."

He walks to the back of the shed and grabs the empty shelf and slides it out of the way, revealing the back wall.

There's a small quarter-size hole near the left side. He sticks a finger inside and pulls.

A hidden panel opens, revealing a dark, closet-size space.

"Come take a look," he tells me.

I turn on my light, and he steps aside so I can see.

The small room is completely empty except for a dirty twin-size mattress lying on the ground.

It's stained and worn down to the point that stuffing is coming out of a corner.

It's the stains that bother me the most. They're dark brown—the color of dried blood.

I aim my flashlight at the floor, walls, and ceiling: tiny dark specks cover the surfaces.

"This isn't good, Hughes. This isn't good at all."

I feel a surge of anger and disgust. I've seen enough crime scene photos to have an idea of what kind of abuse went on here. The blood spatter is especially concerning.

"What do we know about Mazer?" I ask.

"Not much. He was politically connected. He died in 2000. When the trust he set up went bankrupt, this land became property of the county. Although a law firm working for it insists that the land wasn't to be developed."

"Any criminal history?" I ask.

"None that I could find."

"What about the teachers?"

"I couldn't find anything about them. One of the articles mentioned that they hired men who'd gone through criminal-justice reform."

"That doesn't sound good. We need to talk to Solar."

I also need an excuse to step outside the shed and catch my breath. That mattress is a nightmare made real.

"What's up?" asks Solar when I call him.

"We're at Skolnick Farm. I'm going to send you some photos. We found something disturbing."

"Let me have it."

"The graphic term would be a potential 'rape room' at the back of the property. We found a bloody mattress that looks like something out of a serial killer's basement."

"How recent?" he asks.

"My guess is that it's been sitting here for decades."

"Any connection to Stafford?"

"None that I'm aware of. But this case is only getting weirder," I admit. "Who knows?"

"Okay. I'll call the sheriff on my way and also clear something with the governor's office."

"What's that?" I ask.

"I just want to make sure we don't have any roadblocks. It seems like Mazer was a good ol' boy who may still have some supporters. I don't want any surprises."

I hang up and start pacing around the field in front of the shed. Hughes emerges and walks toward me but keeps his distance. He's still trying to process what he saw.

It's difficult enough to imagine a young child abandoned by their parents and then thrown into a desolate and lonely place like this. It's another thing to imagine that child having to go through beatings that constitute torture—and likely repeated sexual abuse.

Mazer may be dead, but I plan to speak to every person I can find who worked here—I don't care how old or infirm. We also need to track down the victims and make sure they tell their stories and get some chance at justice. God knows what it would be like to carry that trauma for so long.

"Hey, McPherson," says Hughes.

"What?" I snap. "Sorry, what is it?"

"You know Dr. Theo Cray, right?"

"Yeah. I've spoken to him a couple times."

"Do you think you could give him a call?" asks Hughes.

"I guess so." I scroll through my contacts to find his number. "Do you think he might know something about this?"

"He has this interesting theory about vegetation growth . . ."

I dial Cray's number and wait as it rings.

Hughes is staring at the grass beneath his feet. "He says in some situations you can—"

"This is Theo," Dr. Cray answers.

"Hey. It's Sloan McPherson. Sorry to bother you," I reply a little nervously.

"Not a problem. What can I do for you?"

"My partner has a question."

"Can you put him on video?" Hughes asks.

I give him a confused look.

"Not a problem," Cray replies, overhearing the request.

I turn on FaceTime and Theo Cray's steel-blue eyes look back at me. The flecks of gray in his hair make him look perfectly professorial.

"Pan the camera around the property here," says Hughes.

I point the camera at the weeds and grass, still unsure what he is looking for.

Then it clicks.

What Hughes was about to tell me was that Dr. Cray has shown that in some situations you can spot unmarked graves through the pattern of vegetation growth.

"Jesus Christ," says Cray when he sees what we're seeing.

CHAPTER 31
RAPID INVESTIGATION TEAM

Hughes and I are helping Gayle Pinnesky, a record keeper for Okeechobee County, take old filing boxes from the back of her station wagon and set them on a table under a tent in one of the makeshift workspaces that have been set up on the grounds of Skolnick Farm.

We found the evidence of a mass grave only six hours ago, and there are already more than forty people here, including an FDLE forensic team and agents from the FBI.

When the UIU was disbanded, Solar worked behind the scenes to put together an interagency response team that could act quickly when needed. The two biggest hurdles he'd observed were getting the legal authority necessary in place quickly enough and the laboratory work processed as fast as possible.

His solution was convincing the governor to use discretionary funds to pay for two RVs—one with a mobile attorney's office for quickly navigating all the potential legal minefields and one with a mobile lab that could process evidence on-site.

The special-response teams were comprised of staff Solar had hand-picked from the FDLE and state prosecutor's office. They are almost all under thirty or have a reputation for getting things done fast.

Solar convinced the governor by pointing out the amount of time we spent getting warrants and waiting for lab results on some of our high-profile serial killer cases. But behind closed doors, he also made the case that in order to go after public corruption, you have to move faster than the legal teams of the bigwigs you're pursuing.

Literally being able to drop an RV full of rabid young idealist lawyers on the doorstep of a city hall or a corrupt police department would be the law enforcement equivalent of a SEAL team that could land anywhere in the world within hours.

While there's an argument to be made that you can sometimes move too quickly, Solar believes that it's better to get your evidence processed quickly and incriminating documents out in the open fast than to let them be buried by court motions.

While waiting for the others to arrive, we used a methane probe I keep in the back of my Suburban for cases like this. It's a long, hollow tube you shove into the ground that gives you a reading of how much methane is present—higher methane being an indication of a body decomposing.

We counted at least fourteen spots where there was enough methane to indicate a body was buried. The probe couldn't tell us how long ago they were buried—we'd need the team in the mobile lab to tell us that—but unless this was a cemetery for farm animals, it seems a certainty that there are human remains to be recovered.

None of the vegetated patches looks recent enough for Stafford's body to be buried here, but I wouldn't rule it out entirely.

Solar asked Gayle Pinnesky to bring whatever documents she had on Skolnick Farm so we wouldn't have to wait to do records searches. Gayle's no youngster, and that's no coincidence: Solar's task force members include a large number of senior citizens from across the state, ranging from retired state troopers to small-town librarians.

"I started in the county office when I was twenty-three. That was back in 1958," explains the spry octogenarian as she carries a heavy box and drops it on the table with a thud. "I had a bad feeling about Mazer the first time I met him. He was what you call *oily*. All smiles and laughs, but phonier than a three-dollar bill. He was always buddying up with the police chief, the mayor, whoever was in charge. Anyone running for office knew they could go to him and get a campaign donation. Where it came from, I don't know. He didn't have a penny until he showed up one day as the trustee for the Skolnick family after Olga passed away with no heirs."

"How involved was Mazer with the farm?" I ask.

"Very. He lived a half mile up the road in a big house that became a horse farm after he passed away. He came here all the time." She points to a window second from the end on the left wing. "That was his office."

"Would you say he had a good idea what went on here?" I ask.

She locks eyes with me. "He *was* what was going on. I tried to tell people there was something *off* about him. People who knew him told me that's just the way he was. Well, I didn't trust him or what was going on here—that's why I kept every record, every document . . . anything that came through the records office that related to him or the farm." She winks at me. "I have an old shelf in the back of records storage where I kept all this. Knowing one day somebody would come asking. Just like what happened at the Florida School for Boys up in the Panhandle," she says, referring to one of the darker chapters in Florida history.

The Florida School for Boys, also known as the Arthur G. Dozier School for Boys, was a reform school that operated from 1900 to 2011. During its one-hundred-plus-year operation, it generated scores of stories about abuse, rape, and even covered-up deaths. While there had been sporadic investigations and attempts to reform the school, the full scope of what was going on wasn't realized until a little over a decade ago, when investigators found the remains of dozens of boys in unmarked graves.

Survivors who endured abuse through the 1960s came together to share their story and sue the state. They called themselves "the White House Boys," taking the name of the place where much of the abuse happened.

When I walked out of the shed, I felt especially sickened because I'd already heard a version of this story before. Being one-tenth of the size of the Florida School for Boys could be how Skolnick Farm avoided scrutiny for so long. That and Mazer's political connections. From Donna's gas-station stories to Gayle's accounts, it seems like Mazer was using both the Skolnick estate and the fund for the school to enrich himself and others with influence.

"Did you know Mazer never passed the bar?" asks Gayle.

"How was he able to practice law?" asks Hughes as he sets the last of the boxes down on the table.

"He had a certificate that said he passed the bar in Nebraska. I looked it up, but there was no record. When I told this to the county magistrate, he laughed it off and made some comment about Mazer operating under pro hac vice, which didn't make sense. I think that's why Mazer never set foot in an actual courtroom and had his lackey lawyer Kyle Tibbet do his legal work."

"What exactly is in these boxes?" I ask.

"Like I said, anything I could get that related to financial documents, permits, what have you." She taps a dark-brown file box different from the others. "I got to talking one day with Nora Kleinrock, a nurse who worked in Dr. Hofferman's office, about how Mazer gave me a bad feeling. She said the same thing. Hofferman had a contract with the state to provide medical services to the school—something Mazer arranged, of course. Mostly just making sure they have their shots and get checkups. They needed those records to keep getting funding. He was also the doctor on call, although Nora said he didn't make too many visits to the school other than when it was time to give them their shots and do physicals.

"Anyway, she didn't like Mazer and thought Hofferman might be doing something he shouldn't have. So when he passed away, she took all the records for the school and gave them to me."

Hughes and I look at the box like it could hold kryptonite. There are strong federal rules regarding patient privacy—including for minors.

"We might need to go ask the RV about this," I reply, referring to the vehicle filled with young attorneys.

"Check if you feel like you need to, but I looked up the law on this and checked it with an attorney. Patient records of children in the protective care of the state can be shared with authorities if there's suspicion of child abuse. I think this fits the bill, don't you?"

"Good enough for me," I say as I sit at the table.

"I'll go double-check with the lawyers," says Hughes. "Read fast, in case they say no."

"Walk slowly and grab some coffee first," I advise.

"Now, I don't have anything like a smoking gun," says Gayle, "other than Hofferman double-billing by performing two annual checkups. But as far as I know, this might be the best record of what boys went there because neither Mazer nor Hofferman would miss a chance to make a dollar."

I pull out a binder filled with lists of immunization and checkup records. Each page has a list of names filled in by hand and a checkbox regarding whether they had a physical and which shots they were given.

I flip through the binder, searching for Fred Stafford.

I find it in the last third.

8/22/1976
Fredrick Anson Stafford
Age: 15
Race: Caucasian
Notes: Patient treated for broken arm. Fell from playground equipment and landed wrong, resulting in a fracture of the ulna. Bone reset on premises and plaster cast applied.
Cost: $812

"Did you ever see *any* playground equipment around here?" I ask.

"No. That's not the kind of thing Mazer would have thought was conducive to a child's education. You'd see the boys running laps and playing football, but nothing like that." Gayle taps the binder. "You'll notice that more than a few boys got fractures falling from invisible monkey bars," she replies. "And Hofferman overcharging. I don't know how much of that was for keeping quiet and how much went back into Mazer's pocket. Probably a little of both."

It's bad enough that these boys were being abused, but even worse that every broken bone put money in Mazer's pocket. I want to find his grave and spit on it.

"What other records do you have?"

"Just these, but I've called a few other people to see what they have. I told them to bring 'em on down. It's time for a reckoning."

"Hey, McPherson," says Hughes as he approaches the table.

"What did legal say?"

"Same as Mrs. Pinnesky. But that's not what I want to tell you. Ground-penetrating radar has confirmed our methane probe. They've brought the necroscope and are about to look at the first potential burial."

CHAPTER 32
GRAVE ROBBERS

An archaeology teacher once told me a story about an amateur collector who invited her to his home to show his private collection and tell her about his discovery of a previously unknown cultural practice of an ancient tribe in Central America. Since the collector was a friend of a trustee of the college, plus a donor, she obliged.

Over dinner, the collector told her about his trek to a remote jungle and how he acquired several pieces of clay earthenware from a previously unrecorded archaeological site. He said that upon inspection he noticed a practice that made him think that this group was somehow connected to the Navajo.

When Navajo (or Diné, as they're also known) weavers create rugs, they create an imperfection known as a "spirit line" to prevent their own soul from being trapped in the tapestry. The donor brought the professor into his collection room and showed her eleven different pottery items in display cases. He believed the makers had imparted this spiritual belief into the vessels.

"You'll notice that in every single item there's a small flaw—a hole punched into the ceramic," he explained as he flipped a switch that turned on tiny spotlights to illuminate the location of the holes.

She noticed that each one was about the diameter of a quarter.

"Did you collect these yourself?" she asked.

"I acquired them near where they were found."

"But you didn't see how they were found?"

"No. They were dug up, I presume. But you'll notice each hole is almost exactly the same size. That's too perfect to be random."

"It is," she replied. "It's the exact diameter of the sharpened stick grave robbers shove into the ground to try to find artifacts like this."

The professor told me that the donor didn't understand at first, then it all made sense. He hadn't found some unknown cultural feature connecting tribes across thousands of miles. He'd paid grave robbers for artifacts they'd damaged in the process of stealing.

The amateur archaeologist didn't realize the process of acquiring the pottery was what had created the unusual feature. He was also completely unaware of one of the oldest grave-robbing tricks: shoving a stick into the ground and seeing if it hits anything.

Modern methods have become less destructive, but they still amount to using something to see if there's anything there.

Delusional amateurs walk around historic battlefields with dowsing rods and get excited when they find a bullet close to where their rods cross—not realizing you'd find a bullet at just about any random location.

When trying to find out what's under the ground in a suspected unmarked burial site like the one we're on, it's important to make sure the excavation methods don't destroy what you're looking for. The problem is, the less destructive the method, the slower the excavation. In a proper research dig, you can spend months or years meticulously removing layer by layer with brushes and tiny trowels.

For a criminal investigation, you have to find a happy medium, which can sometimes mean using heavy construction equipment to clear as much of the soil as possible, *then* using slightly larger brushes and shovels.

For his forensic operation, Solar convinced the military to lend him state-of-the-art gear that's not even used in civilian research.

Brenda Jules, a physicist from Florida State, is working with a postdoc named Kevin Tsang to use the most advanced version of the grave robber's stick: in this case, two sticks.

These sticks are narrow carbon fiber tubes that are screwed into the ground using a power drill. Their placement is determined using ground-penetrating radar. GPR can show you if there's something with a different composition in the dirt below, but without much precision.

What makes the tubes useful is the long instruments Jules and Tsang place into them. One has an X-ray emitter, the other an X-ray sensor.

By moving the tubes deeper into the ground, the system can image a one-inch by one-foot cross section. To image the next section, another pair of tubes are drilled into the ground adjacent to the last ones.

This lateral movement is what takes the most time. But in field tests it only takes an hour to get a complete scan of the skull and half that for the teeth—which are what we're really concerned with at the moment.

Exhuming bodies can be fraught with legal difficulties, even on government lands. For anything older than seventy-five years, we have to coordinate with the state archaeologist and give them two weeks to decide how to proceed. If they determine that the remains may belong to an indigenous group, they'll make sure that the appropriate practices are put into place.

For a rapid investigation, that can make the "rapid" part difficult. Thankfully, with the necroscope—the rather spooky nickname for Jules's side-scanning X-ray—we can capture enough data to ID a body, assuming we have dental records for comparison.

Hughes and I walk over to the small crowd gathering around a display connected to the necroscope.

"We used a predictive algorithm with the GPR to try to find the jawbone," says Jules as she steps through the curious crowd to the screen. "Kevin, go ahead and start."

Tsang is kneeling by a case with cables running to the two probes. "Please clear the area if you have a pacemaker. The ground should absorb the X-ray, but we don't make any promises," he explains. "Okay? Three, two, one."

The screen is filled with a gray blur.

"Did you take the lens cap off?" asks a forensic tech in an FDLE jacket.

"Funny, David. Give it a moment. The X-ray uses an achromatic lens to give us depth. The computer is still processing."

The image suddenly changes and reveals a solid white shape.

"Back it up two centimeters," Jules calls out.

A moment later the image pans out and we see the edge of what looks like a molar.

"Gotcha," says Jules. She steps closer to look at the shape. "That's definitely a tooth. A human tooth."

The excitement is immediately followed by the sad realization that we're standing over the graves of at least fourteen young people who were likely murdered.

"Get the verticals, then let's set up for the next lateral," says Jules, cool as ice.

She's not being indifferent. She simply has a job to do and no time for emotion.

Twenty minutes later, we have a complete X-ray of the mouth. A computerized reconstruction will help match it to a person if we find the dental records to compare with them.

"How are we coming with dental records?" asks Solar.

A young woman working on the RIT research team speaks up. "We're getting the database of missing-persons' dental records."

"What if these poor kids weren't reported missing?" asks Solar.

"We'll have to check the state to see if they have the student records archived," she responds.

"Oh Christ," he groans, clearly realizing that his rapid-investigation proof of concept may have hit a not-so-rapid wall.

"What about Dr. Vincent's records?" asks Gayle Pinnesky.

"Who's that?" replies Solar.

"He was the dentist for the school."

"Can we get him down here?"

"Oh, he's long dead," she says. "But I have his files in my station wagon."

CHAPTER 33
NEXT OF KIN

"We have a match. Jason Jackson," calls out Dr. Bill Karp, a dentist who showed up on short notice with a police escort provided by the Okeechobee County Sheriff's Office.

He's sitting at a table with the dental records Gayle hauled out of her car, sifting through small X-rays and documents almost as fast as Jules and Tsang are able to assemble the images from the necroscope.

At a table in another tent, the FDLE researchers are typing away on laptops, looking up family histories, court records, or any other details they can to connect the names to something other than a body.

"Checking," calls out Larissa Simone, a lawyer working for the FDLE. "Jason Jackson, no next of kin."

This is the third victim we've imaged. As with the other two, there's no living relative to claim him. Which also implies the other sad truth— he's buried here because there was nobody to miss him.

"Reported as a runaway in October 1972," calls out Xan Hoy, another FDLE researcher.

I'm sitting at a table with Solar as the information comes flooding from the ground below us and through the thousands of documents his team is poring over.

"I'm going to call it and say we're gonna keep seeing this pattern the whole night," he tells me. "The boys were chosen exactly because they have no relatives. That's the difference between an orphanage and a reform school. At least kids in reform schools usually have someone out there who cares."

The records show that as orphanages declined in favor of the foster program by the late 1970s, Skolnick Farm started taking in juveniles who had been processed through the justice system but had no home to return to. Because these boys hadn't had much parental guidance to begin with, they were too difficult to place with families.

The Florida School for Boys was able to carry on abuses for almost a century because it housed dangerous juveniles convicted of violent crimes, including rape and murder—kids the public had no empathy for. Any child who complained of abuse was disregarded as a lying psychopath. It took fifty years for anyone to take those claims seriously.

Much like our anger at criminals makes us blind to the real abuses taking place in prison, we ignore what happens to "disturbed" kids.

Skolnick Farm was different. It was much smaller than the Florida School for Boys and housed children with no families. Only the locals knew they even existed. Other than an annual report sent in by Mazer to the state, nobody was checking on their welfare. While there were state employees whose job was to check in on facilities and monitor the progress of each child, that process clearly fell apart.

It still fails them to this day. Hundreds of children vanish from foster care programs every year. Some leave to live with other family members. Some live on the street. Others become victims of sex traffickers or people looking to exploit them.

"Donatello Capaldi," calls out Karp as he holds up a file folder.

"No next of kin. Reported as a runaway in March 1968," says Hoy.

"That's four so far out of fourteen graves," I note.

"Fourteen that we know about," says Solar. "There's a lot more property to cover. I want to know what Reesman knows about this place. It wouldn't surprise me if he knew Mazer. But I'm curious as to why."

I'm convinced that Reesman never would have breathed a word about this place if he thought there was a remote possibility it would get back to Gwen.

"Does Mazer have any . . . inclinations in common with Reesman?" I ask.

"Underage, probably. Male, not that I've ever heard about. I also suspect that whatever was going on was just between Mazer, the guards, and the children." Solar calls out to the research table, "How are we coming on teaching certificates for the employees?"

We're trying to track down the people who worked here. Because they weren't employed by the state, there aren't any records we could find. But as part of its licensing agreement, the school was required to have at least one full-time teacher on staff. And those records we can look up.

"The last teacher was Travis Busman," says a woman from research. "He lives in Cutter Bluff, Arizona."

"Check with the sex-offenders registry," says Solar.

A moment later she replies, "Affirmative. Arrested for lewd and lascivious with a minor under the age of fourteen in 1993 in Georgia."

"Where did he teach before here?" asks Solar.

"West Miami Junior High School. He was a music instructor from 1973 until 1975. Then he came to work here."

"Find somebody from there. I'm sure there's going to be a story. Get me the number for the sheriff where Busman lives now."

"Did Mazer hire him because he knew about Busman's past or because he'd work cheap?" I ask.

"Probably both. I'm sure we're going to find a profile for teachers who worked here. Mazer probably kept his ear to the ground for the right type. Or they found him."

"I've got another teacher," says Hoy. "Robert Drucker. He was the staff teacher from 1968 to 1975."

"Where is he now?" asks Solar.

"Dead. He was murdered in November 1975. Shot in the face after leaving a bar in West Palm Beach."

"Any priors?"

"He was arrested for solicitation of an underage prostitute two weeks before he died. Charges were dropped after he was found dead."

"That's convenient. Drucker could have used what he knew about Mazer to cut a deal," says Solar. "I suspect the other staff probably left the state after working here. Mazer was a ticking time bomb."

"Do you think—" I stop midsentence.

"Fredrick Anson Stafford," calls out Karp.

I run over to his table. Karp has an X-ray film on a portable light table and is comparing it to an image on his computer sent to him by Jules.

"Are you sure?" I ask.

"He had a bad filling done here. A chipped incisor here, and you can see this molar is at a bad angle."

Karp places the slide on a white area of the screen and uses his touch pad to rotate the computer rendering until they line up exactly.

He turns to me. "That's as close as you can hope for."

Larissa Simone calls out from the research table: "Fred Stafford, no next of kin. Reported as a runaway in October 1976."

"Damn," I say quietly.

"Do you know who he is?" asks Karp.

"No. No, I don't."

I walk away from the tables and the harsh blue tint of the overhead work lights.

The name and birth date are an exact match. The Fred Stafford I knew certainly isn't the Fred Stafford who was murdered and buried here.

Then who the hell *is* he, and why is he using the name of a dead boy?

CHAPTER 34

JACQUES CERF

"So, who is claiming to be Fred Stafford?" asks Solar from the end of our conference room table.

A television on a mobile cart displays Stafford's passport photo—or rather, the man I knew as Stafford. This has been the question haunting me since he was called out by the team identifying the remains of the boys buried at Skolnick Farm. We still don't know the cause of death of the real Stafford. His body hasn't even been exhumed yet. But I think I have a general idea of what killed him.

The simplest way to assume an identity is to use the name and birth date of someone who's dead but born near enough in age to you to make it credible. Then you request a copy of the person's birth certificate. There are a lot of complications that go with that, chief among them that there should also be a death certificate. But if you do manage to get the birth certificate, it will enable you to acquire multiple other forms of identification.

Identity theft is a regular occurrence for living persons, but in those situations, the thieves typically want to establish lines of credit or steal funds—not to *live* as the other person.

"It's interesting that when we were looking into his background, nothing came up about the real Fred Stafford being sent to Skolnick Farm," says Hughes.

"My guess is that Mazer had someone pull his records from the state archives after Stafford—the real Fred Stafford—was killed," I suggest.

"Can we just call our asshole John Doe or . . . Jacques Cerf?" suggests Gwen. "Jacques for his hero and Cerf because it's the French word for 'deer'—as in John Doe?"

"That works for me," says Solar. "A major question is does Cerf know the source of his fake name? If he does, that could tie him into other potential criminal activity."

Cerf was living openly as Fred Stafford. If he'd stolen the identity of a living person, he would have been more careful and gone by another name that didn't match the government documents—or at the very least, gone by a nickname.

"Mazer had a fake law degree," says Hughes. "And one of the judges he was friendly with was exposed for faking his college record."

"We need to dig into that more. Maybe talk to Reesman. It sounds like he had an idea of what happened there," says Solar.

"Maybe Cerf was a student there?" suggests Hughes.

"I've been thinking about that," I reply. I spent the entire car ride back trying to figure out an explanation that would make Stafford out to be the bad guy, but I didn't have much luck. "There were some big clues out there that I ignored. Clues that Stafford—Cerf—wasn't even born in this country. We have his old book with the US country code imprinted on the cover. That's not much by itself, but there's also the way he spoke. He had a slight accent that sounded like he was from Minnesota or some other place with a Scandinavian influence."

Hughes and Solar nod.

"*And* his girlfriend said she overheard him talking to a sister. Her name was Petra—which is way more common in Europe than in the US."

"I think that makes the most sense. He may have been living somewhere else in the US before moving to South Florida. Possibly he overstayed a visa and needed an identity," says Solar.

"I can do a search of visa violations," offers Gwen.

"Can I point out something I think is at the back of all our minds?" asks Hughes.

"What's that?" asks Solar.

"We know that Cerf had a very old mummy in his storage unit, implying he's been involved in something illegal. Improper storage of remains being the least of them. We also know that he was using a stolen identity and even got a passport with it—which is a felony. Clearly, he's a criminal," Hughes concludes.

I hate to have to agree, but he's right. Stafford may have been a good guy in general, but those are all serious crimes.

Hughes looks around the table to see if we're keeping up. "And all we have is a fin and a diving weight in an underwater cavern that would seem like a pretty good place to fake your death."

I realize that I'm only now catching up with my partner's train of thought. Of all the possibilities, I hadn't considered this one—even though it was right in front of me.

"I'm not saying he did or didn't," Hughes adds hastily. "We found out that he was gambling more and had lots of cash—until he lost it. Maybe he was up to something and decided to cut and run."

"There'd be easier ways . . . ," I say, thinking.

"Yeah, but this felt the most believable. Instead of up and vanishing, he left behind just enough evidence to imply an accidental death."

"Well, he certainly didn't make it easy to find where he went," I point out. "Assuming he did it, though, why?"

"Maybe he thought the walls were closing in. Either from an investigation or the people he was dealing with. You tell me: What's the first thing you think about when you hear a scuba diver came into a lot of cash?"

"I think it might be drug related," I admit.

"Maybe he was working for somebody and ripped them off. Or he could have stumbled upon a dropped shipment or cash bundle while diving off the coast."

"Plausible," Solar replies. "But it doesn't explain the mummy, among other things. We have to stick to what we know. I'll talk to the other agencies and see if *our* Fred Stafford was a focus of inquiry. I'll also ask if there's been any word about money or drugs going missing. In the 1980s, scuba divers would find bales of coke in lobster cages so often that it became an excuse to take up recreational diving."

"Can we check the other sinkholes?" I ask.

"It's on the list. But right now, I want us to talk to Reesman and see if he's willing to give anything up. If Cerf bought the identity, it was likely through Reesman. That also suggests Reesman knows a lot more about him."

Gwen speaks up. "I don't want to reveal my source. Going to Reesman directly could reveal how we knew where to look."

"I've thought about that," Solar says. "The news is already starting to hit about the bodies found at Skolnick Farm. There's no way to hide that. For the record, we're telling the press that a maintenance worker for the county found the bodies."

"Jerry will know that's too convenient," Gwen says.

"Actually, if he suspects your informant, the smartest thing he can do is to leave him alone. I'd say warn your person, but our hands are tied here. Let me know if you want any help for them."

"Ugh. I understand. I'm sure he'll understand too. When this is all out in the open, I want him to get credit for breaking this case. He deserves at least that. It'll make him almost as happy as nailing Reesman."

Working with informants—especially law-abiding ones—is notoriously difficult. When you have actionable information, you have to take care that it doesn't lead back to the source. Sloppy or overzealous investigations have led to more than a few killings of informants. Some cops take a cavalier attitude about it, dismissing them as snitches. But even terrible cops feel a little bad when an innocent informant pays the ultimate price for their assistance.

"Hey, Hughes!" Gwen calls out and points to her laptop screen. "Your notes from last night. You wrote down the name Kyle Tibbet?"

"Yes. The woman who brought all the records said he handled Mazer's legal filings because Mazer didn't have the license to practice law. Why? Do you know him?" asks Hughes.

"I know of him. He's got to be pushing eighty. He's still got a practice in Port Saint Lucie. Mostly probate," she says. "I know the name because he's served as counsel to Reesman on numerous occasions."

"That's certainly suspicious," says Solar, understating things as usual.

"When do we talk to Reesman?" asks Gwen.

"I want you here keeping track of developments at Skolnick Farm. The less he connects you to, the better."

"Yeah. He's probably expecting my gloating face," she admits.

"Should we call him in for questioning? Maybe at some other police station, to confuse him?" I suggest.

"He'd have his attorney with him. Let's drop in on him, although he might be panicked already." Solar pauses for a moment, then says, "Hughes, I have something for you to do."

CHAPTER 35
INSIDE MAN

Reesman spots Solar from across the pool deck and starts to gather his belongings. He turns to seek an exit in the opposite direction, only to find a Broward sheriff's deputy standing in his way.

Trapped, Reesman drops his iPad and newspaper back on the table and sits—no doubt planning to talk his way out of whatever Solar's up to.

"George Solar," he says, looking up at my boss as we approach the table. "Retirement doesn't look very good on you. You seem tired."

"You know I'm not retired," says Solar.

"That's right." He nods to me. "You're chasing after this one all the time. That will wear you down."

Solar takes a seat. I do the same.

"Please sit down," says Reesman.

"We were curious if you were able to remember anything else about Fred Stafford," asks Solar.

Reesman looks at me. "So, you realized that bringing Wylder wasn't such a good idea. Bringing him is even worse. You should have just come by yourself. You could have brought your bikini, had a few drinks, and seen if that jogged my memory."

"We have a witness who says they saw you with Stafford three days ago," Solar alleges.

It's a bluff. Reesman will assume as much, or that we had a bad tip. Solar's real gambit is to see what Reesman chooses to say—or, more accurately, what his face says.

Gwen has been studying the man for years, watching videos of him being questioned by the police and giving courtroom testimony. She's gone through all of his statements and concluded that Reesman has three tells, which she described to Solar and me:

"If you ask him a question and he says, 'I wouldn't know anything about that,' that usually means he knows enough to incriminate himself. If he says, 'I have no idea what you're talking about,' he probably doesn't. See, Reesman doesn't think of himself as a liar—he thinks he's really clever at playing a game with hidden rules. 'I wouldn't know anything about that' can also be interpreted to mean, 'You don't want to know anything about that.' Which is how we feel when we're asked something that could implicate us. Whereas 'I have no idea what you're talking about' is a specific statement. 'No idea' and 'don't want to know' imply different things, at least with this guy.

"Finally, if you tell him something he knows isn't true, he can't help but gloat in a minor way. He'll say, 'Ooh, that's interesting'—which is him being sarcastic because he knows it's bullshit."

Reesman sits back in his chair at Solar's allegation, raises his eyebrows, and says, "Ooh, that's interesting."

Solar and I don't flinch, but we're thinking the same thing: because we know it's not true, we have a baseline.

"Do you deny that?" I ask.

"I haven't seen him. I've been either here or my condo all week. Ask around."

"Do you know if Stafford was involved in anything illegal?" asks Solar.

"Like what? I don't know the guy, as far as I know, but I love this kind of thing. It's like one of those true crime podcasts just sat down at my table."

"Is anyone you know involved with Stafford?" Solar asks.

"Kinda vague, don't you think? Either way, I wouldn't know what you're talking about," Reesman replies—which, according to Gwen, is a yes.

"Are you aware that Fred Stafford was using an alias?" asks Solar.

"I wouldn't know what you're talking about. It's the kind of name a reporter in television has, don't you think?" He turns to me. "You'd be good as a TV news reporter. You're cute but not too cute, just the right amount. I know some people at WSVN, I could talk to them if you wanted."

It takes every ounce of strength not to say something back. But I know that's what he feeds off. I won't even give him the chance at repartee. I simply pretend like I didn't hear anything.

"Didn't a female reporter file a claim that you were stalking her?" asks Solar.

"What? That was like thirty years ago. And she was a crazy bitch. She left town and moved to Iowa or something." He twitches. "Who the fuck remembers that kind of thing except for you, Solar? Jesus Christ. I could tell your assistant here some things about you that I heard . . ."

"I'm sure they were all told to you by fine, upstanding citizens," says Solar.

"Actually, a couple of guys on the force you knew, then snitched on to save your own ass. Grant Hoffslaw? Ty Wilson? You remember them. I saw them not too long ago. They can't wait to catch up with you. Hoffslaw made some interesting friends in prison. He got himself a nice tattoo with a big red *A*," says Reesman.

He's hinting that Hoffslaw joined up with the Aryan Brotherhood, a white supremacist gang deeply rooted in the US prison system.

"You hang out with quality people," says Solar.

"I'm a lot of things. Rat ain't one of them."

"That's good to know. Although all your enemies who were anonymously snitched on by someone from a pay phone by the Elbo Room would be interested to know that each of those calls came five minutes after a surveillance camera caught you leaving. What are the odds?"

Reesman falls silent for once. Solar dropped something he wasn't expecting.

"Real good talking to you. Is your boy back there going to put the cuffs on me?"

"What boy?" asks Solar.

Reesman turns around and sees the deputy isn't there anymore. He's now thinking he should have just walked away when we approached.

"You're a slippery bastard, Solar. I'll give you that."

Solar gets up and I follow him out.

The whole time I was waiting for him to drop some bombshell on Reesman about Skolnick Farm, but he didn't.

"That was interesting," I say after we get into Solar's car.

"I assume you picked up on the same tells I did."

I nod. "I hate that guy more and more each time I have to talk to him."

"He does not grow on you. I assure you."

"All that bullshit about calling you a snitch. You know I know that's not true."

"I know what I did," he says stoically.

Solar has a clear idea of right and wrong, but loyalty also means something to him. He was jailed in a unit with some really bad cops. He dealt with it the best way he could.

He takes his phone from his pocket. "Hughes is calling." He accepts the call, then asks, "How did it play out?"

"He kicked me out of his office right after his secretary came in and said she had Reesman on the line," says Hughes over the speaker.

Solar doesn't play three-dimensional chess—he invented his own game.

While we were talking to Reesman, Hughes was in Kyle Tibbet's office, asking for legal advice about some made-up zoning issue he was dealing with. Getting a phone tap on a lawyer's phone is fraught with legal issues—but sitting in their office and casually overhearing a caller is a different matter entirely. Mostly.

But it's a totally legal move in Solar's game.

CHAPTER 36
HUGO MAN

"Good work," I say to Hughes as he walks into the office.

"All I did was ask him if he did legal work on zoning restrictions. He then proceeded to tell me everything about a bass fishing trip he went on in 1974 to why he can't eat apricots anymore," says Hughes with a shrug.

"Did he seem concerned about the crime scene at Skolnick Farm?" asks Solar.

"He seemed like he pretended not to be aware. Although I did notice an empty bottle of whiskey in his trash can, and he was very happy to hear that I was just some businessperson looking to acquire a commercial space."

"He probably burned all the files when Mazer passed away. Less to trace back to him," says Solar.

"Anything more come out from the scene?" asks Hughes.

"Nine bodies identified so far. They may have found a separate grave site farther back. Two staff members have no public records after having worked there. Mazer wasn't taking many chances," Solar replies grimly.

"Jesus. Can we go assist? There have to be others besides Tibbet who knew what happened," I tell him.

"No. I think you need to meet up with Stafford's diving group. You *and* Hughes," he reminds me. "They probably have no connection to Skolnick Farm, but they're connected to him, and he was clearly up to something shady. Or still is."

"I talked to Stacy a little while ago," I reply. "I asked her if she could remember anything else. She's still getting over what we told her about finding his truck."

"Normally we'd surveil the girlfriend in case the suspect tries to make contact. But since she was the one that reported him missing and also indirectly led us to the body in the storage unit, I don't think she knows anything, nor will he go to her. But call her periodically under the pretext of keeping her updated. Just in case. If she stops taking your calls, then we worry," Solar explains.

"Hello, Sloan?" someone calls from the front.

I bolt up out of my chair. "Back here, Nadine! You all remember Dr. Baltimore, my permanent PhD adviser?"

"Is this a good time?" she asks as she steps into the office.

Nadine is in her late fifties and has a polite and retiring manner that disarms you until you realize how brilliant she is. She grew up in the US Virgin Islands, where both her parents were teachers. She came to the mainland to study and ended up staying and becoming a professor of archaeology.

She notices the television monitor. "Can I plug in?"

Hughes hands her the cable, and she takes over the screen a moment later with her desktop.

"I have a preliminary report on the body you found in the storage unit. While the coroner will have his report and the state archaeologist will be weighing in, I wanted to talk to you first," she explains.

A photo of the desiccated body lying on an autopsy table appears on-screen.

"The first thing you'll notice is the advanced age of the body. Also, that it hasn't undergone much decomposition. It looks almost like a mammoth that's been pulled out of a glacier or Ötzi, who was found in the Alps.

"For a body to be preserved this well in Florida requires special circumstances. While it's not uncommon to find some tissue, brain, skin, and organs, something this well preserved hasn't been seen before," she explains.

"How do we know it's from Florida?" asks Solar.

"Good question. And the answer lies in how we think it was preserved so well. If you look closer, you'll see dark-brown flecks that resemble dry skin at first glance. That's actually mud. A type of mud only found in Florida. This person was covered in it and it dried on their skin, creating a kind of natural mummification. The chemicals in the surrounding peat also helped.

"Whoever found the specimen apparently washed off the mud or exposed it to water long enough for it to fall away. But thanks to the mud, a number of features were really well preserved, including a rock or weapon in their hand, along with dried blood. We're awaiting a DNA sample on that."

"Wait, Professor. You didn't say how old this specimen was. Are we looking at something several hundred years old?" asks Solar.

Nadine pauses for a moment. "Didn't they tell you?"

"We've been a little preoccupied," I inform her, sheepishly.

"I'm sorry. We used radiocarbon dating from three different labs to make sure. This specimen is close to thirteen thousand years old. It may be one of the oldest remains ever found in North America. I thought you knew," she apologizes.

"Wait, *what*?" I ask.

Nadine shrugs. "It's unlike anything I've seen before. I'd like to know everything about where it came from."

"So would we."

"I can tell generally that it came from somewhere in Central Florida. It's different from the Vero Man site. I suspect maybe a large cenote—that's an hourglass-shaped sinkhole where the limestone floor of a natural pool erodes away and exposes a cavern underneath it."

She pulls up an image showing a diagram.

"This is Warm Mineral Springs. You can see where the pond above collapsed into the cavern below. For thousands of years the lower chamber was open air. Stalactites formed and animals and artifacts collected in there. Hugo Man probably came from something like this, but in a location we're unaware of."

"Hugo Man?" repeats Solar.

"Sorry. Temporary name. Normally we call something by the location where it was found. Since you found it in Hugo Storage, we're calling it that for now."

"Makes sense," says Hughes.

"Pardon my rather vulgar question, but how much is something like this worth?" asks Solar.

Nadine seems taken aback by the question. "These are prehistoric human remains. You don't sell them. This is the find of the decade—maybe the last fifty years. It's priceless."

"Okay, but if you had to name a price, how much?" asks Gwen.

"It would be illegal. No self-respecting collector would buy it," she says.

"What about one that wasn't so self-respecting?"

"I don't know. I've heard of some eccentric Russian and Asian collectors that buy rare specimens for their personal collections," she says with distaste.

"Millions?" asks Solar.

"Tens of millions. I don't know. This is one of the most important archaeological finds you could imagine. You price it."

"I'll start looking up rich douchebags who buy this kind of crap," says Gwen.

"Start with ones who dock their boats in South Florida," Solar adds.

"A step ahead of you."

I'm dumbstruck. I don't know where to begin or what to ask. I have a thousand questions. I've been diving underwater archaeological sites my whole life. To think that there's been something like this so close? I can't even wrap my head around it.

"How many people know about this?" asks Hughes.

"Just me and the coroner and the state archaeologist. We're all keeping this quiet because of the investigation and the scientific questions."

"Okay. Let's keep it that way for now. If Stafford was going to sell this, we don't want the buyer to know we have it. And if Stafford is still out there, we don't want him to know either."

"The camera we put in the storage unit hasn't caught anyone yet," Hughes informs us.

"I doubt Stafford will be coming for it," says Solar.

"Because he got spooked?" I ask.

"That or he's dead. But this discovery just raised the stakes." Solar leans back and thinks things over for a moment. "Instead of interviewing his Dive Rat friends officially, use the dive trip with them. But bring Hughes with you. They'll probably be a bit freer if it seems cordial."

"Okay," I reply. I'm uneasy with using a friendly invitation to spy on potential suspects—but they're not my friends. And if they are involved, they're certainly not friendly.

"You all right with this?" he asks.

"Yeah, I'm good. It's complicated, but we'll handle it," I reply, missing the simplicity of sharks and stinging jellyfish.

CHAPTER 37
SLOAN'S GAME

Hughes and I are at a restaurant called the Lobster Tale, across the street from Liza and Pete's dive shop. Besides Pete and Liza, Ed Buelman has met us here, along with four other people whose faces I saw in photographs from prior Dive Rats outings. While Stafford, Pete, Liza, and Ed are the core Dive Rats, it's apparently a loose group of people who like to drink and dive together.

Hughes and I are trying to look like a couple of off-duty cops who decided to hang out and not two undercover cops trying to find out who knows what.

I called the dive shop after my meeting with Solar yesterday and told Pete Langshire I had some news about Stafford.

The plan was to tell them that we'd found his truck in a rural setting and saw no signs of foul play. I didn't tell them about the fin and dive weight, that his truck was near a sinkhole, or any hint about the body we found or Stafford's stolen identity.

Langshire's reaction didn't give me much to go on. Instead, he'd asked what that meant, based on my experience. He seemed like someone genuinely curious and not quite processing the idea that Stafford could be dead or even murdered.

I've learned not to read too much into those reactions—especially when someone has plenty of time to rehearse what to say.

"Are you guys still doing the dive on Friday?" I asked.

"Do you think we shouldn't?" Langshire replied.

"I don't know."

"We'll talk about it at the dinner the night before. You have any interest in coming up?"

I'd been rehearsing my own lies. "Yeah, and, actually, my coworker and I have been wanting to do some recreational diving. Mind if he comes along?"

"Scott Hughes? That would be great. You two are celebrities."

And just like that, Hughes and I are sitting at a restaurant in Central Florida, undercover as ourselves.

I don't have a personal connection to anyone here, so I don't feel completely horrible. It's not like Hughes and I are going to slap hand-cuffs on someone if they toke up a joint in the parking lot without a doctor's note.

We just want to find out what happened to Fred Stafford / Jacques Cerf.

Pete asked me if it was okay to tell Liza and the others about Stafford's truck being found. I said that was okay as long as they kept it to themselves. The press was about to run an item about it anyway, so there was no point to keeping that an internal secret within the investigation.

By the time I reached the restaurant, everyone at the table had heard the news. I got basically the same reaction from the others as Pete Langshire: "What does that mean?" and "Did he run off?"

I spent a lot of time shrugging and saying "I don't know" until Hughes showed up an hour later. (We had decided a staggered entrance would make us less suspicious as opposed to two people they knew were cops walking in at the same time.)

The extended Dive Rats don't seem fazed by our presence at all. Jennifer Wasser is a police dispatcher and Kevin McCord works with the Orlando Fire Department. The presence of two cops doesn't cause a batted eye among them.

That said, when I made my intro, I told a lot of Fred-this and Fred-that personal anecdotes. I want them to see me as a friend of Fred's and not the cop investigating his disappearance.

After we'd finished the conch fritters and calamari and started into our entrées of mahi-mahi and other seafood dishes, Pete got up and addressed the table.

"So you've all heard from Sloan here that nobody has any idea where the hell Fred is and whether he's alive or, well . . . ," he begins.

"He's probably on some island taking a break from Stacy," says Liza.

"Maybe so. But one of our members is gone. It might not be good. We have to face that. Let's all toast Fred and hope he finds his way home."

Everyone clinks beer bottles and mugs and takes a swig.

"Next question. About tomorrow's dive. For Sloan and Scott's benefit—last time we spotted a new section in Neptune's Labyrinth that had just opened up. As far as I know, nobody has gone in yet. It's at about thirty meters down and a good two hundred meters from the main chamber. Are we still on?" he asks the group.

"Fred would never forgive us if we didn't," says Buelman.

"He's probably waiting down there so he can pop out and scare us," adds Reed Faisse, an airline pilot who doesn't quite know how to read the room.

He gets a polite laugh, but you can tell that everyone has been holding back the image of Stafford dead in some underwater cavern.

"I'm in," says Alissa Zarez, a high school science teacher.

"Me too," echo the others.

"Have either of you dived the Labyrinth before?" asks Buelman.

"Nope," I reply.

"Then we'll buddy you up with people that have. Sloan, you'll be with Liza. Scott, you can dive with Pete."

"We place tanks by the underwater entrance to the cavern and then run a line with glow sticks through the passage," says Pete. "We keep contact with our buddy the whole time. In narrow channels, the designated lead goes first. One hand on the line at all times. If you have to check your tanks or do anything, you attach a carabiner. We also keep extra belts at intervals. It's a pain to have to carry the extra weight—but it's even more of a pain to be at depth and suddenly find yourself rising too fast."

While Ed Buelman seems to be the organizer, Pete Langshire is the one with the technical expertise. I respect the fact that he's explaining their methods to Hughes and me, regardless of the fact that we're probably the two most experienced divers in the room. Maybe not in total hours, but definitely in dealing with dangerous situations.

"This sound good to you?" asks Pete.

"I think so," I reply after catching a glance from Hughes.

"Absolutely," he adds.

We both know this could be a very bad idea. We're about to trust our lives to people who could be involved with Stafford's disappearance, or working with him. Besides having to worry about the elements killing us, we have to worry about our fellow divers.

This means taking extra precautions.

CHAPTER 38
WHEELS UP

Part of the allure of Neptune's Labyrinth is that it's hard to get to. Other locations within an hour's drive you can walk to from a parking lot. The Labyrinth requires a thirty-five-minute hike, pulling your gear in carts through brush, sawgrass, and mud.

The reason I agreed to the dive wasn't the dive itself—people can only reveal so much when sucking air through a regulator and communicating through simple hand gestures underwater. It was to see what these people are like before and after the dive.

The moment I pulled up (Hughes and I drove separately and stayed at different motels), Reed Faisse, the pilot I met last night, and Morrison Crick, an attorney, were already there and eager to help me unload my gear.

They were like enthusiastic kids asking me about my equipment. (The back of my Suburban is practically a high-tech dive shop.) Hughes and I even have our trucks equipped with high-voltage systems so we can power portable air compressors for our scuba tanks and work self-sufficiently in the field.

Crick is thin and seems intelligent. He was the first to offer to unload gear.

Faisse helped, but the second question out of his mouth was whether my husband dives—a blatant ploy to learn my marital status.

Fortunately, I had a ready and honest answer: "We dive a lot. He had to work today."

Faisse accepted this answer and proceeded to help place my gear into the cart and made no more non-dive-related inquiries.

As I finish loading my cart, Buelman pulls up in an SUV with Liza and Pete.

Liza climbs out of the back seat. "Sorry we're late. We had to go back to the shop to get Ed some fresh tanks." She walks over to me by the tailgate and looks inside. "Pete, you got to check this out!" She takes in the fins, weights, suits, two ROVs, the drone, multiple toolboxes, and a huge parts chest.

"Hughes and I kept adding gear over the years," I explain. "We've been meaning to go through and simplify things. But you know . . ."

"Oh, I do. The dive shop is a mess. We still have cases with dive computers from the 1990s, when my dad ran the place."

So that's how they came into the dive business. I probably could have looked that up or asked my father; I'm sure he's been in there a dozen times, but it didn't occur to me.

"When did you take it over?" I ask.

"Almost twenty years ago. He decided he didn't want to do it anymore and called me up and said I could have it. My sisters, none of them dive, so they didn't care."

"And Pete? Were you two together at the time?"

"We met a few years later. He was coming into the shop to rent gear. We went on a few dates, then he just started showing up and helping out. We got married, and now, well, this is what we do."

I gently probe a little deeper. "How has business been?"

"We picked up a few contracts providing gear to the theme parks. We've also got two trailers we send to dive sites. We hired a couple local dive masters to run those. They do pretty well. Wear and tear on the gear is a constant problem. And people using their Apple Watches as dive computers is cutting into what was a good margin. But we're making it up with classes." She sighs. "I hope Staff figures himself out and comes back. He's our most requested teacher."

I can't tell if her apparent disbelief that something bad happened to Stafford is a sincere admission or a calculated statement to get me to dismiss her as a suspect.

"You think he's hiding out?" I ask.

"Staff hates conflict. I think he and Stacy had run their course and he decided to take a little time off."

"Why not tell any of you?"

"You know Staff, he's honest to the core. He wouldn't want any of us having to lie for him. It's easier if he does the Irish Goodbye and shows up some other time."

I can't ask her how she'd reconcile the fact that this honest man has been using the identity of a murdered teenager for forty years. So I shift the conversation to what she does know.

"And just leave his truck?" I ask.

"He left his last truck parked in our driveway for three months when he was in Dubai laying down some fiber optic for one of those islands. He came back from the airport, went straight to the car deal-ership, and bought a new one with the wad of cash he had in his bag. We had to remind him about his last truck. That's Staff for you," she says with a laugh.

Pete overhears us as he sets his tanks in a mud-covered cart he pulled from the back of his truck. "You talking about Staff forgetting his car at our place?"

"Yeah," says Liza.

"Fred could tell you how many cubic inches of air you have in your tank or where you set down your snorkel ring but leave his wallet sitting on top of his car as he rushed to catch a flight."

Hughes has joined us and is watching out of the side of his sunglasses. I can tell he's wondering if that comment about Stafford forgetting his wallet was a little too on the nose.

Ed is leaning on the front grille of his SUV watching us. He's quiet, observing.

"I'll never figure that man out," he says after a pause in the chatter.

"You know him better than any of us," says Liza.

"He had a lot of secrets," Ed replies.

"How do you mean?" I ask.

"I joked that he must be working for the CIA because he'll just vanish for weeks and fly back from some place with a suntan and never speak a word about it. Other times he'll come into the dive shop to get his tanks filled and not mention where he's diving. Can one man spend that much time at the bottom of the redneck pool in his backyard?"

"Let's get this expedition moving," Pete calls out. "Everybody ready?"

As we pull our carts into the trees along a tiny path, Hughes walks alongside me and whispers, "I'm going to have a minor emergency after we reach the bottom. It's planned. Don't worry. Understood?"

I hear Jennifer's and Alissa's carts getting closer, so all I can do is nod.

CHAPTER 39

TREK

We take a few breaks along the way to the Labyrinth to avoid getting too exhausted before our physically demanding dive begins.

Hughes uses the breaks to talk to the other divers and get a sense of who they are. Alissa and Jennifer seem as sincere as can be. Faisse and Crick talk among themselves, while Ed and Pete lead the way and get into deep conversations about college basketball.

Liza moves around, talking to the others and asking McCord, a firefighter, about his kids.

The conversations aren't that different from what you'd expect at a backyard barbecue, except we're hauling dive equipment so we can explore an uncharted branch of an underwater cave.

Jennifer Wasser strikes up a conversation with me when we're out of earshot of everyone else.

"So, who's your main suspect?" she asks.

"I'm sorry?"

She uses her free hand to point to the line of people ahead of us. "Come on, somebody knows something."

I decide not to play completely dumb. "About Stafford?"

"Who else?" She lowers her voice. "I saw the bulletin about his truck being found and that the Park Service was looking into a possible missing diver."

Wasser is in her late twenties and has inquisitive eyes. Last night I noticed how she'd spent more time observing than talking.

"Then you know about as much as I do."

"I doubt that," she says with a laugh.

I want to hear more about what she has to say, but I don't want to lead her into any particular direction.

"Who's *your* suspect?" I ask.

"Stafford and Ed were tight. I think Pete was a little jealous. If anyone was going to help him, Pete would jump at the chance," she says.

"Help him . . ."

"Vanish. Especially because of the Liza situation."

"And what's that?"

"You must be playing dumb. You had to notice. She's infatuated with Stafford. I think it's a daddy-issue thing, to be honest. She keeps calling him 'Staff' 'cause it sounds like 'Dad.' Well, sort of."

I wince inwardly at the lame pop psychology. "Do you think the two of them . . . ?"

"She would if he'd given her the chance. But Stafford doesn't like anyone getting too close. That man-of-mystery thing."

"What do you mean?"

"You know he didn't grow up here, right?" asks Wasser.

I don't want to reveal what I know. "Oh? Where did he come from?"

"He was born here, but his mother took him back to Germany after leaving his father. That's why when he's really, really drunk, he sings German songs."

Dad never mentioned that. Maybe there are degrees of drunk for Stafford.

"I never knew that," I say.

"Your investigation must have pulled up his school records and all that from Germany?"

"I don't handle that part. We have a woman in our office who does that. I just drag things out of the water."

"Yeah, right. So, Stafford calls up Pete and says, 'Hey, I need to lay low for a while. Want to help me out?'"

"To get away from Stacy?" I confirm.

"No. The debt."

"What debt?"

"Stafford loves to gamble. He apparently made a wager that he couldn't pay, and he's trying to outrun that."

"Who told you that?"

"Pete told me. But don't ask him about it. He says Stafford told him in confidence."

"Do you have any idea who he borrowed from?" I ask.

"No. Other than the kind of people you shouldn't borrow money from."

"You heard anything around the police department?"

"No. This is just group gossip."

"You guys ever find anything while diving?" I ask, trying not to be too obvious as I steer the topic elsewhere.

"Like what?"

"I don't know. My dad's a treasure hunter. I'm always curious. I found a penny-farthing in a canal once. That's one of those bicycles with the giant front wheel," I explain. "I mean, I find a lot of weird stuff, but that was the most unexpected."

"We've found some junk. Soda cans, but not much exciting. We like the spots that other people don't go to."

"What about the Labyrinth? Seen anything here?"

"No. This one was dived out a bit in the 1980s from some kids at UCF. Pete and Liza make it out like it's this unknown place, but people know. It's just that most aren't willing to make the effort, what with the Blue Grotto and other spots close by."

"Do you know if Stafford was looking for new spots?"

"Stafford? All the time. That was his dream—finding some new dive location nobody ever heard of. He talked about what it must have been like to be the first diver in the Blue Grotto or one of those really deep holes in South Africa." She turns to me. "See, that's why it would make sense for him to leave his car near a bunch of sinkholes. People who knew him would assume he'd gotten lost. But people who really knew him and how he dived would know better. You know what I'm saying?"

"Maybe not," I confess.

"Well, I know what you found in that sinkhole, and I know what you didn't find—besides Stafford."

"You got me, Jennifer. What am I missing?"

"There was a fin and a weight found, according to the police report I saw. What about the extra tanks?" She tilts her head toward a cart being pulled by Crick ahead of us. "We always keep extra oxygen down there in case we run out and need more to decompress. Stafford never dives at depth without a backup."

Damn it. She's right. I did the dive with just one backup—but I had Hughes on the surface ready to bring down extra air if I needed it. Or to pull me out if we broke radio contact.

Stafford was the most thorough of divers. He'd have put extra tanks down there. Hell, there were three full ones in his truck.

Was he in a hurry and forgot? And would that have been in a hurry to find something in the cavern? Or a hurry to fake his death?

"Beware, brave explorers, the mouth to Neptune's Labyrinth is upon us," Ed shouts to us from the front of the line. "From this point on, there is no going back . . . except for beer, snacks, or anything else we forgot. But other than that—we're here!"

Hughes and I park our wagons and lay out the tarps we use to keep our gear from getting wet and dirty. He doesn't remind me about the "accident" he's planning because people are all around us. But when nobody's looking, my partner points at his mask.

I think I know what he's planning, but I don't know why.

CHAPTER 40
SAFETY STOP

We're gathered in a circle, kneeling on the floor of the cavern seventy feet underwater, staring at each other in the dim light. I'm looking at Pete as he makes hand signals, explaining our next move, when Hughes's mask explodes off his face in a cloud of bubbles.

This provokes a series of slow-motion *What's going on?* gestures from the group.

He holds his mask out to show a bent buckle, then pulls out a tablet from his vest and writes:

GETTING SPARE. BACK IN 10.

Hughes hands the mask to Pete and doesn't wait for a thumbs-up. He instead starts swimming toward the surface with one hand on our safety rope.

Pete makes the gesture for us to stay in place. There's no need for all of us to waste more air going to the top, wait for a safety stop, then come back down again.

I look up and watch Hughes getting smaller as he nears the light.

I feel a tap on my shoulder. Ed has his face in mine. He's pointing to my mouthpiece.

I'm confused, then realize I'm hyperventilating . . . breathing too fast.

I hold my breath to slow down—compounding one mistake with another.

Finally, I force myself to relax and give him the okay sign.

He looks skeptical. So I take out my pad and write:

TRYING TO CLEAR EARS

It doesn't make sense, but he knows I'm an experienced diver, so I should know what I'm doing.

He gives me the okay sign in return, then aims his light at the walls and shows us the different features of the cavern while we remain in the circle.

You can see the layers of limestone that were worn away to create this environment. Small silver fish, not much bigger than a half-dollar, swim around and between us when we've settled.

At this depth, it's not completely dark, but it is otherworldly.

As Pete casts the beam from his flashlight into the walls, you can see deep crevices that look like they continue forever. This is broader and more open than the cavern where we found Stafford's fin but not as big as the Blue Grotto. Still, I see why the Dive Rats like it.

I'm involved enough in Pete's light show that I miss the fact that Hughes has made his way back to us.

I check my watch. He was gone for eight minutes. Either he got what he needed done in a hurry or he blew right through the safety stop so he'd have more time.

Hughes is a pro and has an uncanny internal sense of time and how much he's breathed, but mistakes can be made. I would like to keep an eye on him, but I'm paired up with Liza.

After we're all accounted for, Ed takes the lead, using a reel to unfurl line behind him. Crick, his dive partner, follows.

They vanish into a crevice not much different from the others; then, one by one, we grab the line and follow them into the dark recess.

Back in the main chamber, our eyes were adjusting. Now, as we swim through the passage, we navigate more by the glow of the lights ahead of us than our own.

It makes me think about the glow of an anglerfish. What makes these fish so unique isn't only the fact they have a flashlight hanging in front of their face—it's the source of the light: luminescent bacteria gathered into a sac at the end of a spine. It's a fascinating symbiotic relationship. The bacteria glow and attract prey for the anglerfish, which in turn provide nutrients for them. Each gets something out of the relationship. The ocean is filled with pairings like that. And it's not always apparent what the trade-off is. Sometimes something is simply a parasite, but sometimes it provides a benefit.

As I swim behind Liza, following her glow, I wonder about her and the others. Was their friendship with Stafford symbiotic? Was someone a parasite? If so, who was the parasite and who was the host?

By the time we reach the end of the section, I realize I haven't been paying attention to the cavern around us. It's easy to go into autopilot when you're holding a line and following the diver in front of you.

The cavern at the end is a small chamber, barely wide enough for us all to fit kneeling in a circle.

My professional opinion so far is that this is indeed an underwater cave, and that's about it.

Pete aims his flashlight upward and directs our attention to a special feature.

A three-foot-long stalactite in the center of a curved ceiling.

Okay, now I'm impressed.

Stalactites don't form underwater. They're the accumulation of minerals over hundreds, thousands, and sometimes millions of years, formed by dripping water in open air.

While I don't know the age of this stalactite, I do know that the last time it could have been in open air was nearly ten thousand years ago, when this cavern was more than three hundred feet above sea level and what we think of as Florida covered twice the land area that it does now.

My mind goes to the ancient body Stafford found. Did it come from here? Or a place like it?

CHAPTER 41

RECAP

"Care to explain your little mishap?" I ask Hughes over the phone as we drive back to South Florida after the dive.

"Yeah. Sorry for the short notice. As everyone was loading up their carts, I saw that some of them had mud on them."

"Ah. Good thinking. So while we were at the bottom of the cave waiting, you were up there getting samples."

"Exactly. And, yes, I timed for a safety stop."

"I wasn't going to say anything. I had my eye on the time too. How many samples?" I ask.

"Three carts had mud on them. The problem is the carts are pretty identical, so it's hard to know which belonged to whom. Although only one had a Diver's Bell logo from the store."

"I saw you talking to Ed and Pete. Any insight there?"

"Not a lot. Just picking up the dynamics of the relationship. Pete seems to want to please Ed. I think he sees Ed as more successful and living his best life."

"But . . ."

"Ed gives off all the signs of someone trying to look successful. A lot of talk about vacations and women. I don't know if you saw, but Ed was wearing a Royal Oak Offshore Diver on his wrist. Pete mentioned that he's getting one too."

That's a thirty-thousand-dollar status symbol for your wrist. You can spend a fraction of that on a more functional watch and have enough left over for a boat to tool around in.

"Anything else?" I ask.

"No. I'll have to think about it. I didn't see anything suspicious. Nobody said anything that seemed like a red flag. Pete talked about Stafford a couple times. Ed didn't mention him. I get the idea that they're all processing this differently."

"You probably saw I got an earful from Wasser. She has more real-world info than the others, from her police job. And she has her theories. She's convinced Stafford faked his death because of some vague gambling problems. Either that, or to escape Stacy. I think she has a thing for him," I explain.

"How come?"

"Because she kept talking about how *Liza* has a thing for Stafford. I've seen that tell before. Like if Run says to me that his friend Justin is really obsessed with a new Yamaha outboard motor, that means he's obsessed with it too."

"Hold on. I need to make a mental note of that. Next time Cathy says someone else wants something, that's code for her wanting it."

"Don't worry. She'll just text me and ask me to pretend it was my idea when you ask for gift suggestions."

"Wait . . . Has that ever happened?" asks Hughes.

"Let's focus on the case. Wasser said Stafford was originally German—or at least spent part of his childhood there. She said he sings in German when he's drunk."

"We'll add that to the list of countries to look for records from. Something else has been bothering me. We still haven't seen anyone come for the mummy at the storage place. If Stafford is out there, I'd think he'd have tried by now."

"He might have seen the body-removal team or got tipped off," I speculate.

"Possibly. But we got in because there was a key to the lock on the key ring he gave Stacy. Do you think he intended for her to have it?"

"Maybe as a backup. He didn't tell her about the storage unit—as far as we know."

"As far as we know," Hughes echoes.

"Let me call her and check in."

"Okay. I'll check in with Solar."

Stacy picks up after three rings. If it had taken longer, I would have been suspicious.

"Sloan?" she asks. "Any news?"

She sounds sincere.

"No. I just spoke to Ed Buelman, Liza, and Pete. No leads."

"Oh."

"I was checking in to see if you'd heard anything."

"No. I keep hoping he'd call. I came home this morning from my sister's place and realized I'd left the front door unlocked. I got excited for a moment and thought Fred had come back. Silly me. I'm kind of losing it," she admits.

A little alarm bell goes off in my head. "Hey, Stacy, do me a favor and don't touch anything. I want to send someone by to look for fingerprints."

"Fingerprints? But I don't think anything's missing. I can look," she offers.

"No. Just sit tight. Literally. Prints could be anywhere. I can get someone out to you right away."

"Do you think Fred was here?" she asks.

"I don't know. You probably did forget to lock the door, but we don't want to take any chances."

I hang up with Stacy and dial Hughes.

"Change of plans," I say. "Let's call Solar together."

Hughes gets our boss on a conference call, and I tell them both about my talk with Stacy.

"Stacy came home after visiting her sister and the door was unlocked. She's not sure if she did it or not. We need someone to print the place."

"Hold on. Let me text the watch officer for her district," Solar replies. "Okay. And nothing was missing?"

"Not as far as she knows."

"Think Stafford came back for the storage key?" asks Solar.

"Maybe. You could get into most places with a screwdriver and five minutes of YouTube instruction."

"Okay. We'll have someone get prints and put a car outside to keep an eye on her," Solar replies.

One of the difficult parts about being a cop is knowing when to chase something down and when to save your energy. While our dive trip to Neptune's Labyrinth gave us a little more insight into who Stafford's friends are, I can't say that anything came of it to get us closer to figuring out his whereabouts.

"There's something else to consider," says Solar. "If someone did enter her home to look for something, who's to say they won't be doing the same to the Dive Rats?"

"Like Stafford?" I ask.

"Like anyone. What happens if they show up and somebody's home?"

"Do we warn them?"

"I'll take care of it," he says.

CHAPTER 42

SPLATTER

"What's up?" I say to Nadine Baltimore when I enter UIU headquarters and see her sitting at our big table.

"I have something I want to show you," she tells me.

"She wouldn't tell me anything 'til you got here," says Solar, at the table with her.

"I wanted your archaeologist to hear this first," Nadine tells him.

Hughes joins us as I sit across from Solar.

"May I?" Nadine asks as she plugs her laptop into our screen. "Remember how I said that there was a rock in Hugo Man's hand? And what might have been blood? It turns out it was. The conditions were just right to preserve it. This almost never happens," she explains.

"Whose blood?" asks Solar.

"That's what I wanted to find out. We were able to get DNA sequences for both the mummy and the blood on the rock. They're two different individuals. And not only that, they have separate haploid groups. The two samples aren't even closely related."

"Do we have a match?" asks Solar.

"A match with whom?"

"The blood on the rock. Did we compare it to Stafford's?"

Nadine seems taken aback. "Stafford? Oh, I'm sorry, George. I should have been clearer. This blood on the rock dates back to the mummy's era. They're both more than twelve thousand years old."

"Ah, right. This is an archaeology thing," says Solar, clearly disappointed.

To be honest, I am too. We needed a break in this case.

"Yes. That's why I was eager to share it with Sloan. There's really nothing quite like this. Not only do we have a nearly perfectly preserved specimen of a Pleistocene-era human, we have a weapon that may have been used in a murder."

"The world's oldest crime scene," I muse.

"Exactly. That's why I thought you might find it interesting. And the rest of you, well, because you investigate crimes for a living," she says, faltering as she reads the lack of enthusiasm on Solar's face.

"Unfortunately, this one is a little out of date," he tells her.

"There's no statute of limitation for murder in Florida," says Hughes, deadpan.

"Yeah, well, I think we already got our perp," Solar shoots back.

"What do we know about the victim?" I ask Nadine.

"Does it matter now?" asks Solar.

I can tell he's agitated with the lack of progress. So am I. It doesn't help that it feels like we were unintentionally pranked.

"It does to me," I reply.

"According to the DNA, the victim was female. Genetically, she appears to be related to one of the earliest groups to settle here. Her attacker was from some group we haven't identified yet. He could have been part of a failed migration or a long-range raiding party," she explains.

In police work you sometimes have to disconnect yourself from what's around you and simply be an observer. When I find a body floating under a dock with a gunshot wound and a T-shirt with a photo of the victim's grandchild, I can't stop and contemplate what the loss means. I have to focus on the physical and get the body out of the water while preserving as much evidence as possible.

Even when I'm back on shore and the body is being carried away in a van to the morgue, I still have to remain disconnected in order to write my reports with a clear mind.

Weeks later, when I'm watching a suspect being interviewed, I have to focus on the logic of their explanations versus the physical reality I observed. Even when the suspect is on the witness stand and I see the faces of the family of the victims in the courtroom—maybe even the same grandchild I saw on the shirt—I remain detached so I can deliver precise and objective testimony.

After the case is over and the suspect has met whatever fate the court decided, that is when I feel connected to the victim and family and feel the magnitude of the loss, which extends well beyond the physical.

But it's too late by then. I'll be consumed by some other case, writing analytical reports about the physical state of things.

The woman Nadine is talking about is as real as any other victim I've encountered. I can't let the thousands of years separating us create more of an emotional barrier to caring than I already have.

I can't solve this one or punish her attacker—but at the very least, I can care.

"How much blood was on the stone?" I ask.

"A lot. And there was blood spatter on Hugo as well. We found some long hairs embedded on his clothing. It appears that she was in a prone position, while he clutched her hair and struck her."

"That's horrible," I say with a shudder.

"I had one of my colleagues use the multiplex methylation SNaPshot method to get an estimate. Best guess is she was between twelve and fifteen years old."

"Jackie's age," I whisper.

From the expression on Solar's face, I can see this is a gut punch to him as well.

Here we are, cops more than ten thousand years in the girl's future, and there's nothing we can do except shake our heads and say that's too bad.

"Part of my job is learning how to disconnect myself sometimes from what I find," says Nadine.

"If you have a good way to do that, I'd love to know how," Solar says.

"Dr. Baltimore, can I ask you about something related?" Hughes pulls the mud samples he gathered from the carts out of his bag. "Do you think your lab could identify these?"

Nadine picks up a plastic bag and stares at the dirt gathered at the bottom. "I don't think I need a lab for this. I was just looking this up. This is an ultisol. Very similar to Millhopper soil. Same as on Hugo Man."

Hughes takes a map from his desk and sets it in front of her. "Can you point to where this came from?"

"Sure. You already have a circle drawn around it."

She places her finger on the map, and we all lean across the table for a better look.

Just beyond her fingernail is the word Hughes wrote in his tidy handwriting:

SIRIUS

Sirius—the northernmost location in Stafford's diving log. One of the spots I didn't get to check and felt childishly relieved that I didn't have to.

It's not the name that disturbs me; it's the location. And the stories Dad told me about the Devil's Cauldron.

CHAPTER 43

MUGWAMPS

"I can take you in about five miles, but I'll have to head back so I don't get stuck after dark," says Ranger Theresa White.

We're standing next to a trailhead that's so hard to spot White had to park her truck next to it so we wouldn't drive past it.

This section of the Devil's Cauldron is called the Spine and is the hardest section to traverse because of the thick brush and marshland. White agreed to take us down the trail to the point where you have to use a compass and a GPS to avoid getting lost.

"You sure you want to bring in all that?" she asks, pointing to the dive equipment and other gear we've piled into two carts.

"No. But I don't know what to leave. Have you ever been out here after dark?" I ask.

"Where you're headed? No. And I wouldn't do it without one of those," she says, pointing to the shotgun Hughes has slung over his shoulder.

"You don't strike me as the supernatural type," says Hughes.

"Supernatural? Shotguns don't work on ghosts. I'm talking about the bears, panthers, and other weird things back in there."

"What kind of weird things?" I ask.

"You come all the way out here and you don't know?"

Actually, Hughes and I listened to an entire podcast series about the Devil's Cauldron on our way up. But I want to hear what she believes.

"I'm curious about your personal experience," I tell her.

"About two miles in I'll show you something," she explains as she leads us down the path.

Hughes and I follow behind, pulling all-terrain carts loaded with our gear.

The narrowness of the trail makes it clear this was cut by animals, not people. My cart is too wide and flattens the grass as we move along. While White speaks, I keep one eye on the wilderness around us and one on the ground for any sign that someone else came through here recently.

"This place started to get a reputation when the Spaniards first settled. It was considered much wilder and more treacherous than other parts of Florida—which were already wild enough back then. Before I share my story, I'll tell you something my supervisor told me when I asked him about all the stories.

"When he first started in 1975, he heard all the tales about mugwamps, Skunk Apes, giant alligators, floating orbs, you name it. All the senior rangers were eager to scare him with the wild tales.

"Well, he's only a few weeks in and he gets a call from the police because a woman living south of here says she saw something leaving her house. He thought he was being put on when the others told him the woman described some kind of ape-man. Turns out they were serious. Her cupboards were open, and it looked like her kitchen had been ransacked.

"Soon other people started talking about seeing some kind of wild man stalking around and stealing food. Then someone reported seeing the wild man club an armadillo on the side of the road, then run off into the swamp.

"Eventually the police decided to do a manhunt, and the ranger tagged along. The dogs finally got a scent and they saw something in the trees. A warning shot was fired.

"The bushes spread apart and out walked a man covered in dirt, wearing rags. Nobody could understand what he was saying.

"They arrested him for burglary and took him to jail. That's when they brought in an interpreter who spoke his dialect of Chinese.

"The man had been a sailor on a ship and started acting erratically. So he was sent to a hospital in Tampa, which he escaped from.

"Witnesses weren't lying or even embellishing their stories. They were just reporting what they saw. I try to keep that in mind when I get a crazy story. Sometimes there really *is* a wild man out there, clubbing armadillos."

"What happened to the man?" I ask.

"That's the tragic part. He was incredibly fearful and ended up hanging himself in his cell."

As we walk down the trail, the trees grow more densely. I can smell decomposing carcasses in the tall grass. The farther we hike, the less this feels like the Florida I know. Some of what we consider wild swampland was cultivated at some point. There were entire plantations and farms that were retaken by nature, leaving what looks like untouched wilds.

This place feels different, though. Any attempts to tame it would have failed. I understand why this sinkhole never was explored like other sites.

"This way," says White. "Leave your carts."

We follow her off the trail and through the grass to a muddy area around a large pond.

"See that spot on the other side?" she says, pointing to a bank opposite from where we are. She takes out her phone and opens the photo roll. "Take a look at this."

Hughes and I lean in for a better look.

The image is a zoomed-in shot showing the head of an alligator.

"How big would you guess it is, from this?" she asks.

"I'd need to see the whole photo," says Hughes.

"In a second. Just guess."

"Maybe nine or ten feet?" I reply.

"I'd say twelve," Hughes ventures.

"Its skull is comparable to a sixteen-footer's," she says.

"That's a beast," I admit.

"You'd know. You swam with Big Bill, didn't you?" asks White.

Big Bill was an exceptionally large and territorial alligator I had a very close call with while looking for human remains.

"Yes. I'd say Bill and this one could be cousins."

"Well, here's the mystery. We don't know how big this alligator was because we can't find the rest of him," White explains as she zooms out on the image.

The head ends abruptly in a pink, fleshy stump.

"I found this right over there. At first, I assumed it was poachers—but they usually take the head and leave the body if they're trying to make some fast money. We had our wildlife experts take a look. And here's where it gets weird. That alligator was alive when its head was severed. It was too decomposed to tell how it was cut off, but the edges were pretty chewed up and the vertebrae below the skull were snapped."

I look across the pond to where the alligator's head was found and try to imagine what fate befell it.

"No evidence of poachers?" asks Hughes. "Despite 'em leaving the head?"

"None we could find. Our best guess is he met a bigger alligator . . . or another reptile," she says.

"A python couldn't eat something that big," I reply. "Or bite its head off."

"Maybe not. We've got anaconda out here now . . ."

"I've heard," I reply. "How pervasive?"

"Hard to tell. We've had old fishermen, guys who go back several generations and fish differently than other folks—much more quietly—say they've seen brown snakes that were longer than their boats swimming in the water.

"At least with pythons, we have fire ants invading their nests and keeping their population low. Anaconda spend most of their time in the water and have live births. It's only a matter of time before they reach a critical population mass and we see them everywhere," she explains.

"Cannibal alligators and giant anacondas," says Hughes. "Wonderful."

"I wasn't talking about snakes when I said other reptiles," White corrects him.

"It's velociraptors? Right? Tell me it's them," I say.

"Nope. It's convenient that we're at a point where you can turn back if you want," she says. "Because I wouldn't want to go anywhere near the water around here after I tell you what one of our herpetologists said when she saw the photo and heard the accounts of some hikers that came through here."

She pauses, making sure she has our full attention.

She does.

"Our expert thinks the other reptile was a Nile crocodile."

White doesn't have to explain the significance of that. Although Nile crocodiles have been spotted in Florida, they haven't been large or plentiful enough to be much of a threat.

But a Nile crocodile large enough to rip the head off a full-grown alligator is a different matter. Nile crocodiles are much more aggressive than American crocodiles.

American crocodiles can lie side by side with other alligators and not mind.

Nile crocodiles, not so much.

They're by far the most dangerous large reptile.

"So, there you have it. Sure you want to go on? I didn't even get into the really weird stuff."

"I think we're good," I reply, but my hand instinctively checks the pistol on my hip.

"Just another day at the office," Hughes affirms as he tugs the shotgun tighter to his shoulder.

CHAPTER 44
SIRIUS

I'm in the lead as Hughes follows. We parted ways with White an hour ago, and while her stories didn't quite unsettle me, they did create a dramatic backdrop for our journey ahead.

As the trees grew denser and the trail harder to follow, a thin fog began to surround us. White told us to expect this. She said trappers called it the Devil's Breath. While, analytically, I know this is the cold air hitting a warm body of water somewhere around us, all the science talk in the world doesn't make it any less unsettling.

I've been trained to handle a variety of situations, including animal encounters on land and in the water—I have no experience with such encounters in thick fog. Hughes and I have tightened up our ranks so there's little gap between us.

"Do crocodiles like the fog?" asks Hughes.

"I don't know. But any croc out here has had a lot more experience hunting in this than we have," I reply.

The problem with Nile crocodiles is that they are the most apex of apex predators. Their only competition for outright ferocity would be hippos. If a senator from Louisiana had his way more than a hundred years ago, we could be dealing with wild hippos out here as well.

The senator's plan was to introduce the hippo into the Southeast to reduce the hyacinths, which were beginning to clog the waterways. He also thought all these nuisance-plant-eating hippos would make a great source of meat that he called "Lake Cow Bacon."

Hughes and I are keeping careful watch on the misty forest around us while also doing occasional stops to listen. Between the sound of our footsteps and the squeaky wheels of our carts, we make quite the racket, making it impossible to know if anything is stalking us.

I feel pretty sure—and Hughes agrees—that there's at least one large animal, probably a big cat, that's been tracking us.

It's hard to know for sure, but you can make an educated guess based on the lack of other noises, a scent you pick up, or an auditory clue. I've had this feeling before and found the tracks on the trail back later, confirming that it wasn't just my nerves getting to me.

Being tracked by a big cat doesn't mean you're in imminent danger. It's just the natural behavior of a large predator when something else enters its hunting territory. The animal wants to know what the potential threat is—or whether it's prey.

Usually humans aren't on the menu. But exceptions can be made.

"What do you think about White's anaconda claim?" I ask after a long silence.

"Everything gets exaggerated by forty percent, but why not? We have wild monkeys, Nile crocs, and god knows what else that got dumped here."

I don't want to be the one to say it, but it needs to be said. "Any extra precautions we should take?"

"Keep the shotgun close," says Hughes. "But to be honest, people have been walking through here for thousands of years—even living out here."

"True. But they knew the bad neighborhoods. Also, the three biggest threats are reptiles that didn't exist back then. The Nile crocs, pythons, and anacondas were all brought in recently," I point out.

"So you're saying we created Jurassic Park."

"Kind of. But the biggest threats are the small poisonous snakes. You're more likely to injure yourself tripping over a garden hose than getting hurt by a python or anaconda. Then again, putting a bunch of different species from different ecosystems into one place can have unpredictable consequences."

"We could just get desk jobs somewhere," says Hughes.

"Not on your life," I tell him.

"Just checking. I've noticed a trait in your family where you guys like to talk about the morbid and scary when situations are already pretty unnerving."

"You have no idea. When I was a kid, we went on an expedition to map parts of the ocean where some crazy eccentric guy was convinced Atlantis was located. He paid my dad to go get depth readings right in the middle of the Bermuda Triangle. While we were out there, we encountered a thick fog that lasted for days.

"Dad kept telling us stories of missing boats and strange occurrences throughout. I'd grab a box of cereal from the cupboard, and he'd start telling me about some ship that was found without a crew and their breakfast still on the table.

"I'm trying to eat my Frosted Flakes, looking out at this blanket of fog through the porthole, and Dad is telling me that a kraken could be reaching a tentacle into our boat anytime it wants. After that, I tied my leg to the headboard at night so the kraken couldn't drag me away."

"That sounds traumatic," says Hughes.

"The crazy part was that we kept begging him to tell us more scary stories. Well, mostly me. I don't think my brothers were as into it as I was."

"That doesn't surprise me."

I check the GPS and see that we're getting closer. The trail begins to narrow even more. I'm essentially following the path on the ground with the least grass.

We travel through thick brush for another twenty meters and find ourselves at our destination.

The location known as Sirius is an irregularly shaped pond with a large clearing to the east of it and a thick copse of trees along the western side.

The fog lingers across the pond, making it hard to see the other side clearly.

It's still light out, but fading fast. Hughes and I use our flashlights to search the ground for any sign of human activity.

"Here," says Hughes as he points his light at the ground.

There are two tracks. One made by a wheel like the ones on our cart. The other by something else.

The single track before me appears elongated and narrow, with a V-shaped arrangement of slender, pointed toes. There are four visible toes, each ending with a sharp, curved claw that has left a distinct mark in the mud. The impression of each toe is well defined, with minimal webbing between them.

Hughes has his phone aimed at the track and is taking a photograph—probably to use in some app that can identify the creature that left it.

I already know the answer before he gets his result.

It's a crocodile print. And a big one, at that.

CHAPTER 45

BOT

As we set up our gear, we spend a lot of time studying the water for movements, waves coming from below, and bubbles rising to the surface.

The water seems perfectly still—but that doesn't reassure us.

As an added precaution, we set up on the side of the pond with the biggest drop-off, leaving the more gradually sloping side open in case disturbed reptiles decide to leave the water.

This might be a foolish wish, given that an annoyed croc or alligator is just as likely to sink to the bottom of the pond and skulk—which would be fine if we weren't interested in what's at the bottom of the pond.

"Ready to free dive this first?" asks Hughes.

"Ha. Right after you," I reply.

He unfastens a case and starts to assemble his underwater robot. "I was hoping I wouldn't have to get Nemo wet. But fine," he says.

"Bots before humans."

Hughes presses a button and the robot lights up. "Nemo, you ready to prove yourself with a second chance?"

I thought this was a rhetorical question until the robot starts to speak.

"Affirmative," says Nemo in his Keanu Reeves–like voice. "On the last dive I didn't keep far enough away from the alligator and came too close to the tail. I'll try not to make that mistake this time."

"Uh, hearing that thing talk like that may be more frightening than any story we told on the way in," I tell my partner, not kidding.

"It's just a large language model interpreting a summary of previous experiences and data tables," he assures me.

"Got it. 'It's just some body parts and electricity,' said Dr. Frankenstein. What could go wrong?"

"Would you rather go in first?" asks Hughes.

"Nope. Point taken. Let's let John Wick have the first look at what's down there."

"I've added some new mapping features. We'll use the cable from the ROV that found Stafford's fin so we can get more real-time data."

I step back and gesture that this is Hughes's show.

He opens a small case with a view screen. I put my dive mat down and sit on it for a better view of the screen—while still keeping my eyes on the water and forest.

"Nemo, what are your instructions?" asks Hughes.

"I'm to survey the pond and look for potential solution holes or other geological formations indicating an entrance to a subterranean chamber," says Nemo.

"Nemo, how will you do this?"

"I'll make a topological survey using my LiDAR and other sensors, then look for the lowest point. I'll also use a thermometer to look for temperature variations," it explains.

"Nemo, what do you do if you encounter a large reptile?" I ask.

"Swim for the surface as fast as I can."

"Good call," I chime in.

"I'm gonna add some kind of deterrent in the future, like an underwater siren or something else that will keep wildlife away," says Hughes.

"You still haven't got over that alligator swatting your toy."

"You'll also notice that I've added lights to make Nemo more obvious and less turtle-like," he adds.

He carries the robot over to the edge of the pond and drops it in, sending ripples across the water.

The robot swims out three meters, then dives with the cable trailing behind.

"What happens if the cable gets cut?" I ask.

"Nemo will surface and await instruction. I can program him to survey, just like we did at the Belt Road pond. He can also detach himself from the cable if we run out of slack or he gets tangled up."

Nemo submerges and starts a spiral search pattern like his dumber cousin did at the Arcturus site. The screen shows the camera view as well as a 3D reconstruction of the pond as it scans more area. The 3D view glitches every now and then, after which more details emerge.

Another display shows sonar, temperature, and various other readings. It's a lot of data to wrap your head around. Fortunately, Hughes's AI monitors it all for us.

The shape of the pond is a flat basin with a deeper section about twenty feet from where we're sitting.

As Nemo spirals around the basin, getting closer to the bottom, I don't see any outstanding features. The bottom is a bit rockier than I expected. There's not a huge layer of sediment. That might be due to the fact that the trees are a bit set back on this side and less likely to drop leaves into the water.

"See anything?" I ask.

Hughes checks the readings. "Nothing. Not seeing an overhang or entrances to deeper chambers. Let me do another sweep."

Nemo moves along the bottom in an outward spiral. The lights bounce off sunken branches and rocks, but nothing like the entrance we've been hoping for.

"You're the archaeologist . . . Could the mummy have been found here?" asks Hughes.

"No. The water down here is too active and not the right conditions. The mud would have come off. He died somewhere dry that filled in with water later," I say, fairly sure I'm correct.

"Nemo, have you found anything like an entrance or exit at the bottom?" Hughes asks the robot via a microphone in the case.

"Negative. The lowest part of the body of water is completely flat with no sign of an entrance," replies Nemo.

"I don't know. Check our maps and look for some other pond nearby?" asks Hughes.

"I don't want you thinking I've gone nuts, but do you *feel* it?"

"Like we're being watched? Yes, since we got here."

"What? No. Wait, you do?"

"Yes. Just my nerves," he says. "What are *you* talking about?"

"This *feels* right. It looks like another pond from the air, but being down in here, I get the sense that this is the place."

"But it's not. The water just ends."

"Wait. Nemo, how flat is the flattest part of the pond?" I ask.

"Let me figure that out. I'm going to take the deepest readings and then group them. Okay. The center meter of the deepest part of the pond has a variation of about three centimeters."

"Nemo, does that sound unusual to you?" I ask.

"Although I'm not an expert in hydrology, that does sound unusually uniform. Would you like me to do a test?"

"Nemo, what kind of tests can you do?"

"I can position myself so my sonar sensor is directly over the flattest section. That could give us some idea about the material. Similar to how dolphins can use echolocation," says Nemo.

"Nemo, you can do that?" asks Hughes.

"Maybe."

"Nemo, do it."

The robot swims back to the lowest part of the pond and settles to the bottom.

"Sending a pulse now. Analyzing."

"Nemo, what's the conclusion?" asks Hughes.

"The bottom of this portion of the pond appears to be solid," it replies.

"Nemo, solid what?" I ask.

"Wood, most probably. This says the uniform thickness of a half-inch-thick piece of plywood."

"Nemo? Are you saying there's a trapdoor?" I ask.

"While it's beyond my abilities to determine, the deepest and flattest portion of this pond would suggest that someone has placed a flat obstruction over a karst window. Perhaps in an effort to protect or preserve the chamber that may be below," says Nemo.

"So, they just covered up the entrance?" I ask.

"It looks that way."

"Can Nemo move the plywood?" I ask.

"No. He's not capable of that," says Hughes. "I'll suit up."

"I'll do it," I reply. "I'll do a free dive to the bottom, move the trapdoor, then come back as quickly as possible."

"What if there's something down there?"

"Nemo did a survey. Just fish," I remind him.

"He wasn't thorough," says Hughes.

"I'll bring a small tank if there's a problem. Besides, I'll have Nemo watching my back."

CHAPTER 46
RAPID DESCENT

I'm standing at the edge of the pond, using both hands to hold a dive belt loaded with weights.

I'm wearing my suit, full-face mask, and a belt around my waist with more weights and two lights attached to it. Also just in case, I have two dive knives. One on my leg and another on my forearm.

Dad once explained to me that a dive knife won't do you much good if it's already in the mouth of a bull shark along with your leg. He was a big believer in having backups.

"You'll see the lights of Nemo from about five meters," says Hughes.

It's thirteen meters to the bottom. I can do forty feet in my sleep and still have several minutes of breath left at the bottom.

Going without dive gear lowers the risk of having a problem with decompression if I have to come up quickly. Normally this is a dumb idea, but when my biggest threat isn't the water but anything that may be in or around it, getting the hell out of Dodge City is my biggest priority.

Not that I plan to panic and surface at the first sign of trouble, but I'd rather be agile and lithe than encumbered if I have to move fast.

Of course, a week ago I had the same thought when I was trying to get the van out of the Belt Road pond.

I take a deep breath and jump into the water feetfirst. After I'm submerged, I twist my body so I'm upside down and let the weight pull me toward the bottom.

The trick is balancing speed with physical exertion. Kicking hard gets you to the bottom faster, but it also burns up oxygen.

I gently move my legs to guide me and see the lights of Nemo as I pass by.

"I have you on camera," says Hughes over the underwater radio.

I don't respond because talking would expel the air in my lungs with nothing to replenish it other than water.

The flashlight on my wrist catches the flat surface of the bottom, and it's clear from here that someone dropped a circular disc on the bottom of the cavern—like a tabletop—and then moved a few rocks to hold it in place.

"Who were they hiding this from?" asks Hughes.

Who are *they*? I ask myself.

I reach the bottom, and my weights hit the board and make a hollow thud I can hear and feel through the water.

I grasp the first stone and roll it away. I then start to move the other one and a thought strikes me: What if they weren't trying to keep people out—but to keep something in?

Okay, let's not panic ourselves too much, Sloan. Save the creepy stories for the next time you take Jackie on a trip and want to pass on a horrible family tradition.

I try to ignore all the possible nightmare scenarios of what could come crawling through and look for an easy place to get my fingers underneath to pull the trapdoor aside.

What if it's not a thing . . . but a someone? I think as I start to lift the wooden disc.

An image of a bloated body floating by comes to mind. I blink that away and slide the cover off.

I can feel warm water flow past my exposed skin, indicating some kind of underground spring.

I push the cover completely to the side, and I'm staring down into a meter-wide hole that descends at least two meters before fading into black.

Nemo whirs, moving in for a closer look and aiming its lights straight down.

I don't know if Hughes told it to do that, or if it decided on its own.

The powerful beams go straight down another ten meters and reveal a conical mound of rough rock.

Now things make sense. The pond floor was obviously too smooth.

This hole, created by the dissolving limestone, formed a kind of garbage disposal at the bottom, and I'm looking at the things that piled up underneath.

There are some sharp and jagged edges, but it's hard to make out much more detail than that. The same goes for how old it is: It formed over thousands of years, at least. There's no way of telling how far back in time it goes.

"McPherson, you plan on coming up?" Hughes asks me over the radio.

I almost answer and exhale the air I've been holding in.

Part of me wants to swim down into the hole and see what's down there right now. The lower chamber has to be much bigger than the pond above. My imagination is running wild with what is at the bottom.

I linger just a little bit longer, then give the robot the okay sign so Hughes knows I'm coming back up.

I let go of the second weight belt and swim for the surface.

Hughes is standing at the edge of the pond, ready to help.

After climbing out, I take a deep breath and wring the water from my hair. "What's with the heat?" I say when I notice he's got the shotgun hanging over his shoulder.

"Nothing. Just being cautious."

The sun has set, and the forest is darker and feels even more impenetrable than before.

I use my flashlight to scan the trees. The beam cuts through the fog and fades into black, revealing nothing.

Hughes hands me a towel. "Ready to take a deeper look?"

"Hell yeah." I unzip my dive suit and pull my arms free, letting the sleeves flap down at my sides.

The parts of my skin not covered by swimsuit appreciate the cool night air after sweating inside the suit.

"Sending Nemo down," says Hughes.

On-screen the robot flies upward and then directly down into the mouth of the cavern. It feels like I'm watching from the cockpit of a spacecraft.

The lights hit the rock-filled sediment as Nemo dives into the hidden chamber. The robot levels off and the lights aim forward, giving us our first look at the size of the cavern.

"It's huge," I reply.

"The front sonar is hitting a wall a hundred feet away," says Hughes. "Let's spin it around and have a look at the rest of the cavern."

I watch the readings as the sensor bounces sound waves off the walls and reports back how long they take to return.

"Sixty-five feet to the north. Fifty-five on the east. Two hundred and forty feet to the south," says Hughes.

"That's over a football field long!" I exclaim.

"And that's just the main chamber. I'm getting fluctuating temperature readings indicating that there's an underwater stream coming from somewhere. This must connect to a larger network of caverns."

"We haven't found anything like this in decades!"

Nemo's lights hit the ceiling, and I see the long shadows of what look like vicious cat teeth.

"Tilt up!" I call.

The robot aims the camera upward, and long stalactites come into view. There are several rows of them hanging like dirty icicles from the ceiling.

"This was open air," I reply. "A long time ago."

"God knows what we're going to find on the bottom," says Hughes.

"Or in the shelves and other parts of the cave," I reply.

"Let's start with the bottom," says Hughes. "Nemo, start a search grid."

The robot descends to the bottom of the cavern and starts sweeping the floor with its cameras as its onboard image-recognition system looks for distinct features.

I see the outlines of bone fragments and squint my eyes to make out the finer details.

I wonder if the body of the woman whose blood we found on Hugo Man's stone is somewhere down here. Did she die in this lonely grave shortly before her attacker did?

My excitement is tempered by the reality that a young woman who was very much alive as my own daughter could be buried under millennia of debris.

Alone and forgotten.

A massive knobby bone comes into view.

"Holy cow. That's a mammoth bone," I say out loud.

"A mammoth?" asks Hughes.

"Pretty sure. They would have overlapped when Hugo Man was walking around and clubbing women."

"The question is—did it fall down here or was it carried?" asks Hughes.

"It may have fallen," I reply.

"That hole was barely large enough for Nemo."

"I think that's the sediment and mud. The actual solution could be much, much larger."

Every square inch is a glimpse into a primitive Florida I can only imagine. It has me lost in thought, trying to picture the history that played out below me. I barely register the text Nemo is displaying on the screen:

Human 74%

"Hughes!"

"I see it," he replies as he sends the robot back to the object it spotted.

For a fleeting moment I wonder if this could be Hugo Man's victim, then realize that's unlikely.

The lights move across the floor, revealing more bones and sharp stones, then fall upon the white backpack of a rebreather unit strapped to an inert body.

I recognize the pack immediately. I don't have to see the face to know whose it is.

"Is that . . . ?" Hughes asks.

"Yeah. It is."

The realization sinks in. The man known as Fred Stafford isn't hiding out from creditors or girlfriends.

He's dead at the bottom of this monstrous chamber.

I don't know how he died. But I do know that he wasn't alone— because someone was here to cover the entrance to this vast cavern of Paleolithic treasure.

CHAPTER 47
THE ROTATION

"We got to get him out now," I tell Hughes.

"We should wait until we have backup divers and more support," he replies.

"We can't wait. Someone put that cover back. That means there's someone out there who knows he's dead. That someone might have been the one who broke into Stacy's home."

"I understand that, but it's dark out, and a body recovery even under the best of conditions is dangerous. We just have to sit still."

I'm losing my patience and want to accuse him of being overly cautious, but I hold my tongue for a moment so I can explain it more clearly.

"Hughes. We don't know how he died."

"I know. And an autopsy will hopefully show us," he responds.

"Yes, but it might be too late."

"Too late for what?"

"If someone killed him, then that someone's still out there. We don't know which of the Dive Rats were telling us the truth and which were lying. We also don't know why the killer felt the need to hide his body."

"Probably to keep the cave a secret," he says.

"Right. But possibly also to conceal a murder scene. If they wanted Stafford killed for some reason we don't understand, they might be willing to kill someone else for the same reason. We're looking at priceless historical specimens down there. This person might kill to protect them. Knowing how Stafford was killed could tell us a lot," I explain.

"Like what?"

I can tell Hughes is starting to listen, but he wants me to convince him.

"Was the killer with him? Or were they up here when it happened?"

"Or was he killed at all?"

"Correct. We don't know. Hours could make all the difference. Our little dive trip may not have fooled a potential killer. We may actually have accelerated things. Stacy's house was broken into after we hung out with them," I point out.

"We don't know that her house was broken into," says Hughes.

"No. But what chance do we want to take?"

"I feel the same way about doing a body recovery. I'm not sure if it's worth the risk."

"I don't know either. But we might just have hours and not days to catch whoever tried to hide Stafford's death. And remember, his truck was parked over forty miles from here along with the planted fin and weight. Someone went to a *lot* of trouble to throw us off. That means they're desperate. And desperate means dangerous."

"Fine. You made the case. First, we call Solar and tell him we found the body and have him send backup," says Hughes.

"Tell him we're recovering the body. Don't ask. He'll say no," I warn Hughes.

"If he says no, we don't do it. But I'll leave that choice up to us if he doesn't say anything."

"Fine." Hughes has a point. As much as it pains me to take the cautious approach, it's the right one.

"And there's another condition," he says.

236

"What?"

"I do the dive."

"I can do it," I protest.

"I know you can. But you also just got over a trip to the hospital, and I've let you do more diving than I should. Let me handle part of it. It's my job too."

"It was an unnecessary trip to the hospital."

"Maybe. But just the same, we're a dive team. That means we both do the diving."

"But . . ." I stifle my own words.

"Better diver? Yes. I know that. All the better to have you as a backup. If something stupid happens, you'll come up with a plan to save my ass."

"But you have a kid . . ." The reality of what I just said makes me pause. "I mean a young child."

"Sloan, let me do the dive," he pleads.

"Okay." I feel a small wave of anxiety like the one I experienced yesterday doing the dive—and when I was in the pipe at Belt Road.

It's not the diving that's making me anxious. It's something else.

"We'll be smart and efficient," Hughes says. "I'll go down and strip his gear first. We'll put that in a bag and use an inflatable balloon to surface it. Then we'll bring the body up in another. Okay?"

"Yes."

As I go through the steps with my partner, I realize why Hughes is insisting on doing the dive himself. It's not about my little mishap in the pipe or that it's his turn. It's because I knew Stafford. Hughes doesn't want me to have to come face-to-face with the dead body of someone I was close to.

"Help me gear up?" he asks.

"Okay," I reply, hoping that Hughes doing the diving is the right decision.

CHAPTER 48
RECOVERY

I watch as Hughes sinks below the surface of the pond, leaving behind only a small wake and a trickle of bubbles.

On Nemo's display screen, a beam of light from Hughes's flashlight flickers by as he descends toward the robot and the entrance to the lower chamber. 3D sonar also tracks Hughes as he sinks deeper into the pond.

All these sensors and technology are so different from how I learned to dive. You had a scuba tank, a depth gauge, and a compass. Everything else relied on common sense.

I worry that the use of this technology comes at the expense of our other senses.

"How you doing?" I ask Hughes over the radio.

"Great. Poor visibility and creepy as heck," he replies. "I'm nearing the entrance now. I'm not sure how well the radio will work down there."

"You have five minutes of radio silence before I come down after you," I explain. "And I'm not using air. I'm free diving all the way down."

"Let's hope it doesn't come to that. I don't want to be down here any longer than I have to. Picking up your weights."

As a precaution, Hughes is using my weight belt to help him stay at the bottom.

Nemo's camera follows him as he enters the hole.

The plan is to have Nemo follow him in after he's made it into the lower chamber. The robot will be there to provide extra light and allow me to keep an eye on Hughes as he prepares Stafford's body to be brought to the surface.

The jagged bones of the mound below the hole come into view.

"It's like a Jurassic Park pet cemetery in here," says Hughes. "I can't wait to find out how . . ."

"Hughes?"

". . . this goes," he finishes saying.

"The radio is cutting out," I call.

No response.

I feel my chest tighten.

This feels like the panic attack I had before.

"Hughes? Can you hear me?"

Nothing.

I realize I'm not afraid of diving.

"Hughes?"

I'm afraid of being alone.

"Here. Lost radio contact. Routing through Nemo. Nemo, track me," says Hughes.

The robot spins around until Hughes is in the center of a yellow box in the middle of the screen. He looks at the camera and gives me the okay sign.

While the radio signal is having trouble traveling all the way to the bottom of the cavern, Nemo's hardwired cable is still able to relay a signal of what Hughes is saying.

"First field test of this. How do I sound?" he asks.

"Loud and clear," I say, trying to conceal my panic.

Putting a radio relay on the underwater robot was one of Hughes's many clever ideas. I suspect it's only a matter of time until we lose my brilliant partner to some oceanographic company or military contractor.

Hughes swims around the pile until he reaches the section of the floor where Stafford lies motionless. I don't envy this part of the dive. It's not the danger factor; it's having to deal with a corpse that's in some state of decomposition. Not to mention someone I know.

"Stripping off the rebreather," says Hughes.

He rotates Stafford's body so that it's facing upward, giving me the first good look at his face since the last time I saw him alive.

I have to look away for a moment. My eyes have been staring at the screen for so long, all I see is black beyond the pond.

Something glitters for a moment in the distance, then vanishes.

I stare into the void, trying to discern a shape but seeing nothing but darkness.

I take my flashlight and aim it across the water and search the trees. Nothing.

"Holler if you're out there. I'm very well armed," I call out.

There's no response.

I click the comms. "Hughes. It may be just my eyes adjusting, but I could have sworn I saw a light across the pond. Like a cell phone."

"Need me to surface?"

"No. I'll just start shooting," I call out loudly.

Our partnership is tight enough that he doesn't ask me "Are you sure?" He only wants to know what I need him to do.

I whisper now, "It's possible I saw a reflection or maybe a wildlife camera light come on for an instant. Just keep doing what you're doing."

I grab the shotgun and stand. I flick on the light attached to the barrel and use it to probe the trees.

I see only the slow swaying of leaves in the gentle night breeze.

I listen closely for the sound of a breaking branch or footsteps. All I hear is croaking frogs.

"I have him out of his gear. Putting him into a pouch," says Hughes.

We've practiced this more than anyone I know, so there's no need to observe every step of the procedure. I keep my attention on the darkness and only occasionally glance down at the screen.

I probe the corner of the pond to my left that connects to the trail we hiked in on. If someone is out there, that would seem like the most likely place they'd enter or leave from, but I still see no sign of movement.

If there really is someone out there, I have no reason to assume that they're hostile. It could be a curious hiker who saw me sitting at the shoreline watching a computer screen and then moved on.

"Backup team just texted. They're almost here," I project loudly—but without pressing the comms button. The lie is exclusively for the benefit of anyone who might be listening.

"I've got the body secured. I'm now putting his gear into a bag," says Hughes.

I turn back to the monitor to check on my partner.

He's sliding the rebreather and dive equipment into another bag that he'll send to the surface for lab analysis.

"You okay?" he asks.

"Yeah," I reply, turning my attention back to the trees. "Just keeping an eye on things."

"I'm more worried about the things out here that don't use cell phones," says Hughes.

"Well, there's that. I've been keeping an eye on the sonar to make sure there's nothing large in there with you," I assure him.

"Sonar won't tell me if there's something sleeping on the bottom."

"Fair point. Just let me know when you send the body up. I don't want the scent of decomposing meat to get the attention of anything."

We both know that just because we haven't seen any sign of an alligator or an alligator-killing Nile crocodile, that doesn't mean one isn't around.

A Nile croc can stay submerged for two hours, and I haven't seen any movement on Nemo's sensors to tell me one's in there. That said, a croc or an alligator is perfectly capable of hiding in foliage and waiting for the right time to attack.

One could be behind me right now and I wouldn't notice. Being anywhere near the water puts you in their danger zone.

"Sending the gear up first. I'm going to guide it to the opening and let the air in the bag take it the rest of the way," says Hughes.

On Nemo's screen I can see the flashing light of the strobe attached to the end of the bag. It's bright enough to illuminate everything in a ten-foot perimeter like a camera flash.

In between flashes, my imagination conjures up images of nightmare creatures in the dark.

I start to hyperventilate a little, then catch myself.

I can still see Hughes. He's right in front of me . . . well, a football field away underground.

The strobe light pops to the surface as Stafford's dive gear surfaces.

"Bringing the body up now," says Hughes.

I stare out into the darkness, trying to see if we're being observed.

"Affirmative," I reply.

"Holding at the dive stop," he says.

I feel an anxious surge of energy as I wait for Hughes, but my nerves begin to relax when I see the bubbles from his scuba equipment boil close to the surface.

Stafford's body bag bobs up, then Hughes pokes his head out of the water.

He gives me the okay sign, letting me know everything is fine.

I return the gesture.

Now that my anxiety has subsided, I can think more clearly. There is no doubt in my mind that someone was out there and they were watching us.

We did this dive because time was critical. I'm convinced more than ever that it was the correct call.

When Hughes rolled Stafford over, the look on his face wasn't that of someone who had died from an accidental drowning. The skin was discolored—almost jaundiced, with blue blood vessels and bloodshot eyes—the way that someone who had been poisoned would look.

CHAPTER 49
AIR MIX

Hughes, Solar, Gwen, and I are in our office, talking to Dr. Ernesto Gravis via video. Gravis is the FDLE medical examiner responsible for determining the cause of death for Fred Stafford.

Gravis took the extra step of meeting us at the pond after Solar arranged a helicopter to fly him in and retrieve the body. His reaction was the same as mine the moment he saw Stafford's face.

Right now, he's showing a close-up photograph of that very face. The blood vessels around his nose, mouth, and eyes are ruptured and almost blue in color.

"As we saw at the scene, the deceased's skin had discoloration that's consistent with a caustic substance—most likely potassium hydroxide or sodium hydroxide—and massive carbon dioxide exposure caused from a failure in the diving apparatus. His lungs were a wreck," he explains.

"You people are insane," Gwen says, looking at Hughes and me.

"Do you think this was accidental?" asks Solar.

"There have been about seven hundred rebreather fatalities where a malfunction or defect was considered the contributing factor. Given that the deceased's apparatus was homemade, I'd normally suspect that it was accidental, but from my understanding of the deceased's experience with closed-circuit diving, I wouldn't automatically assume that. I'd leave that question to someone who knows more about the equipment," says Gravis.

"Hughes?" asks Solar.

"We sent it over to the FBI, but when I opened the case, I noticed that a gasket around the inner cylinder had been worn through, and there was a crack in the plastic," he tells us.

"That's not the kind of thing Stafford would overlook," I point out.

"I agree," says Hughes. "He had to open the case to add the soda lime before the dive. The crack should have been evident."

"This isn't my area of expertise," replies Gravis, "but is it possible the crack formed when he was at depth?"

"Absolutely. But it had to start from some kind of hairline fracture first," I tell him. "Stafford wrote the book on testing for those."

"You could weaken the plastic," says Hughes. "When I built underwater housings, I learned the hard way not to let materials cool down too quickly when using a heat gun. Someone could have done something like that beforehand."

"This all suggests that someone had access to Stafford's equipment. Which means it was either someone he knew or someone who was able to get near his rebreather," says Solar.

"And someone who understands rebreathers," adds Gravis.

"I'm pretty sure that rules out his girlfriend—although I shouldn't be too quick to judge," I add.

"Thank you, Dr. Gravis." Solar ends the call. "Okay. Let's walk through motives."

I begin by stating the obvious. "That cave is a gold mine. Hugo Man may be only one small part of what's in there."

"All of it illegal to sell," says Solar.

"In the United States. But in the rest of the world? They just don't care," says Gwen.

"That motive assumes that whoever killed Stafford had a connection to buyers. We need to chase that down a little more," says Solar. "So, hypothetically, Stafford—rather, the man we know as Stafford—and someone else were looting the cave. This person kills Stafford, then conceals the cavern. They knew enough to tamper with Stafford's equipment, and they possibly had a buyer. So, let's ask again: Why kill Stafford?"

"Greed," I say.

"Maybe. But you and Hughes said you have no idea what's down there. Why kill the one person who can best help you retrieve it? You generally don't kill the other bank robbers while you're still in the vault filling your bags."

"Maybe Stafford's stolen identity factors in?" I speculate.

"How do you mean?" Solar asks me.

"I have a lot of mixed feelings about the guy right now. He didn't seem like the kind of person who'd steal the identity of a dead kid or get involved in plundering archaeological artifacts. While I can't explain the former, maybe it provides the rationale for the latter?"

"Go on . . ."

"Stafford buys an identity for some reason and keeps this secret to himself for decades. The one person we know who knew about the identity is Reesman. And when it comes to all things shady, Reesman is your guy."

Solar nods for me to continue.

"Reesman couldn't dog-paddle, much less dive to the bottom of your pond," says Gwen.

"No. He's also a middleman. I'm pretty sure he knows the killer. He might have also told the killer about Stafford's shady past," I add.

"And the killer used it to blackmail Stafford?" asks Solar.

I wanted him to say it so it didn't look like I was trying to exonerate Stafford.

"Yes. Remember, Stafford had already moved Hugo out of the cave. Maybe he didn't trust this person. He could have been using it as a bargaining chip."

"We're back to why kill Stafford," says Hughes.

"The killer clearly didn't know the mummy had been moved. Maybe he was worried Stafford was going to say something to the police, so he kills him in a place he's sure nobody would find.

"But just in case, he goes to the effort of moving Stafford's truck and gear to some other location where he could have drowned and been unrecoverable," I explain.

"All right," says Solar. "And because the mud from one of your Dive Rats is a match for the murder scene, we can be pretty sure it's one of them. Do we call them in for questioning?"

"Maybe. But I think our killer might bolt and lawyer up," I reply.

"Okay. Then what?"

"We set a trap. We can be pretty sure the killer never knew about the storage unit where Stafford hid Hugo. That means they may not know *we* have it."

"You're saying we should use Hugo Man as bait?" asks Solar.

"Yep. The killer never came looking for him because they didn't know where to begin. Let's make it a little easier for them."

CHAPTER 50
DERELICT

Hughes and I are sitting inside what looks like a derelict van parked near the last row of storage units at Super Storage, outside Lakeland, Florida.

The van is actually an undercover narcotics vehicle we borrowed from the FDLE and the storage yard a DEA-owned property used to make drug buys.

Solar put this together in short order. Right now, he's sitting in the manager's office behind a desk with a shotgun in arm's reach. We don't expect anything to go bad, but you never know. A facility like this comes in handy when you want to make sure there aren't any civilians to get caught in the crossfire.

Two more undercover FDLE units are parked at either end of the block for backup. Just in case.

Five hours ago, I used Stacy's phone to send a group text message to all the members of the Dive Rats:

Fred mailed me a letter with an address and a combination for a storage unit. I can't read the rest of the writing. Do you know what this was about?

Super Storage in Lakeland

Gate: 1993

Unit: 23

Combo: 23-33-22

The first person to respond was Kevin McCord:

Weird. I can take a look if you want.

Ten minutes later, Faisse replied:

Happy to check it out when free.

The first people to respond to the message aren't necessarily our suspects. They might just be eager to help. I sent the code and the address to everyone because it gives the suspect plausible denial. Whoever did this might not want to reply to Stacy because it would leave a trail. We had to make it easy for them while also providing a modicum of anonymity.

"Any guesses on who shows up?" asks Hughes.

"No. I've made that mistake before. Everyone is suspicious to me," I reply.

"Fair enough."

My panic attack from the other day has lingered at the back of my mind. I think I've found the pattern.

"Are you happy in the UIU?" I ask Hughes.

"Yes. Of course. Why do you ask?"

"The robots and all that. I get the sense that you're not being challenged enough here."

"Oh, this is pretty challenging," he says with a smile.

"You have to be tired of the hours and getting shot at."

"Is this about me or you?" asks Hughes.

I decide to put it out there. "You're the only person other than my dad I've felt comfortable diving with. Not my brothers. Not . . . not even Run."

"You solo dive all the time," he says.

"Simple dives."

"I think I get it."

I feel my stomach clench at the thought that he's misinterpreting what I'm saying.

"Sloan, there are about three people on the planet that I trust enough to do the kind of work we do," he says. "Two are guys I did missions with in the navy. The other is you. It's hard to put it in words. I have friends I know who would take a bullet for me. But that's not it. I only really trust the ones who'll know when I need saving. I bet for you that would be your father."

"Yep."

"I wouldn't do this job without someone like you backing me up. To be honest, I was eager to join because you reminded me of my buddies—only without the shaved heads and tattoos."

"I can look into that if it would put you more at ease," I joke.

"I think Run might have questions."

"Probably. But you kind of avoided my question. How long do you see yourself here?"

Hughes turns his attention away from the monitor he's been using to watch the storage unit. "It won't be forever. But right now, there's nothing like UIU for testing my gear."

"And then?"

"I'll give you plenty of notice. And," he quickly adds, "talk you into coming with me."

"And Solar and Gwen?"

"Did you see those mobile units he put together? That man has many eggs in many baskets. When we hang up our fins . . . if we hang them up, he'll be fine."

"A large black Expedition just pulled into the complex using the gate code," Solar says over the radio. "Rental plates. Looking them up."

"We can see them now," says Hughes, back to watching the monitor.

The SUV's windows are too tinted to see who's driving. We'll have to wait to see if anyone gets out.

The truck heads straight toward us and then stops near the storage unit.

The driver waits a moment, then pulls around to bring the hatch close to the roll-up door. No doubt to make it easy to move what's inside the unit into the vehicle.

We'd wrapped a mannequin with dive weights into plastic to make it look like Hugo Man. As long as the driver doesn't take too close a peek, it should pass.

We can't stop them from going into the unit. We have to wait for them to take the property out. That's when we can swoop in and make the arrest.

My group text didn't explicitly ask anyone to remove property from the unit. Which means that anyone taking anything from there is committing a crime. It's not the most solid foundation for a case. But all we need is a reason to make an arrest and get a search warrant to look for more evidence.

"The door is opening. Someone's getting out," whispers Hughes.

I've got a grip on the handle to the van's sliding door, ready to jump out the moment Hughes or Solar calls it. I can feel my fingers start to sweat.

"Didn't see that coming," says Hughes.

I look back over my shoulder at the monitor for a clearer view.

It's Liza Yurinov. She's wearing a dark baseball hat and hoodie.

She kneels to the combination lock and enters the code. A moment later she slides open the door. She stares at her phone for a moment, then walks inside.

We put the dummy on a rolling cart to make it easy to get it out of the storage unit.

Through a camera inside the unit, I watch her push the cart toward her SUV, open the back, and then heft the body-size package inside.

"Now we have burglary," says Hughes.

Liza pushes the cart back inside the storage unit, then closes the door. She climbs into her Expedition.

"Go!" Solar shouts over the radio.

I bolt out of the van with Hughes behind me. We race to reach her before she can start the vehicle and get it into gear. If we'd had more personnel, we would have boxed her in, but this was the plan we were stuck with.

"Freeze! Police! You're under arrest," I shout as I aim my pistol into the driver's side of the vehicle.

Liza looks back at me with a mixture of horror and confusion.

CHAPTER 51
Pawn

Liza Yurinov sits in the back of an unmarked FDLE car with her hands cuffed behind her back. The look on her face remains pure shock.

Solar is talking to her while I stand outside her sight line, near the rear bumper. I don't want to distract her while Solar questions her. This isn't a good-cop/bad-cop routine. It's about letting Solar do what he does better than anyone else.

"What brought you here?" he asks.

"I was asked to pick up what was in the storage unit," she replies.

"Asked by whom?"

"K-Kevin McCord. He told me to come get this. He s-s-said it belonged to him," she stammers.

"What is it?" asks Solar.

"Something Stafford meant to give him. He said it was a dive-rescue dummy."

Hughes, standing across the alley, gives me a glance. It's not the worst lie.

"When did you talk to McCord?" asks Solar.

"A f-f-few minutes ago," says Liza. She looks over at her vehicle.

"What did you tell him?"

"I texted that I had it," she replies.

"You texted him?"

"Yes. I don't understand. I was only doing him a favor!"

"Whose truck is this?" asks Solar.

"I rented it this afternoon. Pete . . . my husband was out with our truck, and my car was too small. Kevin told me to rent a truck and he'd pay me back," she explains.

"Excuse me a moment." Solar motions for an FDLE officer to watch Liza so we can step out of earshot.

"What do you think?" he asks.

"She seems genuinely baffled. But I've been fooled before."

"McPherson, you need to get that sociopath Riley out of your head," says Solar. "You had your suspicions about her. It just took you a while to act on them. What about Yurinov? What does your gut tell you?"

"She's not a sociopath. She asks everyone about their kids. I don't know how good a liar she is either."

"Hughes, you spent some time with her," says Solar.

"I'm with McPherson. She might be involved, but I don't think she killed Stafford."

"Okay. I got one more trick up my sleeve." Solar walks back to the car where Liza is sitting. "Thank you for clearing that up, Ms. Yurinov. Would you mind standing up so I can take the handcuffs off?"

"I'm not in trouble?"

"I don't think you've done anything wrong. McPherson and Hughes vouched for you," he explains.

Liza looks in my direction and gives me an appreciative nod—forgetting that ten minutes ago I had a gun in her face.

"Could we check your phone? Just as a precaution?" he asks.

"Of course. I'll give you my passcode."

That's either a sign of innocence, stupidity, or another phone hidden away.

Solar pulls the phone from an evidence bag and has Liza unlock it. He then hands it to me.

Under McCord's photo in the conversation history is a back-and-forth exchange. The most recent one started this morning, soon after I sent out the group text about the storage unit.

McCord: Hey Liza. Crazy big favor to ask. I'm in the air right now. Can you go pick up Fred's item from the address Stacy sent? Long story but it belongs to a customer of Staff's. I need to get it sent off ASAP.

Liza: I don't have the truck. Pete is out running errands.

McCord: I'll pay for a rental. It's really urgent. It's some dive dummy thing Stafford promised to a company.

Liza: Okay. What do you want me to do with it?

McCord: I'll text you an address near the airport. I'll meet you there after I land. Thank you. Thank you. Also. Don't tell anyone yet. It's complicated. I'll explain.

Liza's text message history could be faked, but it looks to me like she's been set up by McCord. I show the messages to Hughes and Solar. They quickly come to the same conclusion without us having to discuss it.

"The drop-off point is an industrial area near the airport," Hughes says. "I think there're a couple shipping companies nearby."

"What do you think?" I ask Solar.

"It smells bad."

"Think she's putting us on?" I reply.

"I don't think so. Why would McCord send her?"

"In case of what just happened. Right now, we don't have much to go on. If we arrest him, he could just say that it was a simple mistake. He thought it was the dummy that it is, and he thought he had Stafford's permission to pick it up. Without Stafford to say otherwise, we don't have much. We can hold him like we did Liza, but if he's smart, he won't say anything or just play dumb."

"We should probably take him in and question him on that," Solar replies.

"It may not be enough. What if we have her do the drop-off?"

"I'm not sending her anywhere other than home after this," my boss tells me.

"Okay. What if *I* do the drop-off? You can't see the driver in that SUV. If I have Liza's hat and hoodie, McCord would have to get real close to know it wasn't her. Getting him out in the open might be better than knocking on his door."

"It still smells bad," he says.

"He's expecting her to be there in less than an hour. If we push it or she doesn't show up, then he'll know something's up. If we go to him at his house right now, he'll be on the next plane out of the country, if he has any sense. And from the look of this, he's thought things through."

"All right." Solar reaches for his phone. "Let's get this over with."

CHAPTER 52
DROP BOX

Highland Industrial Park is almost completely deserted. A half dozen box trucks illuminated by the few lights still functioning loom at one end of the long parking lot.

Hughes is crouched behind my seat under a blanket. Solar is following me fifty meters behind, not closely enough to seem associated with our vehicle.

If McCord is acting alone, which seems likely given his use of Liza as a pawn, he doesn't have a lookout and is already here or about to pull in.

"How does it look?" asks Hughes.

"Sketch as hell," I tell him.

While driving here, McCord had texted Liza's phone telling her to meet at the loading dock behind 701 International Freight—which is a bit suspicious because it's closed right now and won't open until six in the morning.

An airplane flies overhead with a loud roar that shakes the SUV slightly.

"Imagine working here," I reply.

"They probably look at us swimming in a dirty canal and think the same thing," says Hughes.

"We're almost at the drop-off," I call into the radio.

"I have you in sight," says Solar.

"Backup here yet?" I ask.

"I'm told they're still on the way."

We had to send the FDLE agents who helped us out at the storage facility back home. The cold, hard reality of overtime.

"Pulling into the back," I say over the radio.

"Keep your eyes peeled. This person is a killer," says Solar.

"A greedy one that wants the mummy," I reply.

I drive the SUV along the road that runs in front of the rows of nondescript businesses. I see my silhouette in the reflection of the mirrored glass. I'd believe it was Liza if I were watching me.

At the end of the building, I make a left and then another left into the area behind the complex. It's a large parking lot with enough room for tractor trailers to back into loading docks. At the opposite side is the outer fence for the airport, runway lights and the tarmac visible in the distance.

701 International Freight was the third building from the end. The loading dock isn't hard to find because there are three empty air-freight containers stacked up next to the ramp.

I park the SUV outside the lamplight. I want to be visible but have the benefit of some shadow to conceal myself.

"Here we are," I say into the radio.

"Okay. I'm going to the far end and parking near the box trucks," says Solar.

"About that backup . . . ?"

"On the way. I have no idea what that really means," he admits.

"I thought you had more pull."

"Even I have my limit. Anyway, if anything weird happens, just get the hell out of here. Okay?"

"Define 'weird.' We've already found a stolen mummy, a mass grave, and a bunch of mammoth bones guarded by a Nile crocodile."

"McPherson . . ."

"Got it. Bug out if it gets really weird."

I keep waiting for headlights to appear at the far end of the loading area or in my rearview mirror.

Ten minutes go by with no sign of anyone approaching.

"Think he got spooked?" I ask Hughes.

"If it were me, I'd probably do a patrol around the perimeter and look for suspicious vehicles. Unmarked vans loaded with SWAT, that kind of thing."

"How about a cranky Dirty Harry–type sitting at the far end of the parking lot?"

"I'm pretty sure Solar is invisible right now. He's had some experience doing this kind of thing."

"Fair enough."

My ears pick out the sound before I see the light in the distance.

"We got something," I tell Hughes.

One headlight approaches our SUV.

"You got that?" I ask Solar.

"Almost missed it. They took a back road. I thought it was chained off," he says.

"One light is out," I reply as it gets closer.

"That's just asking to be pulled over," says Hughes.

"Wait. It's not a car. It's a motorcycle," I say as the rider brings it to a stop under the light of the lamp. He's wearing a helmet, so I can't see the face. "Did McCord mention riding a motorcycle?" I whisper.

"No. But I wouldn't be surprised."

The rider waves to me. I wave back.

He steps off the bike and motions for me to get out of the SUV.

"He wants me to get out," I whisper.

"Text him and tell him you're scared," says Solar over the radio.

I use Liza's phone to message him.

Liza: Is that you? Can I see your face?

The rider takes his phone out of his pocket and reads the message. He nods his helmeted head and motions for me to get out.

I sit still.

Frustrated, the rider texts me back.

McCord: I sat next to someone on the flight who may have been sick. I don't want to get you sick. Bad enough I have to bring this home to Jenny and the kids.

I text back:

Liza: Understand. This is just so weird.

The rider pockets his phone and walks around his bike toward the driver's window.

In two seconds, he'll see I'm not Liza.

He passes the windshield column on the left, entering my blind spot, and has a gun drawn a moment later.

"Gun!" I yell as I lean into the passenger side.

Bang!

Broken glass shatters over me.

Bang!

I hear the right-side rear passenger door open as Hughes exits the vehicle, followed by a thud as he hits the pavement.

Bang!

Bang!

The motorcycle engine screams as it races past and away.

"Hughes!" I scream as I bolt from the vehicle.

"Fuck . . . ," he moans.

I race around the SUV and see him on the ground, holding his side.

"Solar!" I scream into the radio. "We need an ambulance, now!"

CHAPTER 53

PRESSURE

I've got my hands on Hughes's upper chest trying to prevent further blood loss. A black pool of it is already soaking the fabric of my pants at my knees.

"Ambulance is on the way," shouts Solar as he comes running from his car with a first-aid kit in hand.

"On a scale of one to ten, I give this a five," says Hughes through gritted teeth.

"Well, shut up and concentrate on not bleeding so this doesn't become a ten," Solar tells him. "How's it look, McPherson?"

"I think it grazed his rib cage above the vest," I reply.

"Not a good-enough shooter to hit the chest, but enough to get you. How are you breathing?" asks Solar as he rummages through the kit for a large bandage.

"I feel like the wind got knocked out of me. But no gurgling," says Hughes. He does sound winded.

"Okay. Just stay alert. I'm going to slap this over the wound right now so you don't keep leaking. It's not that bad," says Solar, lying.

"What about the rider?" asks Hughes.

"We have a bulletin out. We'll also send cars over to McCord's house," Solar assures him.

"What was the plan?"

"What do you mean?" I respond, trying to force my attention away from all the blood my partner's spilled onto my hands and clothes.

"Why a motorcycle?" he says.

"Fewer words," Solar orders him.

As long as he's talking about the case, at least he's breathing.

"I'd rather not think about the pain," Hughes tells him.

"I think the plan was to kill Yurinov and take the vehicle," says Solar.

"Jesus. McCord didn't seem like the type. Not that I got to spend much time with him," I reply.

"Did that look like McCord at all? Did you get a good-enough view?" asks Solar.

"No. He kept his helmet on."

"That could be for the security cameras. It could also be that we're not dealing with McCord. If we are, then he was definitely planning to kill Yurinov," says Solar.

"I'm sorry I didn't return the favor," replies Hughes.

"If you hadn't returned fire, you'd be sitting here holding my brains in your hands right now," I reply.

An ambulance siren is audible in the distance.

"Sounds like the relief crew is almost here," says Solar.

"I need to call Cathy," Hughes says suddenly.

"Let's have the paramedics take a look at you first. Then I'll talk to her."

"If it's bad, I want to speak to her," Hughes insists.

"Son, if it was that bad, you wouldn't be jabbering like you are right now. It ain't pretty, but you're going to be fine. I'm going to have you at a desk next week if I have my say."

I don't know if Solar is giving him an honest pep talk or trying to keep his spirits up until he can get real medical treatment. Solar seems to sense my uncertainty and gives me a small nod.

"Here I am worried about Nile crocodiles and it's some asshole in a back alley that gets me," says Hughes.

"You're not got yet," I reply. "Still plenty of time for the crocodile to show up."

"You two are morbid," Solar sighs.

The flashing lights of the ambulance bounce off the buildings as the driver finds us in the loading zone.

I hear footsteps and two paramedics materialize on either side of me.

A woman with short hair gently moves my hands out of the way. "We got this."

I back up and step a few feet away but keep Hughes in my view. He gives me a half grin as they strip off his bulletproof vest and shirt.

Solar's on his phone talking to someone.

I feel a twinge of anger that he's not giving Hughes his full attention but realize that he's thinking several steps ahead.

"Do we need a helicopter? We've got one on the other side of the airport that can be here in five minutes," Solar asks the paramedics.

"No arteries appear to be hit. I think we can stabilize him and have him at the hospital in the same amount of time," says the female paramedic.

Red and blue lights flash all around us as the personnel we requested earlier pull up.

"Looks like our backup made it," says Solar. "McPherson, you ride to the hospital with Hughes while I get this straightened out."

"No," says Hughes.

He tries to lift his body up, but the paramedics push him back down.

"You want me to go with you?" asks Solar.

"No. I want you guys to get McCord. If he was ready to kill Liza, then he could kill any of Stafford's other friends."

"We've got people on the way to McCord's," Solar reminds him.

"I know. But it feels off," says Hughes.

"Sir, we need you to relax," says the paramedic.

"And I need you to shut the fuck up," Hughes yells back.

I've known this man for years and I've never heard him snap like this. Sure, he may have dropped an asshole with a punch, but this is a new level.

Hughes's eyes plead with our boss. "Sloan doesn't have to kick in the doors. But I think one of you should be there. It's all wrong. Nothing has been what we thought."

"Fine. McPherson, take my car," says Solar as he tosses me his keys.

CHAPTER 54
BOXED IN

There are two police cars parked at either end of the block where Kevin McCord lives. Solar instructed them to wait until I arrived and keep a tactical team on standby.

The neighborhood is an upper-class suburb with large lawns separating the houses. McCord's home is a beige stucco-style house with a covered entryway.

He has a wife and kids. We don't want him to use them as hostages if things go down hard.

The plan is for me to call and ask him to meet me out on the street, where I'll have two uniformed police officers with me.

His best strategy is to come outside and surrender. I never saw his face back at the industrial park. If he got rid of the gun and his phone, there's not much I can do even if I see a motorcycle in his living room.

The smart approach for McCord would be to come outside and act baffled.

The smart approach for me is to ignore my anger over Hughes being shot and find the most peaceful resolution possible.

"You ready?" I ask Sergeant Fong.

"Tactical's around the block. We'll keep everyone inside," he confirms.

I dial McCord's number on my phone. He answers after the second ring.

"Hello?" he replies.

"Kevin? It's Sloan McPherson. Sorry for bothering you. Can you come outside and talk?" I ask.

"What?"

"I'm outside. I have some questions about Stafford, and I didn't want to disturb your family," I explain.

"Yeah. Sure. Let me get my shoes on."

In the background I can hear him calling out to his wife that he'll be right back.

McCord's front door opens and he steps into the light of his covered porch. He's wearing gym shorts, a T-shirt, and no shoes.

He doesn't look like a guy who just raced here on a motorcycle. But that could be the plan.

He looks around, then steps out onto the sidewalk.

I'm leaning on the other side of Solar's unmarked car. Just in case I need it for protection.

"Kevin, would you mind raising your hands for me and stepping over to the driveway?" I ask.

"Huh? What's going on?"

"It's just a precaution. It's for your safety and mine."

I have my hand on my hip near my gun but haven't drawn. If he doesn't feel threatened, then nobody gets hurt.

"Step over to the driveway," I say a little more firmly.

He raises his hands and moves into the center of the driveway.

"Kevin?" his wife calls from the doorway.

"Mrs. McCord, could you step back inside for a moment?" I ask.

"What's going on?" she replies.

"I'll explain in a minute. Please step inside."

"I demand—"

Her words are cut short by McCord. "Jenny, would you go back into the fucking house?"

She gives him a shocked glare, then slams the door.

McCord looks exasperated. "What should I do now?"

"I want you to just use your fingers to pick up the end of your shirt and raise it so I can see that you're not armed, and then slowly turn around."

McCord lifts his shirt and shows me that he's not hiding a weapon.

"Sergeant Fong is going to place handcuffs on you. These are only temporary. Is that okay?"

"Am I about to be arrested?" he asks.

"I have no cause right now. This is just for everyone's safety," I explain.

"Okay."

McCord stands still as Fong places the handcuffs on his wrists behind his back and gives him a quick pat down.

I open the door to the back of my car, and Fong walks McCord over so he can sit down on the seat.

This keeps him boxed in and out of sight of nosy neighbors—who I can already see peeking out between curtains.

"Have you been home all night?" I ask.

"All day. It's my rotation off from the fire department. Angie will confirm it," he tells me, rock steady.

"Do you own a motorcycle?"

"What? No."

"How about a firearm?" I reply.

"I have two guns in a safe in my closet."

"Do you mind if we check your garage and look at the guns?" I ask.

"What's going on?"

"There was a shooting tonight. Someone texting from what looked like your cell number and fired on me and my partner."

"Oh god. *My* phone? *How?*"

"It was a Telegram text message."

"Telegram? I don't even use it. You can check my phone. That wasn't me. Is Scott okay?" asks McCord.

"He's at the hospital, but I think he'll be okay."

"How did you know her partner's name?" asks Fong.

I give the sergeant a friendly smile, trying to tell him gently to let me ask the questions. "We've both dived with McCord. Who do you know that uses Telegram?" I ask McCord.

"Liza and Pete Langshire. Pete goes on about it."

"What about Buelman or any of the others?"

"Maybe. Wait, did one of *them* shoot at you?" asks McCord.

"We don't know. Sergeant, would you stay with Mr. McCord while I talk to my supervisor?"

I step into the street and call Solar.

"What's the status?" he asks.

"We've been played. We have McCord in handcuffs, and he seems genuinely baffled. He gave us permission to search the house. I'm going to have them do that and do a gunpowder test on his hands. But I know what the results will be."

"We've got a unit watching Pete Langshire and Liza's house and one watching Ed Buelman's place," says Solar.

"Have they seen anything?" I ask.

"They just got there a little while ago. None of them saw a motorcycle," he replies.

"How visible are they?"

"Probably too visible."

I can hear radio chatter over the phone.

"Damn it," says Solar.

"What is it?"

"It appears we have a hostage situation. Ed Buelman just called 911 and said that Pete Langshire is holding him at gunpoint."

"I can be there in fifteen minutes."

CHAPTER 55
THE NEGOTIATOR

From the sheer quantity of red and blue lights splashing the neighborhood, it appears that every police car in Hillsborough County is parked near the Buelman residence when I arrive.

A police helicopter is flying overhead with a spotlight aimed at Buelman's two-story luxury home.

I park my car at the end of the block and flash my badge at the cops barricading the street. Ahead, a row of police cars line the front of the house with a tactical van off to the side.

I spot two majors in bulletproof vests standing on the other side of the truck away from the house, conferring with a SWAT team commander.

"I'm McPherson with the UIU," I explain after I make my way over to them.

"You one of Solar's?" asks a man whose vest identifies him as Major Vennheiser.

"Affirmative," I reply. "What's going on?"

"We got a 911 phone call saying that someone was in the house with the caller, threatening them," says Vennheiser.

"That would be Ed Buelman?" I ask.

"Affirmative. He said that someone named Pete Langshire had a gun to his head."

"Have you heard from him since the phone call?" I ask.

"No. We're waiting for our negotiator to call."

I spot a deputy with a long-range microphone aimed at the front window of the home. It works by bouncing a laser off the glass and picking up vibrations from the sounds inside the house.

"Have you heard anything?"

"Just a television at full volume," says Vennheiser.

"Are we ready to call?" asks a woman in a dark-blue business suit and tactical vest.

"This is Dr. Edina. She's our negotiator. This is McPherson. She's familiar with the suspect."

Edina and I shake hands.

"What can you tell me about either man?" she asks briskly.

"Pete Langshire is married to Liza Yurinov. Just over two hours ago, someone shot at me thinking I was her."

Edina's eyes widen, but she absorbs the info with no other expression. "Is it possible Buelman may have been having a romantic relationship with the wife?"

"Sure. Maybe. She didn't say anything about that. But it could be."

"Is Langshire a violent person?"

"I have no idea. He's a potential suspect in a homicide, and he may have taken a shot at my partner earlier."

"Yeah, Solar told us that. Okay. I'm going to call Buelman's number. We'll see if Langshire lets him pick up."

She puts her mobile phone on speaker and dials.

After five rings, Buelman answers. "Hello?"

"Mr. Buelman, are you on speakerphone with Mr. Langshire?" asks Edina.

"Y-yes," Langshire chimes in after a long pause.

"Mr. Langshire. My name is Dr. Edina. I'm a licensed psychologist. I'm not a cop. May I call you Pete?" she asks.

Another long pause.

"He's nodding," says Buelman.

"Pete. I want to make sure that this is all resolved safely. I don't want any harm to come to you. Can you help me with that?" she asks.

The seconds tick away like years.

"He's nodding again," says Buelman.

"I'd like to hear that from *you*, Pete. Could you tell me what you'd like me to do so this can have a peaceful outcome?" asks Edina.

The call abruptly disconnects.

"Should we call back?" asks Vennheiser.

"Give him a moment. This all went off script for him. We don't want to panic him," explains Edina.

"I'm pretty sure Buelman is panicking right now," he says.

"When Langshire stepped into that house, he may well have been planning to kill Mr. Buelman. The fact that he hasn't done it so far indicates that he's not that determined. We don't want him to think he has to make a decision in a hurry." Edina turns to me. "What else can you tell me about either of them?"

"We think the suspect may have killed a man named Fred Stafford—or rather, a man using that name. There could be some kind of love triangle—or rectangle. I don't know. Everyone's motives are a bit conflicted," I admit.

"Were Buelman and Langshire friends?" she asks.

"Yes. Close ones, I think."

"Okay. This sounds like a bit of a spiral," says Edina. "Let's try to convince Langshire to let Buelman go." She dials the phone again.

"Hello?" says Buelman.

"Hey, Ed. This is Dr. Edina. Can Langshire hear you?" she asks.

"I think he's looking out the window," whispers Buelman.

Vennheiser calls into his radio. "Anyone have a window shot?"

"Negative," someone replies over the radio.

I look behind me and see two snipers on the roofs of the houses across from Buelman's. I suspect there's at least one more on the roof of the house behind his, covering the back.

"Put Pete on the phone," says Edina.

"He's listening," says Ed.

"Pete, I'd like for you to let Ed come outside," she says.

The line goes quiet, and the TV is no longer audible in the background.

"I think he muted it," whispers Edina. She speaks up. "Pete, if you can hear me, I want you to know there's a peaceful path out of this. I've talked to a lot of people in situations like this. The stress can be a lot, but a better outcome is possible.

"The first step is trust. I don't want any harm to come to you or to Ed. I need you to let Ed go. You can still stay inside the house, and we won't go in there. But I'd like to know that I can trust you," says Edina. Her voice is so calm and soothing. I suspect she's had a lot of training to make it this way.

She presses mute on her phone. "Do you think your snipers can take the shot if we get Langshire into the doorway?" she asks Vennheiser.

Correction: she's calm and soothing like a rattlesnake.

"Maybe. I'd rather get Buelman clear. We've got Langshire boxed in. We can wait him out."

The sound of the television in the house becomes audible again.

"He says he'll let me go if you can bring his wife here," says Buelman.

Edina looks at me. I shake my head.

"We can work on that," says Edina. "In the meantime, Pete, could you send Ed out here?"

I notice that Edina never uses the word "hostage" or anything that implies Langshire is committing a criminal act. I suspect this makes it easier for him to rationalize his behavior as reasonable and keep him from thinking he has to act criminally.

"Pete? Is there anything else I can get you? Food? Is there someone else you'd like to talk to?" she asks.

"He says he just wants time to think but will let me go," says Buelman.

"Thank you, Pete. That's very gracious of you," says Edina.

"What should I do?" asks Ed.

"Go to the front door and step outside."

"He says that's okay," replies Ed.

I watch the front door through the side windows of the tactical van. The door begins to slowly open, and Ed Buelman steps through with his hands over his head.

He looks nervously over his shoulder, then takes a step onto the porch.

He glances back and takes another step.

Two of Vennheiser's SWAT team members run from the corner of the house, away from the door, and throw an armored vest behind Buelman and rush him away from the doorway to a nearby ambulance.

Edina jogs over to him and I follow.

"How are you doing?" asks Edina.

Buelman is sitting on the floor of the ambulance with his legs hanging out over the edge as a paramedic gives him a quick examination.

"I've never seen Pete like that before," says Ed, shaking his head. "I don't get it."

He looks over and sees me. "Sloan!"

"I'm glad you're okay," I tell him.

"I'm worried about Pete. What happened? Is Liza okay?" he asks.

"She's fine. Did he mention Stafford?" I ask.

"About him missing? No."

"Where was Pete when he was holding you hostage?" asks Edina.

"We were in the upstairs hallway. He was paranoid about being near windows. He was freaking me the hell out."

"What kind of weapon did he have?" asks Edina.

"He had a bag and a handgun he pointed at me. I think there were more guns in the bag. I didn't get a look."

"What did Pete say when he entered?" asks Edina.

"He pulled out the gun and aimed it at me. I thought he was joking. Then he asked me if I ever slept with Liza."

"And you said . . . ?"

"Of course not! Pete was my friend."

"McPherson, I'd like you to talk to Langshire," says Edina.

"Me?"

"I can't bring Liza here. Maybe he'll listen to you. Right now, he's probably contemplating suicide. I don't want that to happen," she says. "Ed, would you excuse us? They'll take care of you."

Edina and I walk back over to the tactical van parked in front of the house.

"Buelman says the suspect is in the upper hallway of the house. Think you could get a shot?" she asks Vennheiser.

"I thought I was here to talk him into surrendering," I cut in.

"You are. But if he starts shooting, I don't want any of our people getting hurt," she says.

I take out my phone and dial Pete Langshire's phone.

It keeps ringing and goes to voice mail.

"Pete, this is Sloan. Call me back so we can talk," I say before hanging up.

"Give him a few minutes to listen to the message," says Edina. "He might have the barrel of the gun in his mouth right now."

"What's the longest one of these hostage situations has ever gone on for you?" I ask.

"Not counting my last marriage?" she replies.

I give her a grin.

"Two days."

"What was the outcome?"

"Everyone lived. That's why it pays to be patient," she tells me.

"I'm going to call my supervisor and update him."

"Do you have another phone you can use, in case Langshire calls back?" asks Edina.

"I think there's a spare in the car," I reply.

I hand her my phone and walk back to Solar's car.

As I head down toward the end of the block, I pass the ambulance and see one of the paramedics.

"How's Buelman doing?" I ask.

"He'd been in there so long he said he couldn't hold it anymore. William took him over to a neighbor's house to use the restroom," the EMT replies.

A knot forms in my stomach, and something in the back of my mind screams at me.

"Which house?" I ask calmly.

She points two doors down. I start walking in that direction, not quickly enough to cause a commotion, but briskly.

I'm such an idiot.

I've been played again.

CHAPTER 56
PATIO

A deputy is standing by the front door of the house. I flash my badge to him as I walk up to the porch.

"Is the paramedic in there?" I ask.

"Yep. With the victim," he replies.

"What about the homeowners?"

"They're down the street," he says.

I put a finger to my lips, draw my gun, then point to the doorknob. The deputy understands and slowly opens the door.

I enter the house with my gun down, back to the wall. I clear the living room, then head toward the left hallway.

The paramedic is standing near a doorway at the end of the hall.

I put my finger to my lips again and motion for him to come close to me.

"When did you last see him?" I ask.

"A minute ago."

"Go outside and across the street," I tell him.

I wait for him to clear the hallway, then try pulling on the bathroom sliding door. Like many Florida homes, this one has a bathroom that connects to the pool area. Convenient for changing—and also making a run for it.

It won't move.

I could try to break through, but it'll be quicker to run outside.

I race out the front of the house, past the deputy and the paramedic, and around the home, slowing my pace as I reach the backyard.

I can see the patio and the pool from the corner. I can also see the light from the bathroom door spilling onto the pool.

A low fence and a row of palm trees divide the backyard from the neighboring home. A few houses away I hear the sound of a dog barking.

I run for the trees, vault the fence, and land in the other yard.

A metal gate to the right hangs open. I race through it and into the next block. Cars are parked in almost every driveway. The lights of the police cars flash at the end of the street, where a small crowd has gathered.

I don't see any sign of Buelman.

I spot another open gate across the street. I hurry to it, then slow to a walk as I enter a path between the two houses. My feet hit gravel and make crunching sounds.

BANG!

Pieces of the house ricochet and sting my face as someone fires from a shadowed cluster of bushes.

I don't think.

I aim and fire into the dark.

BANG! BANG! BANG!

Ed Buelman falls forward and rolls onto the ground. He clutches at his chest with his hand still holding the gun.

I point mine at his head and pry it from his bloody fingers.

"Make a move. Make a fucking move," I taunt him, wanting an excuse to finish him for almost killing Hughes.

Instead, he looks at me with hate-filled eyes.

"Over here!" shouts someone as a flashlight finds me standing over Ed Buelman with my gun pointed at his face.

"You arrogant son of a bitch. You wanted me to know when we first spoke. You pretty much came out and told me, didn't you? Only you didn't think I'd find Stafford's body."

Buelman sputters something unintelligible.

"Is Langshire alive?" I ask him.

"I need you to clear out," says a paramedic as he kneels by Buelman's body.

"Is he alive?" I yell.

Buelman doesn't answer. He's still conscious but clearly wants that guilt to hang over me for as long as possible.

Guilt because, if Langshire is dead, it's because I was too stupid to realize that it was Buelman all along.

Sure, I had a feeling Ed was an asshole, but I didn't have facts—or rather, I didn't see the facts that were right in front of me.

The first words out of his mouth were that Stacy never understood Stafford's lifestyle. Besides trying to frame Stafford as a risk-taker and hinting at the man's gambling and secrets, he used the past tense: *understood*. Not that Stacy doesn't understand, that she never *understood* . . .

But if bad grammar were a crime by itself, I'd be serving a thousand life sentences. It's what he said afterward that remained in the back of my head, unexamined.

It was a dumb little joke for his own amusement. He told it thinking that his secret would be safe forever, hidden under a plywood trapdoor in the sinkhole.

When speaking of Stafford, Buelman said sometimes people "crack under pressure." Which is what happened to Stafford's rebreather when Buelman tampered with it.

He told me what he did with a goddamn dad joke, and I never saw it.

CHAPTER 57
RELIC

"Langshire's gonna make it," says Solar from across the conference room table after he ends his call.

Shortly after Liza left the house to retrieve Hugo at the storage facility, Buelman showed up at her dive shop (motorcycle helmet and all) and shot Pete in the chest. He then drove to a storage facility where he kept the motorcycle and got into his car.

"Why did he go to Liza and Pete's?" asks Hughes over my phone's speaker. "I'd have just kept going."

"Aren't you supposed to be convalescing?" asks Solar.

"I have questions," Hughes says.

"Buelman is a smart guy. But he's not as smart as he thinks he is. When the plan didn't go the way he wanted, he had to improvise, and he was bad at that," I explain.

"So what was the plan?" asks Gwen.

"The original plan was to steal everything they could from that cave. Then Stafford got a conscience or didn't like being blackmailed. Buelman decided to kill him but make it look like he died somewhere else so we wouldn't find Stafford's body.

"He'd probably found someone to buy Hugo Man and was desperate to get the specimen back. When I sent the text message to the group, he jumped on it."

"Why try to kill Langshire and Yurinov?" asks Hughes. "Sorry if you explained this. Solving crimes is really hard with a head full of painkillers."

"It's okay. My guess was that he planned to kill Liza but dump her body somewhere it couldn't be found. If that had worked, it would have looked like she killed Pete, took the specimen, and vanished. There'd be no need for Buelman to go into hiding. He might get questioned, but there would be nothing to directly link him to Pete's homicide or Liza going missing. She would have looked like Stafford's secret partner and potential killer."

"A lot of things could go wrong with that plan," says Solar.

"And they did," I say with a smile. "Buelman's in ICU with tubes connected to every part of his body because of it."

"He might have gotten away with it before," Gwen says soberly.

"What do you mean?"

"When I did a background search on him, I didn't find anything this serious. But I just did a search of unsolved crimes that he could be connected to. Remember that college girl that went missing in the US Virgin Islands a few years ago?"

"Caroline something, right?"

"Caroline Lineas," says Gwen. "The bar where she was last seen was a quarter mile from a home Buelman was living in. He was a regular there. Police questioned him because someone matching his description was seen in a car with a woman matching her description, but nothing came of it."

"Looks like we'll have more questions for Buelman," says Solar.

"Quite the scumbag," Hughes pipes in.

"Do you think he saw Hughes and me at Sirius when we found Stafford's body?" I wonder out loud.

"Maybe. But if you're thinking that's why he tried to kill Langshire and Yurinov, don't go down that route," Solar replies. "I think he was planning on killing them a while ago."

"Why?"

"For the same reason he killed Stafford. They might not have known what was going on, but each one of them had enough of the puzzle for it to be put together eventually."

"What about Reesman?" Gwen reminds us. "Let's not forget that bastard."

"We'll sort that out. He tipped his hand too much with the comment about Skolnick Farm. I think this will stick to him. The team working on that will make sure we charge him with something," Solar assures her.

"How many teams do you have running around Florida?" asks Hughes.

"You're it. The mobile FDLE teams are just a pilot project. That's it. Well, that's if you don't count a couple of librarians I have in Tallahassee sifting through cold cases."

"Sound like my kind of people," replies Gwen.

"You'd get along real well with them," says Solar. "If something they're working on pans out, you'll be talking to them soon. In the meantime, Hughes, I need you to hang up and get some rest. Gwen, keep digging into Buelman. And McPherson, I have people waiting on that instruction manual."

"What people?" I ask.

"The FUIU," says Solar.

"The Florida Underwater Investigation Unit? That's us. Hughes already knows everything I know. That hardly counts as *waiting*."

"No. The other FUIU. I'm talking about the Federal Underwater Investigation Unit," he tells me. "Turns out there's water everywhere. The Department of Justice is interested in scaling this up a bit."

"What does that even mean?" I ask.

Solar shrugs. "We're about to find out."

CHAPTER 58
COLD CASE

Nadine is waiting for Jackie and me in the parking lot of Broward College. She waves to us as we pull into a space.

"Hey, Dr. Baltimore!" says Jackie as she gets out from behind the wheel.

"You're driving now?" says Nadine as she gives her a hug.

"Only from the campus entrance," Jackie says.

"Small steps. Small steps," I say as my nerves begin to calm.

At the end of the parking lot, a girls' beach volleyball match is taking place on the field.

"Okay, so the mystery is we're here to watch a volleyball game," I reply.

"Not quite. Follow me."

Nadine leads us through the entry gate and into the stands off to the side. We take a seat and watch the game.

Broward is playing against the team from West Palm Beach. The girls spike and hit the ball back and forth aggressively. Each one of them is a virtual giant; their height would dwarf mine.

Jackie's already my height and watching intently.

"Do you play?" asks Nadine.

"Only in gym. I'm more of a swimmer," she says.

"Shocker," says Nadine with a smile.

Everyone's attention is drawn to a statuesque young woman with long dark hair. She's in the back corner for Broward but manages to cover a wide area and place the ball with incredible precision.

"I wanted to talk to you about Hugo Man," says Nadine. "The state archaeologist is about to announce the discovery."

"That's exciting," I reply.

"I know how you feel. Nobody is excited that Florida's oldest human specimen is also our oldest attempted murder suspect." Nadine whispers to me, "How much does she know?"

"That your troglodyte bludgeoned Jane to death?" Jackie answers for me, catching every word.

"Jane?" asks Nadine.

"That's what Jackie calls the young woman. She didn't think 'haploid group N-88' was a suitable name."

"Well, that settles that," says Nadine.

"Dump Hugo in the landfill," Jackie replies as she watches the game. "I know, the science. Just a figure of speech. Maybe."

Jackie took the story of Hugo Man to heart more than I expected. She kept peppering me with questions about Jane until I finally set a stack of my paleoarchaeology books on her desk and told her to find the answers herself.

The joke is on me. She did. Now Jackie throws nonstop facts at me.

"So your mother explained the blood samples we took from the weapon and clothes and how we're able to genetically sequence them?" asks Nadine.

"And determine approximate age," says Jackie.

"Yes. Jane was about your age. We also had plenty of DNA from Hugo Man. We could trace his DNA back but not forward. It looks like his band died out," says Nadine.

"Yay, good news."

"Perhaps. I'm sure they weren't all bad. But in any event, he was a genetic dead end."

Jackie turns her attention away from the game to Nadine. "What do you mean, he was a dead end?"

"My job is to try to put together a story when I only have a few fragments. This means a lot of guesses—many of them wrong. But sometimes they're right and you find out there's more to it."

"What else is there?"

"I don't think it's fair to call Hugo Man a killer. At least I don't think he killed Jane. He may have wanted to, for all we know, but it doesn't look like he did. In fact, it seems like he died trying. I believe that he died and she survived to live a long life."

"Really? How can you tell that?" asks Jackie.

"There was a mutation in Jane's blood. A slight mutation that was passed on generation after generation. I've seen that mutation in the DNA of people alive today."

"Jane had children?" asks Jackie.

"Lots of them, I think. And they had children, and so forth."

Jackie's eyes light up. "You mean I could theoretically meet one of her great-great-great-whatever-granddaughters?"

"Yes. Yes, you could. In fact, when the game's over, I'll take you over to meet one," says Nadine as she points at the powerful young woman dominating the game.

"You mean . . . ?"

"Yes. Rebecca Abiaka is her name. She signed up to have her DNA tested as part of a Florida ancestry project."

"Does she know her great-great-grandmother was a badass who outran your caveman and lived?"

"Not yet," says Nadine. "I thought maybe she'd like to hear it from you."

ABOUT THE AUTHOR

Andrew Mayne is the Amazon Charts and *Wall Street Journal* best-selling author of *The Girl Beneath the Sea*, *Black Coral*, *Sea Storm*, *Sea Castle*, and *Dark Dive* in his Underwater Investigation Unit series; *The Final Equinox* and *Mastermind* in the Theo Cray and Jessica Blackwood series; *The Naturalist*, *Looking Glass*, *Murder Theory*, and *Dark Pattern* in the Theo Cray series; and *Angel Killer*, *Name of the Devil*, and the Edgar Award–nominated *Black Fall* in his Jessica Blackwood series. He was the star of A&E's *Don't Trust Andrew Mayne* and swam with great white sharks using an underwater stealth suit he designed for the Shark Week special *Andrew Mayne: Ghost Diver*. He currently works on creative applications for artificial intelligence. For more information, visit www.andrewmayne.com.